PROOF

Michael Klaene

Shoal Press

Images are courtesy of:
Library of Congress, Prints & Photographs Online Catalog
CameraWiki (https://www.flickr.com/photos/camerawiki/6834942174), https://
creativecommons.org/licenses/by/2.0
Susse Frére Daguerreotype Camera (http://commons.wikimedia.org/wiki/File:
Susse_Frére_Daguerreotype_camera_1839.jpg), https://commons.wikimedia.org
Historic Mathew Brady Studio Camera, circa Early 1860s-1,   Heritage Auctions,
https://creativecommons.org/licenses/by/4.0/deed.en, image darkened, background re-
moved

Michael Klaene/Shoal Press
Florence, KY 41022
www.shoalpress.com

Proof/ Michael Klaene. -- 1st ed.
ISBN 978-0-692-57757-8

for Jacob and Nicholas

proof

: a test photographic print made from a negative

: the cogency of evidence that compels acceptance by the mind of a truth or a fact

Merriam Webster Dictionary
http://www.merriam-webster.com/dictionary/proof

Prologue

Gardner rose up from the camera box upon which he was seated. "A rain is coming," the picture artist said in his Scottish brogue as he drank down the last drops of weak cider from the tin. He ran a hand down his long beard, stilling it against the dusty wind, then slid a thumb between his checked shirt and bottle green suspenders.

Truman Ash stood from the second box and offered back his cup as he held his slouch hat in place, his brown locks blown back behind his ears.

Gardner took the cup and placed it with his own on the tumbler's corked top, leaving them to dangle.

Together they took in the view from that high vantage. Past the old cottonwood where the artist's docile mule stood tied and twitching his ears, a shelf of gray sky had gone broken where the storm was already wetting the barren and grassless plain beyond Fort Laramie.

The fort itself, a half mile distant, appeared little more than a scattered lot of windswept buildings and squat adobes aside the Laramie River, a narrow ribbon through the desolate land.

"Never again may we see the likes of it, Mr. Ash," Gardner said to so much vastness. He shook his head and turned toward his wooden van.

Gardner put a boot on the leather strapping at the back well and reached into the wagon's black canopy. With the clacking of glass, he set the cider tumbler snug somewhere in that dark interior between his bottled solutions.

He returned to fetch the glass lens atop his camera box that he had been polishing during their ten minutes' talk. Then he hoisted the box itself.

"Mr. Gardner," Truman began.

Alexander Gardner watched Truman slide fingers into his back pocket and take out a wallet. He pinched its band but stopped short of opening it. Truman took pause, then said, "Wanted to show you something."

Gardner said nothing. He had suspected the interest this young man had taken in his work had been more than merely passing time.

Truman had been following the photographer like a stray dog since Gardner arrived with the Indian Commission one week ago. To the half-tent beyond the parade ground, where the artist photographed the hard-scowling General Sherman and the men in dusty suits upon long pine benches. Indian men, and many a warrior who had been killing on the high plains months earlier, sat cross-legged in a half-circle on the dirt ground, listening to the white interpreter before an elder would lower his pipe and rise from the small fire to *touch the pen*.

Truman had watched as Gardner jostled his three-legged camera from point to point. Perhaps Truman understood enough of the mechanics to grasp the image's evolution as Gardner slipped beneath the instrument's black cloak to focus its eye, then placed the light-proof box at back and exposed the glass, holding the cap just above the lens to shield the brightest sun, lips counting seconds beneath his beard. Eight, sometimes ten, twelve, before the cap was replaced, the plate secured to its wooden slip and hurried to his canopied wagon where inside its dark well, he performed his great mysteries.

Alexander Gardner, Fort Laramie Treaty, May 1868

When not about the great half-tent, Gardner was no idler. And on more than one occasion Truman followed the picture artist to the Indian lodges that crowded the trodden river bank opposite the fort to capture on glass the natives in their ragged blankets; men, woman, and children whose spartan appearance told of hard living in this land.

Even when Gardner drove his squat van to the surrounding hills to take full measure of the plain, Truman lurked at a distance.

And so it seemed inevitable that Truman would summon the courage to meet him.

It was there on the bluff that he finally appeared. He introduced himself and offered to help steady Gardner's camera against the wind between exposures. It was better than the contrivance of large stones that Gardner had used to pinch its legs.

Gardner accepted the help and when he had finished his series, he shared his cider as a late-morning sun warmed their faces.

Truman asked about Gardner's work at Laramie, as if he had not been there to witness the greater part of it.

In turn, Gardner asked Truman about the particulars of his recent exploration of faraway western lands. The mapmakers and geologists, Truman, and two other naturalists. Fourteen months before the scientific expedition reached Laramie via an easterly route, ebb against the spring tide of emigrants, to draw stores from the sutler's agent and prepare specimens and samples for shipment east via the rail at Cheyenne. Such a young man to have accomplished so much: two hundred twenty-seven species of bird. Three hundred in all, counting fish, amphibians, and small mammals. Truman revealed that he too was Washington-bound at the expedition's conclusion, to take up his position at the Smithsonian.

The conversation had been pleasant. But now it was time for Gardner to leave, and Truman had seemingly more to say.

The wagon's canopy snapped violently against a chill wind. Truman cupped the wallet in his palm and let it fall to his side as if to take back some previous intent.

Gardner bent down to lift the remaining camera box off the ground.

He heard Truman follow him a step toward the van.

"They say you were a photographer during the war."

He looked up at Truman and nodded after a moment. "Yes. You might say that."

When Truman said nothing more, Gardner started back toward the van.

"I was wondering, did you know Mathew Brady?"

Gardner stopped his gait, his back to Truman.

"The famous photographer. Perhaps you made his acquaintance, Mr. Gardner?"

There was quiet when Gardner turned around to face him. Up to that point, Gardner had been in a fine mood, tolerating the strange boy and his unwanted attentions. But now Gardner felt his face go rigid, helpless to reverse course as his lips closed and jaw set tight beneath his beard.

Truman's eyes showed he registered the change. A look close to fear took hold of his smooth, pale face.

Gardner tugged hard at his beard. "I must get back now, Truman. Excuse me." He set the box on the wagon, then turned.

Truman held out a hand and Gardner pumped it once without meeting his eyes.

Gardner harnessed the mule and mounted his wagon bench. He started back toward the garrison.

He felt Truman's eyes watching him as he went on, the rain squall yet miles distant at his back. The young man standing there, no doubt, trying to make sense of things.

Washington D.C., just after the Civil War

I

The honorable senator from Massachusetts rose from behind his desk in the second row. Tufts of brown hair streaked gray rested upon his high collar. The man amply filled his waistcoat, the result of many years of good Capitol City food and wines.

A glass-paneled roof bathed the chamber in soft light. Senators of the 40th Congress sat at their mahogany desks on the multi-tiered floor, facing the center rostrum. The room's purple carpet patterned floral; its high walls beset in Corinthian pilasters. A wall clock above the rostrum showed a quarter past nine.

In the row ahead, Morrill from Vermont and Anthony from Virginia turned themselves round to stare up at Senator Henry Wilson. Apparently satisfied he had everyone's attention, Wilson took spectacles from around his neck and placed them on the edge of his nose. He retrieved a paper from atop his cluttered desk.

"I present the memorial of Mathew B. Brady relative to a national collection of portraits."

His voice echoed across the cavernous room.

Above, Mathew Brady squeezed the ivory head atop his cane and leaned forward in his gallery seat.

"Mr. Brady sets forth that after the commencement of the war he employed a corps of artists who have taken views of battlefields, military camps, bridges, and other matters of that sort."

Wilson then looked to the rostrum where sat Ben Wade, President Pro Tempore and acting Vice President under soon to be ex-President Andrew Johnson.

"He asks some action by Congress on the subject. I move the reference of the memorial to the Committee on the Library."

Through the thick blue lenses of his spectacles, Brady studied Senator Wade's sullen face beneath a graying head, the sergeant-at-arms stoic at his side while two clerks scribbled at their desks.

U.S. Senate Chamber during the Reconstruction Era

"Motion agreed."

Senator Henry Wilson sat. Another senator took the floor.

Four days earlier, Wilson had submitted a resolution into the congressional record. Among the letter's many paragraphs, it had stated:

Mr. Brady has received since the war many offers for the purchase of his collection by public institutions, but he has refused them all, believing that it should belong to the national government.

The seed had been planted. Now, just as Wilson advised his old friend, they followed it with a formal request to spur action. The Committee on the Library, who approved purchases of artworks, could go to work drafting a bill. The library was the logical destination for Brady's images, where future generations would have access.

But Brady fretted about the timing of his petition. The 40th Congress' days were numbered. In a few weeks, the most turbulent session in history would come to a close; its bitter fight over the impeachment of President Johnson had ended only months ago. And despite the personal relationships Brady enjoyed with so many of these politicians, he knew he could easily be overlooked. He was reminded of this as he watched the throngs of railroad lobbyists crowd the floor before session, weaving through the galleries and cloak rooms. That evening, they would no doubt be plying congressmen with fine meals and private parties in their lavish hotel suites.

It was reasonable for Brady to ask himself if he would have their attention, even if so many owed him for helping shape their public image.

❧

Half past seven, Brady turned his key in the hallway of the National Hotel. A porter in buttons and cap hurried past, a silver tray balanced on his palm. Brady pushed open the door and light spilled in, washing over the dark room. Julia winced from the cushioned high back and raised a forearm to cover her face.

Brady slipped inside and shut the door behind him. He turned up the gas burner at the wall. Brady watched as its glow chased shadows across the sparse room.

"If not for you, my dear, I believe I prefer the dark."

Julia lowered her pale hand. Brady stood admiring her somber beauty; soft round eyes, thick black curls to match the dress. He wondered how she kept her youth while time ravaged all things around him.

Room 306 at the National was the small nook that Mathew and Julia Brady had called home since late '67 when circumstances forced their move there. Their former place, a far more generous suite one flight up, had since gone to some young financier who was making his mark in Washington.

A threadbare settee and chair they had brought with them from New York years before, a spare dining table and writing desk. Their four papered walls held a scattering of framed portraits procured from his studio, some semblance of culture which Brady could afford. Julia had long since accepted this more modest lifestyle. Simple, it turned out, suited her. At least that is what she told him.

"I had no idea you would be so late," she said.

Brady crossed over and leaned down to kiss her forehead. He caught sight of her quick smile.

But that smile vanished when her eyes settled on the bottle of Old Renault that dangled from his left jacket pocket.

He removed the cognac and set it on the oak slab table. He took his place on the settee and patted the cushion beside him with the flat of his palm. "Come. Sit next."

Julia did not budge from her chair.

"I am sorry, my dear," he said. "Things ran longer than expected. I sent Sam with a message. Did you receive it?" he asked, referring to his twelve-year-old messenger who shuttled Brady's messages about the city.

Julia took hold of the arms of her chair, pulling herself up. She crossed over to her husband. "He came by at his usual."

She tucked the back of her dress and sat, then held out the note to the light as if to offer proof.

My dear. Running late. Much business. Excited to tell you all about. Apologies. Must catch night express to Manhattan. Tonight. See soon. M.

"Is it so important to leave this evening?" she asked before casting the card to the table.

It had been nearly two years since Julia had accompanied Brady on monthly visits to Manhattan. In all their years there, Julia had never truly felt New York her home, preferring the capital and its proximity to the Maryland plantation upon which she was reared. Brady kept his studio at 10th and Broadway operational with local management. Though nothing like the boom days of younger years, it still drew a steady if modest business. It kept Brady's name in view.

"Yes. I am afraid so. I shall visit the studio while I am there. But, my dear, you will be happy to know that I have also arranged a buyer for the last parcel of land and will sell it tomorrow morning."

Julia's eyes lit. "You did? That's wonderful. I am happy to hear it. We might buy some new furniture."

"Indeed," Brady laughed.

The parcels of land near Central Park were remnants of her father's estate. They had sold them off, one by one, in recent years. Brady did so grudgingly. It was difficult for him to admit the money was needed. He had used proceeds from the last lot he had sold to buy back his Washington studio from bankruptcy. Each sale was like a doctor's lancing of an abscess, painful but necessary; the land parcels, his shares in the Austin Silver Mining Company, they charted a course on the map of Brady's financial misfortunes. Each required to make the patient well again. Brady was in some ways relieved to be rid of them all.

And this time, the money would serve a most constructive purpose.

"Oh, and I'm afraid that hour is fast approaching," Brady said, holding out his watch and chain. He let it slip back into his merino vest. "But there's time to celebrate."

Brady stood up from the settee. "Share a drink with me?"

Her brown eyes swept over the bottle in front of them, then to him. They seemed to question his judgment.

"I suppose not then."

Brady knew how Julia felt about the nature of his drinking these days but tonight he did not care. After all, there was reason to celebrate.

He took the bottle to the far side of their meager dining table where he reached upon a thin wooden shelf, took a glass, and set it on the table. Brady twisted and poured it near full.

He abandoned the bottle and returned to Julia.

He sat down beside her once more and took a drink, savoring its warmth, the hint of oak and sweet.

"What a day. Honestly, I feel twenty years younger."

"Well, you are not. Remember that."

He tapped her leg and laughed. "Thank you for reminding me."

"I could ring for Winston if you want something to eat," she said.

"Quite alright. I ate a fine meal earlier today. And I haven't the slightest hunger. Imagine that. That's what excitement does to a man."

He removed his jacket and took another drink and prepared to tell her about his day, beginning with Wilson's speech that morning. He would skip over the mundane details of the afternoon. Nor had he any intention of relaying how he spent the last hours at the Willard's smoke-filled bar, cajoling congressmen with drinks, making casual mention of a certain petition recently brought to the floor.

"Just as Wilson said it would go. Flawless."

He continued to tell her about Wilson's speech, painting for her a scene in the Senate chamber, perhaps in strokes a tad more colorful than the actual, as an old Irishman was known to do, even with his wife.

Julia, for her part, was quiet, giving nothing away in her demeanor. From the start, she had taken Brady's idea to petition Congress calmly. In '67, he had come close to selling a portion of photographs to the New York Historical Society. General and now President-elect Grant even wrote a personal letter of recommendation. When the purchase fell through, it hit them hard. Bankruptcy followed. Brady reopened his Pennsylvania Avenue studio in Washington later that year with half the space it once enjoyed.

He understood her tempered expectations. But it still pained him. He took a quick drink.

Eager to win her attention any way he could, he forged ahead into the next tale from his hectic day. One he knew would pique her interest.

"Once the Senate recessed until evening, I raced to find Wilson in the cloak room. My Lord does that room crowd when the session recesses. And, oh yes, there was Wilson, encircled by three men puffing fat cigars and suits that- well one need not be a tailor to see they were of the finest cut. Railroad men. They are everywhere these days. I saw Jay Gould himself just the other day! These lobbyists are shameless in their promotions, but they know how to move legislation. And well-connected senators like Wilson are their favorite target. But I digress. Waiting my turn, I noticed a young man standing behind Henry. He seemed to be waiting on the senator too. The young chap looked decidedly out of place, yet he kept a watchful eye on me that entire time. When the railers left, Wilson greeted me then introduced the two of us. As it would happen the young man was a nephew of sorts to our old friend Wilson, though not by blood. No. A family friend from Massachusetts I believe. A naturalist at the Smithsonian of all things. And he knew of me right off. I blush to say it seemed to give the young man quite a thrill to meet *the Mathew Brady*."

He took another swallow of cognac and pinched the wetness from his goatee before he caught Julia's puzzled gaze and laughed out loud. He knew well his story had meandered.

"I am sorry, my dear. I will get on with it. Wilson and the young fellow, not his nephew but something like it mind you, had lunch plans which the senator had to most regrettably cancel right there in front of me, due to pressing business. Well, standing there next to the poor chap with lunch in neither one of us, I asked the young man to join me in a booth at the Willard. Wilson seemed quite pleased at my gesture I can tell you."

Julia sat smirking. Brady held up a finger to give pause. He had yet to tell the oddest part of this encounter.

"So Truman and I are, oh yes, his name is Truman. Well, there we are, enjoying a meal and discussing my work, with which this remarkable young man showed a great interest." Brady stopped himself and leaned close. "And you will never guess who happened by."

⚘

Gardner's morning nap had ended suddenly. Wrapped snug in that dusty blanket, he slid from the edge of the sofa and had yet to regain his senses when he crashed against the floor. A piercing shot up through his slung right arm, pinned between his belly and the floorboards. His body shuddered; he rolled just enough to free the arm.

He lay there, lips pressed against the cold floor, his hot breath caressing his cheeks when a knock sounded at the door.

"Everything okay, Alex?"

Gardner scrambled to a seated position and braced himself with his good arm against the wobbly sofa. He ran a hand through his hair. "Yes, John. Be right with you."

"I'm going to start sitting customers. Lawrence has the floor."

Gardner was silent, which soon engendered a reply of its own.

"Gettin' a might busy down there."

"Thank you, John. I will see to it."

Gardner watched light seep through a narrow window.

Dust wafted over the storage room. He sat surrounded by linen-covered furniture, dull canvas backdrops, and props in various need of repair.

He had arrived at his studio in the predawn hours, lit the stove, intent on tackling neglected paperwork prior to what promised to be a busy day. Now two hours later, with the first appointments being escorted to the top floor to pose beneath the skylights, its proprietor was huddled asleep in a prop closet.

Disgusted with himself, Gardner stood. The blanket fell from round his disheveled shirt and vest. He prodded his slung right arm and shoulder. It ached, but he decided he would live. At that moment, Gardner had never felt so old; a discard, like the rest of the pieces in that frosty room.

He shuffled to the rain-spattered window. Four stories below, two men dressed in black hats and overcoats dodged slush pools at the corner of 7th and D. He cocked his head right and looked down toward Pennsylvania Avenue. A street car clanged. Its horse team inched into view as it pulled the vehicle along metal tracks entrenched in rough cobblestone. Looking east, above the row buildings along D Street, Gardner could discern the spires of St. Peter's Cathedral and to its right the Capitol dome, the faint shape of a bronzed Freedom atop her cupola. She stood ethereal in the drab gray of that February morning. Almost an aberration, not really there at all.

Gardner heard a man's bellowing laugh from the floor below. He reached for his suit coat folded over the sofa and pulled his watch from its pocket. Five minutes past nine. He grasped the lateness of things with a new measure of loathing before he raced down one flight to the stairwell entrance.

He put his left arm inside his coat, draping its remainder over his invalid right arm. He tugged once at his lapels before opening the door.

High windows filled the gallery with day's light. Beneath its chandeliered ceiling, patrons admired framed pictures that blanketed the crimson walls, under the watchful eyes of presidents and politicians; the product of Gardner's thirteen years in the nation's capital. Customers hovered over the glass countertop at mid-room where they considered purchases.

But today's special set of clientele formed a line behind a section of laced gold rope. A most unusual sight. Perhaps twenty couples, men and women, coddling infants and bouncing restless toddlers in their arms. A framed poster on an easel faced their way, a slighter version of the one pasted on the street window.

Gardner's Baby Show.
This week only. Make your appointment.
Win Top Prize!

Margaret had suggested the idea. As far as business ideas go, he had to admit it a good one. The past week's receipts proved it to be, which meant nearly every other studio in town would follow suit. The money was all well and good, but Gardner had to ask himself whether he would have even considered it a year or two ago. At least he had the staff capable of bearing the greater burden of such business.

"Mr. Gardner!"

Gardner looked to the middle of the line where a heavy-set man waved, a baby girl with a pink bow atop her head sat in the crook of his arm. Gardner had not the slightest idea who the man was, yet he stepped to and shook the man's hand with his free left arm, forcing the man to jostle the girl to his opposite arm.

"Wonderful of you to come. Thank you."

"My granddaughter. Little Abigail. Isn't she lovely?"

"Yes! How lovely indeed. How are you, Abagail?" Gardner pinched her cheek. The little girl's eyes filled with terror and she burst into tears. The man laughed as he began to bounce his granddaughter back to content-ment. Gardner thanked him for coming and moved down the line to greet others, commenting on how wonderful all the children looked. He did not pinch any more cheeks.

Gardner then did his best to muster enough energy to attend the morning's business. He studied the appointment book. To be expected, the bulk of sittings were scheduled now to noon with the day's strongest sun. It should be a good day. But nature did not always yield. A day of heavy storms and dark clouds might cause delay, as might a string of difficult subjects. Like babies, Gardner thought tetchily. In these instances, it was all about how to manage those restlessly waiting their turn, entertaining them in the gallery with stereo cards and refreshments. So much competition on the avenue these days, the customer's experience had to be first rate, no matter how many years you hung your sign out front.

On this morning, they ran on schedule. He set about his work, shifting between the gallery and the top floor where he helped pose subjects while his operators managed the cameras or worked the developing rooms.

When next he looked at his watch it was almost noon. He crossed the gallery floor.

"Lawrence, I have an appointment. Can you manage for an hour?"

The husky young man brushed brown locks from his forehead and smiled.

"Yes, father."

Gardner bent forward, dipped the pen and put it to paper.

"Congratulations, Alex. You are acquiring a good plot of land."

He glanced up to Hiram Arthur. The lawyer, wearing a gray wool suit and matching bowler, was a fellow Mason, who managed Gardner's investments, and a friend. Gardner signed as he surveyed the crowded Willard dining hall.

Men in white coats and pants rolled carts of steaming plates from the kitchen. Waiters raced over hardwood floors, slipping between tables with all stealth and efficiency. Even at this hour, groups of men took their whiskeys at the bar in a haze of smoke that Gardner could smell over the scent of so many dishes.

"This investment should be a boon to your children. I don't have to tell you the capital is exploding northward. No one will want to live in the city anymore."

Gardner proceeded to sign the last paper turned his way. The lawyer blew dry its signature and placed the stack in his leather satchel. Hiram Arthur drank the last of his coffee and proceeded to light a cigar. He puffed it a few times as the clamor of the room filled their break in conversation.

After a moment, Gardner watched a smirk form upon the lawyer's lips.

"I would like to know what happened to your arm. I was told at the lodge not to ask but you know me, I cannot resist."

Gardner scratched beneath the sling. "A misjudging, that's all. Carelessness."

"Looks quite uncomfortable. Studio mishap? Some camera prop?"

"Street curb," Gardner said. "It was there. My eyes were not."

Arthur's lips parted wide so that he nearly lost his glowing cigar.

The images flashed before Gardner; a rush of hooves from the hack that nearly ran him over before swerving, wheels inches from his face. Gardner rolling over on the street stones, staring vacant at gray sky, icy water soaking his back and a terrific pain in his arm. An elderly woman appearing over him, visibly shaken by the sight of scrapes and blood. These days it seemed Gardner was no longer capable of minding the ground beneath his feet. Mental slackness had finally bit him. His slung, useless appendage was his just and deserved reward.

The lawyer laughed, then coughed as he tapped out the cigar's first ash.

"Forgive me," Arthur said. "Do steer clear of those damned omnibuses, old friend. We would hate to lose you."

Gardner said nothing.

This appeared to disappoint the lawyer who puffed then pulled the cigar from his lips. "Oh, cheer up! You have a lot to be thankful for. Your investments are doing very well. I hear your studio does a booming business. You should be a happy man!"

Gardner forced a smile.

"I am."

Just then two gentlemen stepped to the table. They did not introduce themselves or think it rude to begin an inquisition with Arthur over some legal matter. But Gardner cared little. He saw an opportunity. He rose and said a quick goodbye to his friend.

Gardner cast his heavy coat onto his shoulders and put his free arm through its sleeve. He moved between tables, advancing past high-backed leather booths along the street-side wall. Through pane glass windows, he looked to the gray winter day. Its damp and chill promised at least an end to the smoke and noise.

"Mr. Gardner?"

He stopped and turned toward a booth.

He looked down upon a young man whose countenance bore a perfect mix of surprise and joy. Some part of Gardner recognized him; his clean, round face, long hair wet trailed back behind his ears.

"Truman Ash, sir," the young man said, scrambling up from behind the table's wide form. He thrust out his hand.

Gardner took a moment. He shook the hand. Then it came to him.

"Laramie."

"Yes! Fort Laramie. Why to think it nearly nine months ago!"

He let go Truman's hand, still disbelieving. *That boy from Laramie?* Gardner searched for the words to offer regarding their encounter in that faraway place when, from the corner of his eye, he saw a companion seated across the table.

Gardner turned and his heart fell into his chest.

"Hello, Alex."

Mathew Brady peered up through the tinted lenses of his steel-rimmed glasses. A grin formed above a trim goatee that, like the curls of his hair, were tinged with gray. Perhaps a year, more, Gardner thought, since he'd last seen him. But so much the same, the suit, and lavender scarf, the smell of Atwood's cologne. The same smug expression.

Brady offered his hand.

Later, when Gardner replayed the tortured moment in his head, he could not recall whether he had wits enough to shake it.

"The two of you do know one another then!"

"Yes," replied Brady. He clasped hands upon the table. "We know each other quite well."

Gardner felt the rush of blood to his head. A waiter scrambled past the booth, bumping a platter against the shoulder of Gardner's overcoat with fleeting apologies.

"I thought of paying you a visit these past months," said Truman, still on his feet. "I sent a letter to your studio, but it must have been lost in transit. I should have delivered it personally."

Gardner wanted to say something, anything. But his jaw shut tight.

"Well," Truman continued after a time, "first we meet and now here I am now with Mr. Brady. And I suppose it is a bit of a celebration, isn't it, Mr. Brady? Celebrating your petition to Congress."

Gardner blinked. He turned to Brady, then back at young Truman.

"Petition?"

Julia Brady put her hand to her mouth. "Alexander Gardner? Really?" Her eyes were full. "Oh, how is he? How is Margaret? The family?"

Brady predicted something akin to that reaction. There was a time when Julia and Margaret Gardner were quite close, in the days when Alex Gardner worked for Brady in New York.

And then early in the war, when neither Gardner nor Brady were home for long. For some time after his relationship with Gardner cooled, Brady felt guilty over having deprived his wife of such a true and dear friend. The women still wrote on occasion but saw nothing of each other.

"He seemed quite alright," Brady said with a laugh. "An arm on the mend but he otherwise appeared well indeed. The same Alex, you know. Always a man of few words. As far as his family goes well, I really don't know. We talked so little."

Julia nodded. Disappointment wore heavy upon her face as she batted her eyes to the folds of her dress.

Brady regretted mentioning it at all.

It now seemed all a tease, though he did not plan for it to be that way. A brief, uncomfortable crossing of paths. Nothing more. He took another drink.

To his surprise, Julia lifted her head with a smile. "Dinner!" she announced with a glint in her eyes.

Brady nearly choked on his last swallow.

"What's this?"

"The Gardners. We must have them for dinner. This Saturday perhaps. If they are free." She seized his hand. "To see Margaret would make me so happy!"

Brady held her in his gaze and managed a smile. But he felt ill. A minute with Alex Gardner was a minute longer than he thought he could bare, even for her.

"I don't know. Do you think it a good idea?"

"It's been such a long time. Too long. And now that you and Alex have seen one another it won't be an invitation out of nowhere. It's perfect. We'll have them here!"

"Here?" Brady questioned the surrounding walls. "We are hardly in a position to entertain."

"There is plenty of room here. It will be lovely."

Brady stammered, then surrendered. "Yes, of course. You write the invitation out, my dear. But don't get too excited about Saturday. It's but a few days away."

Julia fell back upon the settee.

Brady held his beaming wife in his eyes, left only with disappointment. He had tried for months to brighten her sullen spirit. He arrived home hoping news of his petition to Congress might do just that. *A return to form.* Financial boon or otherwise, the government's purchase promised a second act in their grand play.

Instead, it was the thought of the Gardners that moved her. All the joy now left him for her, he drank his glass empty. "I must ready to go." he said, rising from the sofa.

"I packed you a small bag."

She rose with him and pulled close. "Thank you," she said against his ear and kissed him, making it almost worth it.

That evening the Gardners gathered in their two-story brick at 485 E Street North, a few short blocks from his studio. Ten minutes to seven and the winter day already done, a candelabra on the table cast erratic patterns of light upon the green-papered wall and its framed oil of the Port of Glasgow.

Gardner watched his daughter Eliza, seated to his right. Already nineteen. He remembered that 31st of July in '49 as if it were yesterday. A young woman now. Margaret Gardner, across the table, revealed the source of his daughter's beauty and buoyant charm. She wore the same cheery face and soft blue eyes. A beauty at nearly fifty years, he knew long ago he won the better deal when it came to their partnership. And Gardner's mother, Jean Glen, sat peacefully, smiling and doting upon them all, as she had done for so many years, even before her deafness and infirmities took hold.

"Thank you, Emily," Margaret said. "Now please come and join us. You can clean up later."

Emily Newman entered the room with a kettle of tea and filled Gardner's cup, then Margaret's.

"Thank you, ma'am. But I've got something special for dessert and I already ate more than I should have when the food was still cookin'! Don't mind me at all."

Eliza laughed and Emily gave her a playful nudge. "You best behave, Miss Eliza, if you want any of my sugar loaf."

Emily had become like family since they hired her in to their home and spare room two years ago. A forty-year-old woman who grew up a slave on a Virginia plantation, slight in form but as strong a woman as Gardner had ever known. Emily Newman likely knew more about hard living than any of them could fathom.

The thud of heavy feet drew Gardner's attention. Lawrence flew past and threw his stocky frame into the lone empty chair, nearly knocking over Emily, who braced herself with a hand on Eliza' chair.

"Lord dear!" Emily said with amused surprise.

"Lawrence! Mind yourself," Margaret admonished.

"Sorry, Miss Emily."

Emily rolled her eyes. "No matter." She left for the kitchen.

Lawrence Gardner wasted no time in lowering his head to the plate of roast beef and boiled onions before him, shoveling in a first mouthful. Two years older than his sister, fate had awarded Lawrence his father's looks, round eyes to match a round face, clean-shaven, that would not quite yet support a proper beard. Busy these days, with a million things and nothing at all. It had been three months since Lawrence left his clerk's position at the Treasury Department. He had helped out at the studio since, and performed dutifully, Gardner had to admit. Long ago Gardner had taught his son the art of photography. Lawrence, in turn, showed a polite disinterest. Yet he contributed in other ways, helping to keep ledgers, working the counter, and managing appointments. It was temporary until the young man found his passion. Margaret told Gardner that his son inherited not only his father's looks but too his restlessness. And Gardner believed it. He could see more of him in his son than he would care to admit.

Gardner took another bite. But even such a fine meal was not his to enjoy. Not after a day like today.

Eliza turned to her father. "Tomorrow, mother and I are going down to the avenue. Breakfast then a visit to the shops. Can you get away to join us? Brother here has already said no. I know you would not have the heart to tell me that."

My heavens was she her mother's child, Gardner thought. Three Scot women under a single roof, Emily too. Many a stronger man would feel threatened by it.

But Gardner resisted the urge to acquiesce. He shook no. "I have business tomorrow. There is much to do these days. Shopping is not one of them."

Gardner wiped his mouth and eyed his daughter's pout, a look mastered and not forgotten from childhood days.

"Oh, father. You and your work."

Lawrence stared a moment at his sister, then shrugged his broad shoulders. He took another slice of bread from the basket and began lapping gravy from his plate.

"No matter," added Margaret. "Perhaps material for a new spring dress, two in fact. It will be here sooner than you think."

Gardner drank his water. Upon setting the glass down, he caught sight of Margaret's icy stare. Her blue eyes narrow and lips drawn tight. He took her countenance to mean that he had somehow erred and would soon hear more.

❧

The hearth fire glowed.

Gardner, alone in his rocker, enjoyed the fragrant smoke of a cherry log. In the last ten minutes, Lawrence and the women had all taken to their rooms, leaving behind a knitting basket, and a book on the reading table beside a creased newspaper. Margaret followed Eliza up the stairs to bid her good night.

Gardner would have liked to retire himself, putting the day to its merciful end. But Margaret would return, and he owed her something of a conversation.

She came down the stairs. He stoked the fire until she returned from the kitchen with two cups of tea. He went back to his rocker. She wrapped a red and green patterned shawl over her shoulders and sat on the rug at his feet with some effort, finally putting her right arm upon his left leg.

"So, tell me," she said, as a schoolmarm might address a mischievous schoolboy, his guilt of some misdeed assumed.

"What do you mean?"

"Alex Gardner. If I knew that, I wouldn't be asking. Only you know what is eating at you."

He sipped his tea. He knew he would not get off so easy.

Margaret had suffered his melancholy these last months, but she knew what bothered him now was more substantial, something tangible. She could read him. No use in pretending.

And so Gardner opened up. He told her about Brady.

She listened in silence, about Senator Wilson's petition which this young man Truman had so innocently made Gardner aware, all the while Brady sitting there idle. Mathew Brady, *Photographer of the late war.*

Gardner's blood was up when he stopped his rambling. Damn her for making him go on in such a way uncontested. And damn Brady.

Gardner seemed destined to live in that man's shadow.

Margaret set her tea on the floor and turned up at him. "So just what is it then that bothers you about all of this? Is it your pride? The money?"

He still would not meet her eyes. And she pressed: "Or do you think that his gain can only come at your expense?"

He said nothing.

"Look at me."

He did.

"You have made something of yourself. And you need nothing else to prove that you've done well for you and yours."

He studied her blue eyes, their look of concern. He took a deep breath and put a hand on her. "Right as ever you are."

There was no arguing with her reasoning. He drank his tea.

As if a weight had been lifted, he did feel better about things. They sat in quiet, watching the fire burn.

"This is nice. We might do this more often," he offered.

"We used to plenty. Sitting. Talking hours on end. If you recall."

"I do. I do."

She laughed, then pulled at his knee. "Remember? That old hovel of ours on Brunswick when we were first married?"

Gardner smiled. It would never have been had he not been so stubborn as to spend a little more money on sufficient lodgings instead of scrimping for his next great venture. And she let him go along with it.

"Sorry place!" cried Margaret with laughter. "Leaky roof and pots everywhere!"

"Never had to go far to fetch the bath water," quipped Gardner, unable to restrain the smile that spread over his face.

They laughed, the laughter to him like a long lost friend. They talked until the fire gasped in short glowing fits, when Margaret rose with the slightest moan. "It is my bed for me."

She turned and kissed his lips. "So then, this silly matter about a petition is settled, Mr. Gardner?" she asked, a smile belying serious eyes.

He smiled. "It is, Mrs. Gardner."

She kissed him, then took away empty cups. He told her he would wait out the fire. And there Gardner sat and thought about the passage of time.

꧁

With the clock's strike at eleven, a new log burned on the fire. On the end table rested an inkwell.

Gardner tapped the broadside of his nib pen to his lips, reading by firelight what he had written so far on the sheet of paper in his lap.

He would rewrite it again; a single, succinct page to make clear his own case to Congress.

II

B rady purchased his ticket at the brownstone depot at New Jersey and C Street, just north of the Capitol. He hurried down the length of the pillared car house. He met a man, outside the first coach, who wore a black hat and coat with gold trim.

Brady pocketed the stub and boarded the New York and Washington Air Line.

The car was warm from a box-stove heater at back that worked to quash the cold outside. Filled to about half, from unaccompanied men to families with heavy-eyed youngsters and restless infants. An attendant slipped down the aisle, issuing baggage checks. Brady sat across from an old woman who cradled in her lap shawl a boy who fidgeted sleep.

The Night Express was to arrive in New York at 6:09 am. He would return home again at nine tomorrow night. A short trip to tie up many things. An appearance at his New York studio, then off to complete the sale of the land parcel.

Finally, Brady would pay visit to the Manhattan warehouse that had prompted this rushed trip in the first place.

He took the last of their letters, received just two days ago, from his coat pocket and unfolded it against the low light of a wall lamp.

Mr. Brady,

As our previous attempts have failed to prompt you into action, be advised that it will be necessary in one week's time to seek legal action in order to take possession of inventory and liquidate in lieu of payment. Contact us immediately to address the matter.

Franz & Associates Storage
361 John Street, New York

He was days from selling his collections to the government and these people would just as soon sell his plates for scrap.

No. He would settle it once and for all, pay the current bill and storage fees a year forward. More than ample time to protect his assets until they transferred to the National Archives.

The train whistled.

Brady tucked away his letter and shifted on the cushioned bench so as to rest his right shoulder against the wall. He shut his heavy eyes and listened to steam's release, the slow chuffing and its steady increase.

He hoped the clack of the rolling train would lull him to slumber.

But to no avail. Sleep would not come to a man of forty-six years who, tired or not, had so much to consider.

He stared out the window as dark and indecipherable shapes sped past. He thought about the congressmen he paid visit to at the Willard that afternoon, the first to hear about his petition. Having known these men for some time, each sounded their approval.

About time. Hear hear! Good for you, Mathew.

Let me know how I can help.

It sounds well and good, but you know I need a bill to cast a vote.

Brady had his clerk start letters that afternoon, addressed to each member of the Committee on the Library who would need to draft the required legislation.

Three senators. Edwin Morgan of New York, who chaired the committee, had not won his reelection. These days were his last in the Senate. The other two, Senator Timothy Howe of Wisconsin and William Fessenden, the old stalwart Secretary of the Treasury and Chairman on the Joint Committee on Reconstruction, would stay on. None of the three House members on the committee had sought reelection: Baldwin of Massachusetts, Pruyn from Albany, and the four-term Rufus Spalding of Ohio. Yet they could still be of use.

All of them had sat for Brady's camera.

But so many congressmen who had served during the war would soon be gone, even old Ben Wade who presided over the Senate with his gavel.

New faces would fill the halls of Congress, many of them younger men; wealthy, privileged, and from new corners of the nation. To them the war was never so acutely felt; a burdensome past that shifted attention away from the future. *Let the county move on, and west, already.*

It was for them and all the future generations that he did this. It was for those who might need their proof of that war.

And Brady knew this might be his last, best chance.

He had a different sort of letter in mind for Senator Henry Wilson. It was a letter of thanks. One of personal gratitude to a friend who came through, even if it took longer than expected.

It seemed fitting that Wilson would be the one to come to his aid.

They had been connected to that war from the start.

Brady shut his eyes once more. He felt himself relax closer to sleep.

His final waking thoughts were about Wilson, and Wade, and others on one eventful summer's day when Lincoln's cobbled army was to end the rebellion once and for all.

Summer 1861

The wagon pulled roadside where a gray mare and two Sorrel horses stood tied in the shade of a towering oak.

The hour approached noon.

A few miles distant over green forested hills, the muffle of heavy guns sounded the other side of a creek called Bull Run.

Timothy O'Sullivan lowered the reins atop the bench of their single-horse van.

Brady took the folds of his white linen duster and climbed down. He removed a straw hat from his head and wiped beads of sweat from his forehead, eyeing blue skies that cradled the blistering July sun.

Morning before last, Brady recalled Julia's laughter at the sight of his chosen wardrobe before their bedroom mirror. *You look the painter* she had told him. He stood there and studied himself. He thought about his instruments and the work that lay ahead of him. *That seems about right then*, was his only reply.

It was a squat and strange vehicle in which they arrived. A wagon, its bed three feet across and four deep. It had a wire-rimmed roof draped in black cloth. The macabre-looking transport had drawn stares all the way from Capitol City.

But it was sturdy in wheel and fit for hard travel, and stowed inside its walls was everything necessary to record history in the coming hours and days.

"Wait here, Tim." Brady cast a glance up the hill before them, its dry summer grass trodden in paths the battery horses had made to reach her crest. "I think I'll stretch my legs a bit."

Tim O'Sullivan plucked his suspenders. The thin Irishman scratched his bristly beard and spat tobacco juice the opposite way in reply.

Brady smiled and shook his head. He had personally trained O'Sullivan, the boy he once found wandering the nooks and dirt byways of

Staten Island. Rugged but thoroughly competent with a camera, Tim was just the man to accompany Brady all the way to Richmond.

Brady pulled free his cane from below the bench seat and started out.

He could see horses beside limbers and detached caissons at the summit. He then saw the four six pounders pointed west, and blue coat artillery regulars aside the quiet guns.

He had found Tidball's battery, just south of the heights at Centerville.

Closer now, Brady glimpsed the backs of a second group of men, civilians standing watch over a panorama of rolling meadow and dense wood. Faint traces of the Blue Ridge Mountains appeared beyond thin smoke that rose and dispersed into clear sky over treetops a few miles distant.

Somewhere, over there, the Union boys were finally giving hell to the Rebels.

For months the soldiers had deluged Washington, their camp fires lit up the surrounding hills like all the stars in heaven. They drilled in every vacant lot and made mischief in the brothels and faro houses that seemed to sprout daily. Their smoked hams greased the marble floors of the Capitol rotunda, and they slept on Senate gallery benches when not amusing themselves by staging mock sessions. *Forward to Richmond* headlined Horace Greely's *New York Tribune*, echoing a nation's anxiousness to scatter the Confederate Army.

They saved some pay for Brady's. They washed through the gallery like a tidal flood. They muddied his crimson carpets and sofas and left fingerprints on the French mirrors and Imperial portraits, waiting their turn before the camera with all the impatience of pampered children. A drum and fife were often heard. A fiddle player would have them in full song. They succeeded in chasing away any self-respecting patron as they rushed to procure their likeness in uniform, while the war was still on.

Brady had watched the Independence Day parade from his studio window. Confetti showers rained from rooftops and raucous cheers greeted those tight unison forms with sunlit bayonets; the kilted New York's 79th

Highlanders, the 7th in resplendent grays, the 69th Zouaves in bright coats and pantaloons. The batteries on the surrounding hills boomed until nightfall to announce the long-awaited push into Virginia, until finally here they were, now, at Manassas.

Brady caught a glimpse of Captain Tidball, his rough beard beneath a blue cap, standing among the hilltop pack. He started toward the captain.

"Halt!"

An artillerist thrust out an open palm to Brady's chest.

Brady held up his hands but could not help a slight grin at the boy's appearance, pudgy cheeks and a mess of wooly hair sprouting beneath a blue kepi with its crossed cannon insignia.

"Mathew! Glad you could join us."

Brady and the soldier boy turned in unison.

Senator Henry Wilson, in rolled white shirt sleeves, stepped forward. Senators Jim Lane of Kansas and Ben Wade of Ohio looked on, holding jackets over their shoulders. The great Senate triumvirate came to witness victory first hand.

Captain Tidball stood grinning beside them.

"Oh, rubbish!" Wilson said in a harsh tone directed at the thwarting soldier. "Do you know who this is?"

The private stepped back. He began to look anxious.

"At ease," said Tidball in a low draw. He ambled toward Brady. A veteran of the Mexican War, the captain had fought beside half the generals now commanding either side of the present conflict. Brady had always found him a genial sort, far more so than his rugged appearance suggested.

"Perfectly alright," said Brady. He ran his fingers into the pocket of his duster until he found the small card of hard stock within. "Have a look." He pulled it out, handing it over.

The private took the note and scanned it. Brady watched the soldier's eyes widen and lips part before he thrust the card out for his captain as if holding a hot plate.

Brady could not help but smile as he recalled the simple, yet effective message upon the card.

Pass Brady
A. Lincoln

⤖

Brady's plan had taken work. It began with a visit to an old friend, General Winfield Scott, at his 17th and I Street headquarters.

He found the heavy-set general, the seventy-four year old hero of 1812 and the Mexican War, in a loose knit shirt and sprawled in a recliner beside a table cluttered with maps.

Brady daguerreotype of General Winfield Scott, Old "Fuss and Feathers"
Circa 1849, a dozen years before the Civil War

There, old Scott confided to Brady in a mournful tone.

"I tell you this Brady, and it is not yet official. No one but my aide knows, but McDowell is to succeed me tomorrow. He will direct the forces in Northern Virginia. He is your man."

But with McDowell holed up in Lee's former residence at Arlington Heights, Brady and the press corps were held at bay. They were told only that they could access the field so long as they bore all costs and did not interfere with military operations.

Brady thought he might do better than that.

Candidate Lincoln at Brady's in N.Y.C, Feb. 1860, day of the Cooper Union Address *The President-Elect, photo by Gardner at Brady's in D.C., one year later*

Then President-Elect Lincoln had first visited Brady's Washington studio in late February. The following month, Brady was allowed to erect a wooden platform on the East Front. From this privileged vantage, Alex Gardner and another of Brady's cameramen photographed the inauguration under raw March skies.

Thousands of onlookers listened, with sharpshooters along the rooftops, as Lincoln spoke of two sides being not enemies, but friends, and appealed to the *better angels of our nature*, before the Marine Band played them out. A half-finished Capitol dome served an apropos backdrop for the nation's perilous state.

Then, one afternoon last week, Brady was hurried into the room at 1600 Pennsylvania Avenue by Lincoln's old law partner and self-appointed bodyguard, Marshal Lamon Hill. The president rose from behind his desk, smiling through a new beard.

"Mr. President. Mathew Brady," Lamon began. Brady could feel the press of the brute's claw hammer suit against his back.

Lincoln laughed and took Brady's hand. "Don't introduce me to Brady. Brady and the Cooper Union Speech made me president!"

True enough perhaps. It was Brady's 1860 photograph of candidate Lincoln at his Broadway studio that had done what no other cameraman had done. A flattering pose, the proper angle and a raised collar to diminish a long neck, had turned the gangly backwoodsman into the dignified statesman seen in photographs and on thousands of election posters.

Ward stayed close as Brady hurried through his plan with the president, without flourish or detail.

And he got his battlefield pass.

⌘

Captain Tidball returned the card.

Brady reached out to take back the pass and watched as the captain's gaze directed elsewhere, somewhere over Brady's shoulder.

"Looks like you came prepared."

Brady turned and realized Tidball's comment was in reference to his van, below at roadside, where O'Sullivan tended to the horse.

"Well, that is a strange site," added Wilson.

Brady nodded. "Necessary I assure you," he began. "My work is done from the light-proof well of the wagon. Everything I need inside it. Chemicals, baths, glass plates. The cameras themselves. We have for two days now taken exposures of troops and encampments. Of course, capturing the battle itself will not be possible. The exposure would take far too long to capture such movement. If you recall, gentlemen, how I trouble you at the studio by placing the backs of your heads in the immobilizer. Stillness is essential to a quality photograph. But-"

Brady formed a calculated grin to accompany a remark sure to please his company, "I believe I'll manage to record plenty from here to Richmond."

Wilson's eyes gleamed bright. He hit Brady across the shoulder. "Yes, by God!"

Wade offered an affirming nod, but Senator Lane's stony gaze held. Wade had a reputation for intemperance, but he was no match for Jim Lane of Kansas, known to many as *Bloody Jim*.

"Two days, you say? Tell me what you have seen so far, Mr. Brady," demanded the wiry Lane as the wind blew back his tousled brown hair.

The three senators stood, awaiting Brady's answer.

Henry Wilson was Chairman on the Committee on Military Affairs, but that afternoon, with the battle now underway, even he was at the mercy of what officers and passing soldiers might tell him. Tidball's battery, part of Blenker's 5th Brigade in Miles' 1st division, were in reserve on this crest until further notice.

The fated battle was being waged far from where they now stood.

And so Brady began his tale as Lane requested. He, along with Al Waud, illustrator for *Harper's*, and two reporters, House and McCormick of the *Tribune* and *New-York Evening*, respectively, had crossed the Long Bridge on the 16th. McDowell's forces had brushed through Fairfax Courthouse and on to Centerville when the Confederates fell back along the far banks of the Bull Run with nary a musket shot or cannonade.

Brady camped his first night in a starlit meadow, bounded by the wood smoke of a thousand campfires. The morning of the 18th, he ventured down the Centerville Road when fighting broke out at Blackburn's Ford.

The 1st Massachusetts and 12th New York were repelled by Rebels gathered in the heavy wood across the creek.

"A shell exploded not fifty yards from me," Brady added with flourish.

For two anxious days, Brady and O'Sullivan ventured out along the turnpike, photographing troops and batteries. A few dozen negatives so far. Brady thought to have the first plates shuttled back to Gardner at the studio to ready them for quick publication, then dismissed the idea. They would be safe enough with him.

"And this morning when shelling began, six or about that hour, we ascended the ridge at Centerville to try and gauge things. But as we all know, at that distance, it was no use."

As the morning wore on, civilians began arriving from Washington. Gentlemen and ladies, wielding bright-colored parasols and picnic baskets, blanketed the hillside. Brady was party to their frustrated spy glass stares and wanton speculation. *Did you hear that? Oh, wasn't that a splendid volley?*

Brady ventured southwest, until he came upon Tidball's battery on the ridge.

"I'm afraid that brings you gentlemen up to date with my adventure thus far."

Lane's tight face and piercing eyes did more than hint at his dissatisfaction with Brady's tepid story. The senator turned west. He took a field glass from his pocket and pulled its length full. He stared out in futility.

"Well," Lane said, lowering his glass to wipe his brow, "I am not about to end this day without some hand in it!"

"We'll get you there, Jim," Wade replied.

⌘

Brady marked the passing of fifteen minutes on his watch piece when he spotted the lone rider approaching from the woods west. Lane waved the man down with apparent success as he crossed the meadow before them and climbed the ridge, stopping some twenty yards from the crest.

Tidball stepped forward to study the young man, a civilian, in a tattered gray frock. His brown mare looked spent from the crossing and hardly fit for service.

"We've got 'em now," the man pronounced from his horse between breathes. "Just cleanin' 'em up!" A toothy grin showed above his blonde stubble chin. "Won't be long and you'll see."

But he did not linger to take questions. He tipped his slouch hat and turned with a kick to the haggard mare, back down the way he came.

The captain scratched his chin. "Wonder where that bugger came from?" he questioned aloud, then turned away.

Brady watched a hack pull up alongside O'Sullivan and the van below. Its two occupants climbed the hill before they were halted by the same private who stopped Brady. They were house actors at Grover's, they announced, as if that accounted for something. Come to see the battle.

Senator Lane decided he had enough. "Ah cuss," he shouted. "We don't know a damned thing!"

Lane pulled Wilson and Wade in close to confer. The conversation was brief. Lane began plodding down the ridge toward their horses. Wade trailed, responding to Lane's back with a comment Brady could not discern.

"Never mind that. I can easily find a musket on the field," Lane barked over his shoulder as he marched.

Wilson took several steps further before turning back. "We are off, Mathew! See you in Richmond."

Brady watched the triumvirate move down the slope and mount horses. They started out, north and west, through tall grass and into the edge of woods that concealed the turnpike.

More vehicles and riders began to pull up behind Brady's van.

They started up the ridge on foot. Captain Tidball went out to meet them. They peppered him with questions for which he had no answers.

They would be just as disappointed as they were upon the heights of Centerville.

Brady thought about his options. It did not take long to decide.

～～

Brady and O'Sullivan backtracked toward Centerville. They would move faster by road and the plates would be safer were they not to attempt crossing the open field. It was twenty minutes before they could turn south and west along the Warrenton Turnpike that led across Bull Run. Steady along the level road, they pulled aside for the occasional riders or band of army wagons. The cannons sounded, not so distant as before.

Troops gathered at various points in the dense roadside wood. Brady recognized New York regiments, sitting in shade from the hot July sun.

"What's it you got in back there?"

"Hey mister, let me buy one of your pies."

"Captain says hush up!"

"Go to hell, George. You said we was fightin' today."

The road opened past the woods upon a rolling country. They crossed a small bridge over a tributary Brady had heard referred to as Cub Run. From there the road descended, snaking through a heavy wood until it cleared and sloped toward a stone bridge where the turnpike crossed Bull Run. The artillery barrage was now deafening at times. A thin smoke wafted over the road; the acrid smell of powder filled Brady's nostrils.

Perhaps a dozen men gathered upon a knoll before the bridge. O'Sullivan pulled off and tied the horse at a maple there. Brady lifted the stereo camera from the wagon and carried its legs and the box itself in the crux of his arm up the face of the slope until he reached the group, among them William A. Croffut from the *Tribune.*

"Morning, Mathew." said Croffut as he licked his fingers, turned the page on his pad and scribbled. "Not far off now. Of course, you can hear, can't you?" The reporter pointed northwest. "Hunter's division crossed further upstream and come down." He then had to shout over a barrage. "Across the bridge and just beyond those hills. But I'd be careful with that camera of yours to go any further just yet. Hot over there right now. Course you can hear it, can't you?"

"I think here is just fine for now, William."

Brady latched legs onto the camera and began positioning for angles. The men watched with curiosity.

O'Sullivan climbed the hill with plates and over the course of a half hour they managed three images of the stone bridge below them.

Brady saw nothing more of the three senators that day. Cavalry and wagon crossed the stone bridge at intervals. Smoke rolled east in clusters. Brady pulled out his watch. Nearly four in the afternoon. He had not eaten all day and now felt the pangs of hunger. He and O'Sullivan returned to the wagon below.

Brady went to his pack, and they split four thick slices of bread and dried beef in the shade of the maple. Between mouthfuls, O'Sullivan proposed he ride down to the creek and water the horse. They would need to do so before they crossed the bridge when the army advanced.

~

Brady had nearly fallen asleep through the din when a closer volley stirred him from the grass.

He stood and brushed his pant legs.

Down through the trees and toward the bridge came two riderless horses. The horses stopped and turned back to wander the far side of the creek bank. This generated a few laughs above from the men still upon the knoll. Brady thought little of it until a band of riders appeared and passed over the bridge and rode on with deliberate speed.

Brady stepped into the road. The next wave of them appeared soon after. Brady hailed them.

A mounted officer slowed, sweat streaked upon his dirty face.

"We're licked. They're falling back. Best you get back to Centerville and fast."

Brady turned sharp to O'Sullivan. The officer did not wait and tore away.

Three men came down from the knoll, one smiling as he approached.

"What'd he say?"

Brady repeated it. One dismissed it outright. The other two snickered but began to saunter for their tied horses. The rest began gathering their things and descending the hill. More riders now. Three to four wagons appeared over the horizon, their pace anything but casual. Then a ripple of arms fire. Brady scratched his goatee and looked to O'Sullivan.

"Get the wagon."

O'Sullivan packed the camera away. He untied the horse and turned the wagon east upon the road. Brady's first look back from the bench at a hundred yards revealed Union soldiers racing headlong toward the bridge. More than a few splashed into the creek to chase down one of the meandering horses drinking there.

O'Sullivan spat a wad; brown juices trickled down into his goatee.

"Looks like trouble if we can't get a move on."

O'Sullivan pushed the mare hard with little to show for it. Riders sped past their lumbering van, even a munitions wagon, and then another.

No time to panic. But Brady feared for their safety, for the plates.

Dozens of wagons and riders now caught up and moved past. Brady lost sight of the soldiers and bridge as the road turned into heavier wood.

They were soon forced to stop, the road ahead choked with supply wagons. Foot soldiers slipped between the gaps. Men began abandoning wagons and the pack tightened behind them.

O'Sullivan drove the van slowly off road at a level stretch as the sound of shell thundered behind them, each volley closer than before.

They found the smaller bridge at Cub Run jammed with the army's remnants. O'Sullivan steered the mare through its maze and managed to inch across it.

They just crossed when the bombardment commenced.

The Rebels had come up and began shelling all along the road. What followed made the exodus until now seem orderly.

Panic ensued.

A shell exploded on the bridge. Brady saw the dust and smoke; he heard screams and the shattering of wood. Soldiers, who had plodded forward in a haggard state only minutes ago, now surged forward from it. A foot race for survival.

Brady glimpsed an overturned wagon and horses splayed on broken wood planks, the panicked mob tripping over the debris and one another. Men bounded into the water and across it, soaking their trousers by various degree. On this side of the creek, white-eyed men grasped at any nearby horse or wagon, tipping them as they climbed aboard and overloaded one side. Men fought to free the horses harnessed to any load for a speedier flight to safety.

O'Sullivan kicked the horse harder.

The first man to reach them leapt onto the well and clawed for something firm. Brady watched him pull back the cloth roof before falling back to earth with the black drape in his fists.

"Faster, Tim."

Brady committed himself to action. He climbed from the bench and inched toward the back, finding his feet between the two jostling cameras and plate boxes.

He slashed with his cane at a soldier who clung to the side of the wagon. A man threw his torso into the back bed but no sooner began sliding away. He took hold of one of the cameras. Brady rapped at the man's fleshy hand with his cane. The man let go with a yell. He showed his sweat-stained face, a look of hurt and surprise in his eyes, as he crashed onto the road.

The first camera slid off the back. Its box smashed and splintered upon the turnpike.

The second camera bounced toward the edge. Men now pulled themselves up and over the wagon. Brady ignored them when he saw a plate box inch toward the lip.

Brady reached for it, but the container slid off. He could feel himself losing balance and he grasped in vain at the wagon's right wall. Corked bottles clanked and fell with him. Brady managed to swing his body round so that his boots might hit first.

No sooner than his feet made contact with the road, they were gone. His left shoulder punched the ground.

He lie dazed a moment, clutching his arm. When he came to, he realized the possibility of being trampled to death. He rolled away into the grass as a wagon sped past.

Brady got up on knees. He felt his face, grateful that his glasses were still dangling there. He fumbled them up once more upon his nose. He spotted O'Sullivan and the van just as the last camera fell out, its brass tube snapping clean from the box on impact. A second box of plates fell open in the road, its contents smashed by shoe and hoof and wheel. One of the soldiers now crowding the vacant bed took extra measure to lift the third and final carton and hoist it over the side.

The mass of bodies brought the wagon to a teeter. It tipped to its right. Brady watched O'Sullivan leap clear of the bench as the wagon spilled over into the roadway.

O'Sullivan picked himself up. Through the shroud of dust, he raced back to Brady.

Brady stood, watching as the traffic beat their work into the dirt. It was no use in staying for glass plates cracked beyond repair. Staying there might even mean capture.

They caught their breath and hurried ahead for a time until the shelling drew out of range.

Union artillery batteries had taken up positions along the turnpike and now sounded a challenge to the Confederate guns.

Brady saw Captain Tidball's battery among them. Those once quiet guns working hot now pointed west at Bull Run.

Panic ebbed, and the great horde beat the turnpike toward Centerville. Brady and O'Sullivan, walked shoulder to shoulder beside the sulking army. At one point, a soldier turned and handed Brady his sword and scabbard with nary a word. The man's dark face, his sad and heavy eyes, seemed to tell Brady that he was done with fighting.

Fears of a Confederate pursuit ended by nightfall. So too settled in the fact that there would be no counteroffensive. Storm clouds passed over a half-moon and a light, drumming rain began. Brady and O'Sullivan joined the thousands of exhausted men who left the muddy road and threw themselves down in fields east of Centerville for a few hours rest.

⌒⌒⌒

Brady and O'Sullivan made the Long Bridge just before noon. They crossed over into a city very much awake to a new reality. The first of the wagons and cavalry had begun arriving after midnight. Now the streets were filled with civilians watching and tending to a battered army. He and O'Sullivan reached the avenue and climbed the stairs to the studio's second-floor gallery. They sprawled themselves upon the sofas, mud-stained clothes and all.

Gardner rushed glasses of water to them.

"Julia has already been here twice," he told Brady.

Brady soon rose and shook the clouds from his mind. Gardner led him down the stairs.

"Wait!" Brady said.

He found the energy to lead the way back up the stairs and to the top floor.

As Brady instructed, Gardner readied the camera.

Brady posed in profile, wearing his matted straw hat, the shape of a scabbard jutting through the underneath of his linen duster.

Mathew Brady, just after Bull Run

III

Gardner hurried through the bronze doors of the Senate Chamber. No sooner inside, he was engulfed by a body of men being herded toward him like sheep to pen. He side-stepped elbows and shoulders as they crowded past; he shielded his slung arm from them. There was the pungent smell of tobacco in their suits, the warm breath of coffee and even whiskey at that early hour.

Gardner's ears registered the pounding of a gavel above the cacophony. Session was about to begin.

"Clear the chamber. Call to order. You, sir. Clear the chamber."

Gardner stared back at the mustachioed sergeant-at-arms in his button down black coat, a crooked index finger pointed his way. A man bumped Gardner's invalid arm. He winced and pulled his arm in and filed out with the last of them.

Gardner followed the tide of men across the hall, up the wide stairs to the Gentlemen's Gallery. He took a seat on the lowest row of gallery benches and looked down upon the chamber.

He saw Senator Samuel Pomeroy was there below, his balding head over top his desk, as he scribbled something on paper.

51

Gardner cursed himself for not arriving sooner. He should have taken an earlier street car, one that might not have made so many prolonged stops along the avenue. He had missed a chance to speak with Pomeroy, the man in whose hands Gardner's dim hopes now rested.

A brief quiet accompanied the Morning Prayer by the silver-haired and bespectacled Reverend Edgar Gray. The body then proceeded to its morning business; petitions, resolutions, and then Reports of the Committees. These items were followed by the resurrection of a tense debate on what to do about the pay of former secessionist senators.

Only six months ago, the present Congress had pondered the impeachment of President Johnson. Thaddeus Stevens himself, the Republican leading the failed charge to rid Johnson, fell victim to those taxing days and died soon after. That sordid and vindictive business now behind the nation, passions still simmered.

And so did the drum politic beat on.

For all their bickering, it surprised Gardner that the body managed to push through any legislation.

Now, corruption seemed the greatest threat to a Union restored only a few years ago with so much bloodshed.

The papers were filled with constant allegations of elicit gifts, free railroad stock, even cash when all else failed.

And it was plain to see the effects of these so-called *lobbyists*; railroaders, the mining interests, and the remainder. New committees had sprouted up just to handle their demands: Mines and Mining, Pacific Railroads. Men like Sam Ward and Collis Huntington spent lavish sums hosting dinners on behalf of their constituents, businessmen and the great railroad czars seeking land grants and charters. There were professional agents; the *Strikers*, who guaranteed legislation in exchange for retainers and healthy commissions. Others, men like Representative Grenville Dodge of Iowa, the former general and railroad engineer, found they could best push forward their agenda by joining the ranks of Congress itself.

It was enough to make Gardner sick, to think the course of national affairs was commanded by the purse strings of the wealthiest, that it could come to this after all the sacrifice.

Over the years, Senator Pomeroy had been a friend to Gardner. The Kansas politician had not escaped accusations of corruption either, but Gardner trusted the man who came to Congress in '61. The Pomeroy he knew was a man of ideals, concerned with the plight of drought-stricken farmers, woman's suffrage, and Negro equality.

It was Pomeroy who called upon Gardner to accept a commission on the Kansas Railway expedition in '67. But it was Gardner who needed Pomeroy now. Today. Tomorrow would not do.

Gardner rose from his seat, climbed the gallery steps and paced the hall to the Press Gallery above the rostrum. He hailed a passing reporter on his way from his desk to the telegraph office behind the gallery, to trouble him for a sheet of paper and pencil. Gardner scribbled a quick note.

Sam. Alex Gardner. Would like to speak to you. Will be in reception room when you have a moment.

Gardner descended the stairs to the western lobby doors and spotted a page about to enter the closed chamber.

"Excuse me, young man."

Gardner waited on a settee in the Senate Reception Room. He fidgeted, too restless to admire the beauty of the place, its intricate plasterwork and bright Italian frescoes beneath a bronze chandelier. At intervals, senators would appear, greeting waiting constituents. Gardner wondered how long he might sit.

"Alex. How are you?"

Gardner stood fast upon his feet as Pomeroy approached with an extended hand, a smile wide beneath his dark beard.

"Good to see you again," Pomeroy said, holding the note card. "What happened to your arm?"

"Long story, I'm afraid."

Senator Pomeroy laughed. "Then we will leave it that. Now, what's this all about? Please sit. Has it warmed outside yet? I have not been outside in nearly two days. I am so very tired of this winter. But forget all of that. Sit. I have just a moment."

Gardner knew that many a haggard congressmen sat all but chained to their mahogany desks in these closing days of Congress. Senator Wade would often announce a midday recess with instructions to reconvene for evening session.

Many never left the Capitol walls, eating in the Senate restaurant near the rotunda, bathing in the marble hot-baths in the basement, tidying in the north wing barbershop. They found moments to relax in the lounge, to talk and smoke and take a whisky. Many sustained themselves through the long sessions with snuff from the boxes that flanked the rostrum.

For all their perceived faults, one had to admire their doggedness.

Gardner almost felt guilty for the bother, but he cleared his throat. "I have a favor to ask, Sam."

Pomeroy nodded, smile unchanged. Not the hint of surprise. It pained Gardner to find himself among that lot seeking favor and patronage.

"I would like you to petition on my behalf. A petition to Congress to purchase my entire collection of wartime negatives."

Pomeroy raised his bottom lip as if contemplating.

Gardner pulled a sheet of folded paper from his coat. "I've written something up."

Pomeroy unfolded the letter and scanned its paragraphs. Gardner could have just as easily recited it for him from memory.

The undersigned respectfully represents that he is a photographer at 511 Seventh Street, Washington. That he has followed the profession of photographing in the city of Washington and in the vicinity of the same for the past ten years. That at the outbreak of the Rebellion he conceived the idea of furnishing of it a consecutive Photographic History.

That he was most of his time with the Army of the Potomac...

...that during that period, he photographed all the important scenes and incidents which in the aggregate compose the only history of the Rebellion...

...In procuring the above views the undersigned devoted much time, great labor, and considerable expense. He has always regarded them as having a national character and has long indulged the hope that they would someday belong to the nation...

...Without wishing to disparage the labors of others, he believes and is so advised that there is no such collection extant...

Regarding the results of his labor as of priceless value, preserving as they do imperishably, pictures of scenes, the memory of which the country will not readily let die, he is prepared to dispose of them on terms that may seem reasonable and just to the Representatives of the People.

"Yes, Alex. This is good."

"Something else, Jim."

Pomeroy looked up at Gardner. "A similar petition was referred yesterday. You might remember? Senator Wilson presented it on behalf of Mathew Brady."

Pomeroy raised a brow. Slowly he nodded.

Like all veteran congressmen, the senator knew Brady well. Perhaps he remembered hearing that petition come to the floor in the flood of yesterday's business. Perhaps in that moment the good senator recalled a different time, when Brady and Gardner were not adversaries, but worked together, allies toward a common purpose.

Pomeroy quietly folded the letter. "Yes. Well, I do believe time is of the essence then."

Pomeroy sprung from his seat. Gardner stood to meet him.

"Jim, listen I hate to-"

Pomeroy smiled and waved Gardner off with the paper in his hand. "Nothing more to say. It's a wonderful idea, Alex. It's only fitting that the nation should take possession of such a historical record. I'd be honored to put it forth. You've been a friend to the state of Kansas, and to me. It will be my privilege."

Gardner squeezed Pomeroy's hand. A great relief swelled inside him. He trusted the senator would follow through. For now, there was only one thing to say.

"Thank you."

Gardner exited through the rotunda, stopping but a moment to glance upward one hundred and eighty feet to *The Apotheosis of George Washington*, its maidens and goddesses surrounding Washington on that brilliant fresco.

He felt good. Inspired.

He buttoned his coat against the cold and crossed west over the barren winter grounds. Not quite noon, the sun would not make much of a show on this day.

Gardner pictured in his mind the spring crocuses and the lush green grass, and the budding ailanthus trees shielded in their white wooden palisades along Pennsylvania Avenue. What a portrait this city in springtime could paint. *Soon.*

He remembered the early days of the war when the Capitol yards were strewn with marble, workmen sawing and hammering beneath their sheds as they worked to complete her. Thank God all their work had been realized.

Gardner boarded a Washington & Georgetown car and paid his five-cent fare. He took a seat on one of two narrow benches that ran the fifteen-foot length of the car. It rolled west along its rails up the avenue. He listened to two men trade guesses on the composition of President-Elect Grant's new cabinet. Out the window, bootblacks busied themselves and boys heralded their newspapers to passersby.

Gardner hoped his time with Sam Pomeroy was well spent.

He remembered when Pomeroy arrived with that irascible Jim Lane in the spring of '61 as Kansas' first elected senators. Lane had corralled all the Kansas men he could find to defend the nation's capital. Pomeroy marched alongside Lane into the East Room of the Executive Mansion where he stood with smoothbore musket, arm in arm with the proud men of Kansas east and Jayhawks west on velvet carpet beneath its chandelier.

But the fiasco at Bull Run changed all that. Gone were those heady days when every man fancied himself a soldier ready to end a quick war.

Decades of bitterness would not be settled at the hands of amateurs.

And so, the president signed his bill, recruiting hundreds of thousands for three-year service. Men like Pomeroy traded in their muskets, realizing they could best serve the nation from Congress, ensuring a professional army had what it needed for the long conflict ahead.

1861, after Bull Run

"Do you realize the opportunity we have here?"

Gardner stared back at Brady across the glass counter yet offered no reply. The crystal gasolier above them turned low in the cavernous gallery room.

Nearby, a scattering of leather-bound catalogue albums lay just as the day's customers had left them. Stacks of cartes de visite sat on display just beneath the glass, the pocket-sized cards with mounted paper portraits featured Major Robert Anderson, hero of Ft. Sumter, and other Union officers.

The wall clock sounded a quarter to midnight.

Brady uncorked the bottle of Old Renault between them. Gardner declined so Brady poured himself a glass, raising it.

"To Union. To the prospect of doing what's never been done before."

Gardner nodded and Brady drank.

By that second week of August, the dour mood had lifted, and the nation was seized with a newfound determination. Enough time had passed since Bull Run that Julia allowed Brady's return to the studio to help Gardner manage the fourteen-hour days. Soldiers. Thousands in their resplendent blues, responding to President Lincoln's call for a half million volunteers on July 22nd, sought out Brady's. They marched to the top floor where they faced the camera, the backs of their heads firm in the metal clamp of the immobilizer.

Gardner persuaded Brady to order the sets of four lens cameras capable of producing several, nearly identical, images from the same exposure. Four prints were cut and sold for a total of twenty-five cents.

It was a business of volume.

A multi-tube camera that produced four images on a single plate

Brady despised the very idea of such mass production. It debased the art. Gardner argued otherwise. But both men agreed nonetheless, whether they made a dime or not, it was fitting that these men sent off to fight have the means by which to obtain their likeness.

And they were making money. Especially once Gardner negotiated royalties from the Anthony's in New York who began to mass produce Brady's images of celebrity generals.

"Opportunity," Gardner said, repeating Brady's chosen word. "Yes. I suppose it is."

He knew Brady was right. But nothing had yet helped Gardner come to terms with the fact that his beloved country was in peril. These United States were now at war. He recalled all those educated men of Glasgow and Britannia with whom he had discussed America over the years, men who scoffed at her ideal.

Fifty years, you wait and see! They will split.

They simply cannot stand on their own.

Liberty? All well and good but there comes a price.

Those opiners and prognosticators of the end of America's Great Experiment must revel now, he thought. But he would have faith that the Union would be restored.

And yes, there was an important role for them to play now.

"Roger Fenton," Gardner said.

Brady grinned; crow's feet spread out from beneath his lenses. It was not the first time Fenton had come up in their conversations.

Roger Fenton sailed for the Crimean Peninsula in '55. Prince Albert sent the former painter to procure images that might bolster home support for an unpopular war. Fenton and his assistant set out in a hulking merchant's wagon, an improvised contraption that would allow him to prepare and develop plates beneath a light-proof canopy; one Gardner and Brady modeled in the recent venture to Bull Run. Outfitted with a camera and glass plates, and skilled in the new collodion process, the Englishmen battled harsh conditions, broken ribs, even a bout of cholera, and still managed a quantity of negatives; officers and soldiers at camp, including the 13th Light Dragoons who survived the famous Light Brigade charge. Fenton's *Shadow of the Valley of Death* depicted a battlefield, a bleak chasm littered with cannonball.

But that war soon ended, as did Fenton months' long experiment. Impressive as the photographs were, few ever saw them. Gardner had managed to get a glimpse of them at a small London exhibition.

Assistant Marcus Sparling atop Roger Fenton's van in the Crimea, 1855

"Better equipment. Improved methods. We'd stand a better chance than he ever did," said Gardner.

"No, Alex. It's more than that." Brady took a long swallow. "We have the means. And the connections. We can get close in every theater of the war."

Gardner studied him for a moment. "That would take a great deal."

Brady nodded his dissent as he swallowed the last from his glass.

"The expense of it, Alex, leave to me. First thing, I'll go to McClellan's quarters on Lafayette Square. As busy as our new general may be, I think I can get a minutes' time."

Gardner stood up from the counter. "And Pinkerton," Gardner added. "He'd be amiss to turn away a fellow Scotsman at his doorstep."

In the coming days, Brady and Gardner put plan to action.

MAJOR GEN'L, GEO. B. McCLELLAN.

Entered according to Act of Congress in the year 1861, by M. B. Brady, in the Clerk's office of the District Court of the District of Columbia.

Brady carte de visite, 1861
Cards of celebrity generals sold by the many thousands

Pinkerton, the gruff Chicago detective who first arrived in Washington aboard then President-Elect Lincoln's night train, had fled Glasgow for America in '42 following the Chartist unrest. Now, McClellan had named him to head his new Secret Service agency. Gardner and he shared a common history.

Gardner could appeal to Pinkerton's character. He paid his visit.

Brady made his case to the general himself. "It would, you see, be not a hindrance to the cause. It might prove a valuable tool."

In exchange for access to the army, Brady's teams were in a position to provide the military with all the benefits a camera could provide; photographs of terrain, copies of maps, and more. Something mutually beneficial. The moment it proves otherwise, Brady promised his men would vanish from the fields and camps as ghosts into the ether.

Brady won McClellan's approval.

⌇⌇

It was late October. Gardner stepped to a pine table in the clearing, the Army of the Potomac camped for miles all around them.

"This is John Wood," he announced.

Neither Gibson nor Woodbury rose from their seat to extend a hand. Gibson scratched his beard. He touched the brim of his gray hat then pushed a lit pipe to the opposite end of his mouth.

The autumn sun cut bright bands through the hardwoods, illuminating leaves that blanketed their camp; the table, a folding chair aside a smoldering cook fire. The morning air was still and cool. The smell of bacon and coffee lingered.

"He's going out with you today. He's been at the studio in Washington two months now. Right after you left. You won't need to hand hold. Will they, Mr. Wood?"

"No sir, Mr. Gardner."

David Woodbury scraped the last of his tin plate with a spoon, grease dripping from the mushed meal. "Our replacements coming to the field now too?" he asked before he swallowed.

"Now Brady's hiring replacements for the replacements," added Gibson.

Woodbury studied Wood. "Well, ain't quite the same in the field, Mr. John Wood."

Wood looked as though he was waiting permission to breath, and this seemed to satisfy something in Woodbury, who plucked black suspenders. "Not to worry, though. Gibs and I, we'll show you how things are done out here. Not much choice we have anyhow."

Gardner eyed Woodbury's smirk meant for him, then took seat on the fireside chair. Not a one had stoked the flames since he left for headquarters to pick up Wood. And he yet to eat. Gardner began working the burnt tip of a hickory stick into the coals and tossed on some kindling to get it going again.

He decided he could forgive their laxness.

This morning was the first he'd seen of them in three days. They made their way in past the pickets just after mess had ended and made a meal on the scraps. He already had new scouting orders for them, but it could wait a few hours. They wanted to fill their bellies, and a few hours to relax. He would allow them that.

O'Sullivan had been first to the field, gone south by ship to the Carolina coast late that summer.

Gardner had joined General McClellan's army in September, officially as a member of the U.S. Topographical Engineers, leaving behind his brother James to help manage the sittings at Brady's Washington studio.

The army afforded Gardner a log hut with three cots and a sheet ironstove in that wood clearing not three hundred yards from McClellan's own quarters.

Brady scoured Manhattan and the nation's capital to hire and outfit new teams south and west. He and Julia took a permanent suite at the National so he could work from Washington, mingling daily with posing generals and politicians who might aid his cause.

So long as McClellan was pleased, Gardner and the Brady men with whom Gardner was charged, would continue to enjoy opportunities to document the war effort.

"See," began Woodbury again, "we let Mr. Gardner deal with the generals and copy the maps and what not. All the while we go out and photograph the fine countryside of North Virginia. Bridges, streams, and whatever terrain it is they care about for reasons they never tell. Best not to ask, 'bout anything. 'Where to, boss?' That's all we ever say, ain't that right, boss?"

Gardner turned a burning log, intent on avoiding the conversation.

Wood stepped forward now. He found gumption to slide onto the bench across Woodbury, who turned up an empty tin and slid it before Wood, then poured him hot coffee from the kettle.

"Now as for the soldiers, give your soldier his due. And oh does he love to pose. You'll take plenty of their photographs. Ask the whole company to pose if you've got the extra time and plate. Mr. Brady likes those pictures too. They make him good money so Mr. Gardner here likes them too. They sell, don't they, boss?"

Woodbury dipped a finger into his own tin, then threw the cold coffee out over his shoulder and poured the kettle for himself. He drank, then held up a finger as if to tell Wood to stay focused. "Now, if you like to eat, maybe pick yourself up some extra socks or whatever else it is you need, you might want to include the quartermaster in your photographs. Make him your friend. You might even get a little whisky from his stash now and again."

"I did not hear that," said Gardner to the fire.

"The boys, they call it a 'whats-it-wagon' when we drive up," interjected Gibson. "We take some good-natured ribbing from time to time. Mostly from the new ones who've never seen the likes of us before. And officers will want to see your papers so keep 'em handy."

"Sometimes you get the entire regiment to pose," said Woodbury, not yet done with his earlier theme. "And Mr. Pinkerton he likes them too.

Don't he, boss? And I'll tell why." Woodbury leaned forward. "They study those group prints and root out Rebel spies who infiltrated the army. And there are plenty of 'em. Course now the smarter ones know now to avoid the camera."

Gardner shook his head, listening as Wood's education continued on for some time.

Only a few months in the field now, his men knew the ropes.

They had also near perfected a process in less than ideal conditions; they understood the critical aspects of field photography. Coating the plate sufficiently, but without the slightest waste. One needed to always mind supplies and keep a healthy reserve; you never knew when more would be needed. From the plate's nitrate bath to its holder and to the camera, it was vital to mind not only the light but wind and dust that would ruin or leave pocked holes on the image. When to approach officers for permission to photograph. The best weather with regards to lighting conditions and time of exposure required in each situation. Take two images if possible; a stereoview camera produced a side-by-side image that could be printed separately or used to create stereocards, the large format camera could create a single, crisp eight by ten glass negative. Try to provide the most options for marketing it later.

Paired images of a stereoview used in popular three-dimensional viewers

Gardner accompanied his men on the larger expeditions. He knew what it was to sleep in a field under cold skies, to huddle beneath the wagon to escape the rain, and to eat a soldier's meager rations. Gardner, like his men, grew more haggard by the week. A metamorphosis was taking place. He was transforming into a leaner, more necessary version of himself.

Just a few of so many thousands taken in the studio and field between 1861 and 1865

He managed to rotate back to Washington every two or three weeks, able to enjoy a night with Margaret and the children. The studio sold thousands of images from the field. Newly promoted generals rotated through Washington to receive commissions and, of course, pay visit to Brady's soon thereafter. Anthony's mass print operation could not produce these cartes de visite fast enough.

Brady, for his part, stayed warm and dry in the city, coaxing officers before his camera by day and, at night, attending elegant parties and dining with politicians who drove the war from behind their chamber desks.

High society busied themselves in theaters and opera houses while bloated corpses clad in Union blue floated down the Potomac after the defeat at Ball's Bluff, where they lodged in the bank timbers and supports of the Long Bridge.

⚬⚬

When December's freeze ground operations to a halt, war's first winter was upon them.

Where to, boss? would have to wait for spring.

Thursday noon

Gardner slipped into his studio's rear entrance to find the gallery crowd had thinned.

"How was business? Any issues?" Gardner questioned Lawrence behind the counter.

"Without a hitch. Business has been good today."

Gardner smiled. Even if his son's heart was not in the work, he had assumed a job, and he was doing it well.

"Good. I'll be in my office. Then I have one more errand."

Gardner climbed stairs and closed the door behind him. He sat. For all his laxity these days, he managed to keep the room looking respectable; a shelf of ledgers in tight formation, stacks of newspapers in chronological order, the *National Intelligencer* and *Evening Star*. A clear desktop with only dip pen and ink bottle.

His desk drawers were another matter.

Gardner reached across and opened the top right drawer with his good arm. He rifled through the heap of discarded mail and letter drafts, many wadded and crumpled.

Amongst the middle of the paper stack, he found it. A letter inside an envelope with a broken seal of the Smithsonian, postmarked twenty-first September, last year.

That morning Gardner had been thinking about Pomeroy, and how the senator had always been there to support him. And Pomeroy was but one example of those who had shown him kindness over the years. Gardner liked to think he would bestow the same benevolence upon others who came to him. But he knew at least one instance where he could have been a better man.

Lord knows he was a busy man, but he wanted to do right. And he wanted to feel better about himself.

He opened the letter for the second time in five months and read it through for the first time.

❦

Gardner left his studio once more, the letter now in the pocket of his winter coat. A hack driver took him west along the avenue and south across the Washington City Canal at 10th. The Tiber Creek fed the canal west before water closets, stale produce from Center Market, and other noxious elements were contributed by city residents. Even from the high cab, the smell of the cesspool below was dreadful.

Against the gray sky, Gardner watched *The Castle* take shape, its gothic sandstone towers and commanding brick façade.

The driver stopped before the Smithsonian's north entrance. Its yard, with its young oaks and maples, lay dormant and browned by winter.

Gardner pulled his coat in against the cold and moved up the walk.

He entered the warmth of the main hall.

A man wheeled a cart of books nearby. Gardner asked for assistance. Agreeably, the man left his cart and passed through a wooden door.

Gardner waited.

Stoves on either side warmed the vast hall so that men and women carried their coats and held hats as they perused the room filled with glass and cast-iron display cases beneath a high arched ceiling. Muted light seeped through the series of elongated windows. Above, Gardner could see patrons who milled about the second-floor displays.

He had not been inside the castle since before the fire in January of '65 when he placed his camera in the north east yard to photograph the Smithsonian's burning. No lives were lost, but the building and towers required extensive reconstruction. Many things were not so easily replaced, among them the priceless Indian paintings of John Stanley Mix exhibited on the second floor. Their destruction was one of the reasons the government commissioned Gardner's journey to Laramie so that his images could help rebuild the nation's visual record of the Indians.

A wooden door opened at the far end of the hall. Truman Ash appeared from behind it. The young man spied Gardner through the modest crowd.

Truman smiled after a moment. He crossed the hall and that smile widened as he inched his rolled sleeves up over his elbows.

"Hello, Mr. Gardner. Excuse my appearance. I've been in the basement all morning."

Gardner shook his hand. "I am sorry for the intrusion, Truman. I won't keep you."

"It's no trouble really! Just a surprise. That's all."

Gardner pulled the letter from his coat pocket. Truman's expression told him the young man knew exactly what it was.

"I've come to beg your apology, Truman. My lack of response was inexcusable."

"No need for apologies, Mr. Gardner. You must be so busy."

"There is no sufficient excuse for it. That I can assure you."

They were quiet a moment and Gardner returned the letter to his pocket. "I did read it, tardy as I was in doing so. And so, I've come to ask if the invitation to lunch still stands."

"Sure, Mr. Gardner."

"Very well but I insist that I pay as recompense. Are you free tomorrow? I think I can manage to get away an hour or so."

"Actually," Truman said, adding a small laugh. "Perhaps I could interest you in something else. How would you like a private tour of the castle? You seemed quite interested in my work when we spoke at Laramie."

Gardner liked the idea very much and told him so.

"Great. That works out well!"

Gardner cocked his head, intrigued. "How so?"

"You see, I made Mr. Brady the same offer. With all the newly arrived shipments, I am remiss to leave the building. But he thought the tour a grand idea so I hoped you would too. I can show you both around as much as I am permitted."

Gardner could not think clearly to utter a syllable.

"Noon tomorrow shall we say then, Mr. Gardner?"

First his mention of Brady's petition. Now this. For the second time in twenty-four hours, Truman Ash had left him without words.

IV

Brady boarded a hack and directed its driver south along Broadway. The Manhattan train had arrived on schedule that morning. Brady first paid visit to the bank, completing the sale of the Central Park lot. He went to his 10th Street studio for a few hours thereafter. The studio's business had been modest but steady the past few years and on this day its operation seemed in good hands, as he knew it would be.

He did not linger. He had time for quick bite to eat, then set out to focus on his main task.

The driver led Brady through the midday bustle, past the vendor's curbside stands filled with fresh fish, produce, and hanging game. Between breaks in the horse traffic, he watched the clusters of people bundled on the walks, breathing white mist into the chilled air.

Brady recalled the city of old, Battery Gardens to maybe five or six blocks north on Broadway. That was all of her. Things were different then. When Brady was someone in this city. *Brady of Broadway* they had called him.

"Here, sir." Brady called out at the intersection of Broadway and Fulton. "I should like to get out."

The driver pulled over. Brady climbed out and paid. He tapped his cane on the stones and began a slow gait. The warehouse on John Street was a block and a half away. He took hold of his hat as a brisk wind blew up from the battery. New Yorkers rushed past him, but a few taking time to meet his eyes let alone flash a smile.

Broadway and Fulton. He stopped to reflect. *Was it really so long ago?*

Brady smiled and shook his head then continued on again, nostalgia weighing heavy on his every thought now.

New York, early 1840s

Against a column along the vast colonnade, Brady stood watch as men escorted parasoled ladies cross the portico and into the lush green court-yard of Congress Hall.

Brady took a blade of grass from his mouth, mush and broken, and cast it aside. He directed his gaze to a nearby table, where a man and woman in a pale yellow dress sat across an artist in shirt sleeves who sketched upon a pad in his lap.

William Page cut his eyes from his work long enough to give Brady a wink.

In the ten days since Page's arrival at Saratoga Springs, Brady had made something of a friend.

Eight months earlier, Brady had left the home of Irish immigrants Andrew and Julia Brady. As a boy, he had worked the fields of their meager Warren County plot and played along the woodland shores of Lake George where the British had fought Indians a generation before.

Brady's scrawny frame was not suited to a life of physical labor and his mother despaired she could not provide him with proper schooling.

But it was the inflammation of the eyes that Brady had suffered from since childhood that was most worrisome.

Costly spectacle lenses grew thicker by the year. Wise to the family's plight, one evening meal Brady raised the prospect of an unaccompanied trip to the springs at Saratoga, twenty-six miles south. There he would take the waters, as they say, and see if it might improve his eyesight. He would find work and send money home. Despite her concerns, his mother agreed. *Spend a few months, and see what comes of it.* But she was adamant the money should not be sent back. It was to serve as investment for an education or some future that relied upon wits and not brawn.

Brady set off on foot with a sack and bedroll. He did not know at the time that he would not return, all of sixteen and perhaps not so wise as his mother.

Saratoga Springs had been a place of convalescence since Indian times. In colonial days, physicians espoused the benefits of taking its bubbling emerald waters from springs with patriotic names like *Columbian*, *Washington*, and *Hamilton*. Now, grand hotels sprouted along the grounds, catering to high society with gardens and exclusive bath houses. Boys carried silver dippers to fill glasses with buckets from the mineral springs, each with its own distinct flavor. With its spacious dining halls, opera houses, and horse racing, Saratoga Springs offered the rich an escape from boredom and city summer heat.

Brady roomed on the edge of town and found work performing menial tasks for a jewelry case maker in a shop along the wide cobblestoned Broad Street.

Mornings, when free for a few hours' time, he would roam about the springs, among the sick and the wealthy. He learned to pity the first group, the invisible and unwanted, and he marveled at that later.

Brady had never seen the likes of them and their carefree existence; days shopping, promenading, the bows and kissing of kid glove hands. They emerged from their private rooms or from the courtyards at the ringing of a bell to dine on omelet breakfasts, then sumptuous dinners and tea at six where they feasted again on Indian cakes, pies, berries, and jellies. Into late evening, they danced in the grand halls and strolled out of doors beneath a summer's moon. All the while the days passed with nothing to show for it.

William Page understood his subjects well. He was there because of them. He took portrait commissions for twenty cents apiece. Page was not at all intimated by that group. He talked to them. He told stories. He brushed back his sandy curls and sketched them as he chanted sonnets of Shakespeare. *But thou, contracted to thine own bright eyes, Feed'st thy light'st flame with self-substantial fuel.* He was a spritely and confident soul as Brady had ever known.

"And we are finished," announced Page, tearing the sketch free from his book.

The seated couple rose. The dandy gentlemen traded Page the copy for coins and a handshake. The pair departed; apparently quite satisfied with the sketch they shared between them.

Page exchanged his pad for a drink from the glass of water on the table. He waved his hand, guiding Brady to the empty seat as he drank down the glass.

"How are those sketches coming, Mathew?"

Brady shrugged.

A few days ago, Page had given him a couple of pages and a bundle of worn colored pencils. *Crayons,* as Page had called them. *See how these feel in your hands.*

"I am not one for drawing, I suppose." Brady sat.

Page laughed as he stared out upon the courtyard. "Practice and patience. Practice and patience, dear boy."

At twenty-eight, Page was twelve years Brady's senior. The artist was not shy about the details of his colorful life thus far, from that of a New York City artist to a studio in Albany where his wife finally could take no more of his carefree lifestyle and left, taking their three young daughters with her. On his own to face whatever meager existence awaited him in the only profession he could ever imagine, Page made do. He sketched and painted likenesses as he charmed with his wit and humor. Every evening, Brady watched Page dine in the grand hall, a guest of this patron or another. Oh yes, William Page moved quite easily in that secret society.

"Tell me, Mathew," Page said finally, his eyes still upon the sunbathed yard, "have the waters helped your eyesight?"

Brady did not answer right away. He studied a gaunt man in a gown who sat upon a bench across the green, before a spring enclosed by a white wooden pavilion. A young woman sat in plain blue dress beside him.

There was no dipping boy there to wait upon them.

"They say that it may take time." Brady pushed his glasses up the bridge of his nose.

"Ah. This would be the experts? Ha! No shortage of their kind in this world, is there?"

Page bent forward his lanky frame. He plucked his straw hat from the planked floor and placed it atop his curls. "Well, I wish you luck, Mathew. I do. As for me, I am away this very afternoon. I have relieved these good people sufficiently from their symptom of excess coin."

Brady watched Page stand up from the chair, stunned by the news. He was losing his friend. Brady nodded, doing his best to hide his disappointment.

"Where to from here, William?"

Page was sweeping pencils from the table and into his leather satchel with haste as if it were now a race to his next destination and the starting gun already fired.

"I need to pick up a few possessions at Albany then it's a steamer for the big city. I have a small studio space awaiting me on Broadway. A grand reunion of sorts, Manhattan, and I. Oh, how I need her now. Her energy! Had you ever been there yourself, Mathew, you would know what I mean."

Page had painted a vivid picture of a New York City sprawl in their many talks. But Brady found it impossible to comprehend such a place. He had never seen more people in one place than the three to four hundred now at Saratoga Springs.

Page swung his long arms around and clapped his hands. "And today is as good a day as any!"

Brady's mind raced, watching Page gather the last of his things. There seemed only one choice. Even he knew it was a moment that would only present itself once and so he summoned his nerve.

"William?"

"What is it, Mathew?"

"Would you mind the company?"

They hitched a ride in the straw bed of a farmer's cart.

There at Albany they gathered Page's meager belongings; shirts, worn boots, and a painter's tools. They bought tickets to board a crowded Hudson River steamer, Brady offering to purchase them from his Saratoga wages.

The ship beat its way south into the wind. A soaking rain fell in the last hour of the voyage and the pair took refuge beneath a second-floor balcony.

At the wharf, as crowded a place as Brady had ever seen, the pair found a ride on a laden wagon, wedged between heaped canvas sacks and barrels that smelled of molasses, and they rolled onto Broadway.

Brady would never forget that June morning when he first set eyes upon that grand kaleidoscope; a thousand or more people before rows of sundry brick buildings, its citizenry crowding the horse-filled streets and walks packed with carts and produce stands. Not even the smell of waste and horse dung that filled the air could diminish the excitement of it.

Page had taken lease on a loft near 10th where the business of lower Broadway thinned, and rent was cheap. He wasted little time in securing his first appointments.

Brady earned keep cleaning brushes and stretching canvas. He watched Page work beneath the soft light of the window, donning a smock and cradling a palette of colors, stroking the canvas before his seated subjects, chanting those old familiar verses. Seemingly random swipes and pecks, in the end, took on the exquisite likeness of its focus.

Page preferred to take work to his customers' homes, their own parlors, where they were put at ease and would be most giving to him. The fact that afterwards they would often feed him and offer their finest brandies and cigars played no small part in the decision. Brady often took meals as a guest of an elderly man and his wife who tailored suits across the hall.

After a few weeks, Page, who must have sensed he had been neglecting his young friend, announced to Brady that he was worth more than a painter's apprentice. He arranged for Brady a position at the jewelry counter at A.T. Stewart; the largest store in Manhattan, just a few hundred yards away at Chambers and Broadway.

In a matter of weeks, Brady's long hours brought in the lion's share between them, and he paid for their meals as recompense. Brady wrote his mother with words of self-assuredness in the outcome of this second act in his young life.

⌒

One summer afternoon, Page met Brady after his shift ended behind his counter at Stewart's.

"We're going to visit a friend on Washington Square."

They walked there. They crossed the green and entered a rookery on the grounds at the University of New York, climbing steps to the top floor.

Page rapped at a door. A lengthy wait followed before a man opened it. He was a sight, lumbering in the doorway.

To Brady, the man had the look of a bohemian, a long, ragged coat and wild brown hair streaked with gray above his drawn face. He stared blankly at Page. He said nothing. *Good friend.* Brady wondered what manner of friend.

Of a sudden the peculiar man's green eyes lit as if someone had wound a crank protruding from his back.

"Master Page!" bawled the bohemian. "Good of you to come."

He waved them inside a cluttered room.

Brady entered, dumbfounded at the sight of thin metal wires that snaked the floorboards. Wires stretched over half-painted canvases upon easels and across several tables. The wires ran into a strange-looking device on a table top, then out and up the walls and continued across the floor over sections of thin, mangled paper. It all seemed to Brady some invading organism whose advance upon the room had too long gone uncontested.

The man pushed aside an easel and kicked at wires with his boot to clear a path. He stopped several paces into the room and scratched his head, eyes flitting about the room like a man whose mind was gone. The man then brushed newspapers from a nearby chair and set it before Brady.

Brady sat and looked up to Page, who did not appear surprised in the slightest by what he saw.

"Dear Professor Morse, I see your telegraph machine continues to sap the artist in you." Page stepped with care among the tangled wires to the table where sat the contraption that consisted of a wooden frame and appendages fastened by iron prongs. From its center, it looked as if a great pencil hung down over a drum where rolled paper laid spread across.

"Yes, so it would seem, William," the man said in a resigned manner.

"Mathew Brady. Samuel Morse. The greatest of American painters. My own teacher at the National Academy," Page continued, never taking his eyes from the instrument on the table. "Painter to President Monroe. Painter of *The House of Representatives*, depicting the chamber in night session, among so many others."

Brady extended an upward hand. Morse seemed not to notice. Instead, Morse used his thin hand to wave off Page's compliment.

"Ach! Why do you wound me with such painful memories?" Morse said, then pulled out a nearby stool and sat upon it.

"Do tell how you fared in Europe with your telegraph," said Page, now probing the apparatus with his index finger. He glanced over at Brady.

"Mathew, come see!"

Brady side-stepped the clutter to reach the table.

"See?" Page began. "The composing stick beneath this leveler. It see-saws and operates the circuit as it receives the wires' current. Electric pulses. Some short. Some long. The register produces a message in pencil on this paper. Did I get that right, Professor?" Page said over his shoulder, not waiting an answer. "One day this machine will revolutionize the world. Wait and see."

"Revolutionize!" Morse snapped his fingers. "Now that is a word I should have used!" He bit a lip. "It might have gone better in Europe with you at my side. As it were, they showed little interest or imagination. I have come to the realization that there are no more men of vision there than in these states."

Morse left his perch on the stool. He stepped beside Brady. His agitated stare had now transformed into a smile. Brady found the toothy yellow grin unsettling.

"But the trip was not a complete waste. Come see."

They followed Morse, past canvases with partial figures and others that contained bright yet meaningless strokes, to a table tucked beneath a windowsill, a musty sheet flecked in wild colors of paint covering it.

Morse pulled the sheet away to reveal a squat wooden box painted black, about twelve inches in height and just as wide and long. Brady stared at the mechanism, far simpler than the unwieldy wire-eating tele-graph. It reminded Brady of an oversized cigar box. Most conspicuous, a silver dollar sized hole was centered at one end. In it looked to be an eyeglass encased in a brass fitting.

"A friend of mine in France, Louis Daguerre, has just revealed his invention to the world."

"A camera obscura of sorts?" replied Page, as he studied it from multiple angles.

In the process of divesting what painterly knowledge he had to offer Brady, Page described various aids painters used to advance their craft. The camera obscura was one of these. The device took an image through a lens, magnified it through a second larger lens, and projected the enlarged image upon a canvas that could be painted directly over. Though a proven technique to achieve scale and proportion, Page disdained the practice for artistic reasons.

"No! No! Not for throwing shadows on the wall. Rather -" Morse opened a drawer beneath the table's top and pulled out a square piece by its edges and laid the diminutive object in his open palm.

The object was at most two inches by three. It flickered brightly in rays of window light. Dark at the edges; a sooty black, and as the blackness fell off in jagged points the body of it held a glittering image on a plate. A church. Beside it was the outline of buildings.

Every minute detail and delineation. *The world's smallest painting* was Brady's immediate thought.

"Taken from the glass shed on the roof atop the university here. I present to you the daguerreotype. Rembrandt perfected."

Morse transferred the piece to the palm of Page's hand.

"Remarkable," said Page, holding it close.

Morse took this camera in his hands and turned it round on the table. Brady stooped to confront its small lens. Morse placed two hands over its top and side and gently pulled back. The camera slid out, extending another four or five inches. Morse pulled a chain at the back and the hinged panel separated and extended down. Inside lay a mirror.

Morse explained how it worked, how the rear mirror was used to focus the light from the lens reflecting back to it. Then, when just right, a copper plate, polished then silvered and light-sensitized, replaced the mirror in back.

"The first images took twenty minutes to expose! Ah, but we've grown wiser since, we few who tinker with this newfound contraption. There are chemical solutions to use, iodine and bromine. 'Quickstuff', we call it. So that now, in good light, an image can be had even in say twenty to thirty seconds."

Early daguerreotype camera, circa 1839

Morse pinched the corners of the metal plate from Page's hand and turned. Brady raised cupped hands and Morse placed it there. The sharpness of its corners poked at Brady's palm.

He could see it was true; this was not the work of some artist's brush or pencil at all.

Morse took him by the shoulders and nudged Brady a few paces to the window. Brady looked out and there, below, stood the very church that he held now in his cradling hands. He half expected a tiny man or horse to come strolling across the plate's shiny surface.

"After the image is exposed, it is carried in a light-proof holder to a dark room where it is fumed with mercury vapors and then fixed. And thus, gentlemen there you are."

"You'll run us artists out of business!" laughed Page.

Brady thought he heard Page continue, as if at some distance. "You must show me how it is done." "Some other time," followed. "Now let me show you something else here".

The world outside had slipped away. Brady was left alone with his senses and the small and shiny something called a *dag-arrow-type*.

Brady knew in that moment he had experienced something wonderful in this world.

❦

Brady saw a great deal of Samuel Morse in the months that followed.

The old painter and his many pursuits outgrew the cramped university nook. Morse accepted his brother's offer to a loft above *The Observer*, his brother's newspaper business at the corner of Nassau and Beekman.

Sidney Morse had a glass roof installed on the top floor of the five-story building so his brother could practice his newfound art. But for the greater part, Morse continued to paint for pennies between fits over his telegraph machine. He seemed to Brady as impoverished and desperate as ever. But Morse was not without pride and soon had an idea to offer daguerreotype lessons as a means to pay rent. He would teach the science of it but also the art, a painter's sense of lighting and composition.

Brady scrimped and saved to be one of his first pupils.

The hours that Brady could steal away from behind the counter at Stewart's, he spent with Morse.

It was no longer a matter of hocus pocus. Brady learned the process.

Coat a sheet of copper with silver, polish and clean. Expose surface in a small box to iodine vapors until silvered surface turns a golden yellow. Five to thirty seconds. Expose plate in camera. Develop, exposing plate to mercury vapors at 167 degrees F. Then wash in Hyposulfite of Soda. Of course, the skilled practitioner knew when to deviate from these hard and fast rules, depending on available light, the day's humidity, and so many other factors.

After two months' lessons, Brady was producing his own images in Morse's haunt.

One evening after the day's light had quit Morse's loft, Brady gathered up his notebooks in the empty ten-chair classroom when he heard a commotion from behind the cracked door to Morse's private quarters.

Brady stepped forward and pushed back the door into the dusky room. He squinted through his thick lenses to find the old codger on hands and knees before a small sofa, running his long fingers in its creases and along the floorboards below it.

Morse straightened and held a small coin toward candlelight. A smile formed upon his weathered face until he caught sight of Brady behind his coin. Morse picked himself from the floor in haste, beating dust from his trousers.

"I am sorry, Professor Morse. I saw the door open and-"

He waved Brady off, saying not a word.

Brady had never felt such pity. Acting on instinct, he thrust his hand into his trouser pocket.

"I just dropped by to pay you an advance on next quarter's tuition. Five dollars if that would do, Professor."

Morse's eyes lit upon the gold Half Eagle Brady held out.

He shuffled toward Brady until Lady Liberty was inches from his bony cheeks.

"Gold," said old Morse in something of a trance. The wretched man swallowed hard. "It is the most wonderful of all colors, wouldn't you agree?"

❧

But a handful of patrons remained, hunched at stools over the bar in the dank tavern. Brady watched Morse stab at potatoes sopped in gravy from across a wooden table.

Brady had never seen such zestful eating from a man. He sipped his coffee.

Morse slowed his eating to gulp water and wipe his chin. "A young man like you doesn't eat?"

Brady told him he had eaten earlier. Morse shrugged before he took another sip of his water then leaned back in his chair. He grew quiet, his eyes fixed upon Brady.

"You are a good boy, Mathew. So, I will ask that you do something for me. Alright?"

"Anything, Professor Morse."

"Don't be a damned fool!" thundered Morse, pounding the table with his fist. Its candle flickered wild.

Brady jolted back. Barflies turned to glimpse the commotion through clouds of tobacco smoke.

Morse laughed until he coughed. He leaned over his plate, closer to Brady and started again, this time nearly a whisper. "Don't end up a fool like the one you see before you now."

Morse settled back into his chair and exhaled. "Morse the artist. The inventor. Ha! A dog who begs for his scraps. Pennies from the rich man's pocket."

Brady said nothing.

Morse waved his fork between them as if to chase his last comments from the air. "A man with passion and ideals is all well and good, but there is nothing admirable about poverty. You must surely see that even through those thick lenses of yours."

Morse lowered his haggard face to the candle at their table.

"I see it so clearly now," he said to the steady flicker. He then looked up at Brady. He must have read Brady's confusion for he grinned and slapped the table once more.

"One must have a plan. That is all I am saying, boy! I see that now. And not a moment too soon! I am not done yet, by God."

Morse laughed again and took a fork to the remnants of his plate.

Brady sipped the rest of his coffee. He thought about his friend's message, for all he understood of it.

⌒

It was the summer of '43. Brady stepped out upon the crowded two hundred block of Broadway, watching the thoroughfare of horses and clattering horse cars pass. The crowds moved past him, close enough that Brady could smell the sweat and tobacco of the workmen and the lavender and sweet jasmine waters of the better-offs.

They all shared one thing in common. Brady's concerns were of no consequence to any of them.

He turned back to the building behind him, to the wooden sign that dangled from it. A small painted red hand on the white wood pointed up at the building's upper stories.

Brady's Daguerrian Miniature Gallery – Three Flights up

He hung the sign with great hope not so many months ago.

In late '42, Brady leased a room at Fulton and Broadway to sell his jewel cases, with the skill he had acquired during his apprenticeship in Saratoga Springs and the little business knowledge he gained behind the counter at Stewart's.

Encouraged by the first two months' results of this modest venture, Brady leapt. He leased the top floor of the building too, installed windows on the roof and opened each morning for daguerreotype appointments.

Sixth-plates, quarter and half plates; three dollars apiece, five dollars with one of his best miniature casings.

But by '43, Broadway already exhibited several daguerreotypists. The cornerstone of John Plumbe's chain of elegant studios was two blocks away. Brady had scaled back the jewel casing business to focus on his daguerreotypes but the surge of customers, presented with plenty of suitors for their business, did not follow.

Expenses mounted.

For all his missteps, Brady did not fault himself in choosing such a favorable location.

Next to his building towered St. Paul's Church and past it stood the Astor House, the finest hotel in the city. Enough wealth passed daily through its doors to make any businessman rich indeed, were he only able to entice them inside.

But it was Barnum's that won the notice of those who happened upon lower Broadway.

Now, watching through the street bustle, Brady looked to the opposite corner where, at this moment, a boy handed out fliers as fast as his hands would allow, his shrill voice never ceasing in its call. "Barnum's American Museum. Unbelievable sights! Sheer delights!"

Barnum's five-story museum towered like a grand obelisk. Its brick walls painted bright with images and letters, its loud display no doubt caused offense to the more pious who attended St. Paul's. Twenty-five cents a visit. At night, Barnum's massive lighthouse lantern paced over the Broadway skyline.

Just then, Brady watched Barnum himself emerge from the front doors of the great building.

If ever there was a bubbly gent, thought Brady, it was Barnum. Pear-shaped with a round belly beneath his coat, the man's squat legs, covered in bright plaid trousers, seemed always on the move.

Brady stood a few minutes, watching Barnum turn to and fro, grasping hands. To those who frequented the area, Barnum's appearance was no surprise. Many an afternoon, Barnum would hawk the street in person, accompanied by his eclectic stars; *Gigantic Woman,* or *Tom Thumb* all two feet eleven inches who sat high upon her shoulder in the smallest of tuxedos. Barnum would shout his latest revelations, his celebrated *Feejee Mermaid* and other creatures hereto unknown to science.

Brady spied a break in traffic and slipped across the street.

He stood, like so many others, watching the odd little man work. Brady felt a poke in his hand. He flinched and looked down to the boy stuffing a playbill in his hand.

The crowd broke and Barnum glanced Brady's way. Barnum smiled. He stepped to Brady. The two stood near equal, but the great man was energy unbounded.

"Mr. Brady! How are you this fine day? Work done so soon?" Barnum asked, before removing a linen kerchief to wipe his chin.

"It is the end of the business day for me, Mr. Barnum."

"Ah yes, I forgot", Barnum said, casting a quick glance to overcast skies. "The day's sunlight must be at its strongest in your profession. That much I understand of it."

"True it is, Mr. Barnum. Lack of sunlight spoils the day," Brady hesitated before adding, "but not so much as the lack of customers."

Barnum's smile faded and the man formed the most serious and sad expression. A moment later, Barnum said "Mr. Plumbe's portrait gallery does a boom of a business it seems. Sat for him myself on several occasions."

"Yes, Mr. Plumbe. He's very good."

Barnum nodded. Then the boisterous fellow narrowed his eyes upon Brady.

Of a sudden, Barnum grabbed Brady again by the shoulder and spun him round so they faced north on Broadway. His arm waved over the busy street.

"Mr. Brady!" shouted Barnum as if he were shouting from across a chasm, "You have competition for the American dollar. That is so."

Barnum spun Brady back around, he ran his fat finger in the direction of the passersby. "They carry their coins just inside their billfolds and pockets. I can hear it jingle as they pass. Teasing me!"

Barnum let go of Brady and stood erect, tugging at his silk vest. He cleared his throat. "So many places for them to spend their time and money. How do we draw them in?"

Barnum's eyes widened. He cast up a finger as if the answer had just occurred. The arm turned and the finger pointed up the towering façade of his own building; banners, reds and yellows blowing. "A bit of show-manship! That is how."

Then Barnum laughed. "Love what you do and let the whole world know it!"

He leaned close until his red nose nearly brushed Brady's cheek. "And do it with gusto, my boy!" He smiled, but his eyes had fire in them. "Gusto."

Thursday, early afternoon

Brady entered the front of the warehouse. He wasted no time as he moved down the tight corridor until it opened upon a musty room.

A single window drew light where drawers and stacked crates hugged the far wall.

The heavyset man behind the desk peered up as Brady approached. Another man of slight build, his back to Brady, turned. This one a boy no more than fifteen with a great beak of a nose upon his thin face.

Brady stared down at the fellow whose belly protruded over the lip of the desk covered in loose stacks of paper. The man worked an unlit cigar between his teeth.

"Good day, sirs. Mathew Brady. I have some business to attend."

Brady took the letter from his frock coat. He held it out over the desk and let it fall amongst the papers.

The man followed the letter down with his eyes. Brady looked down upon his oily head, thin hair streaked across in sheen patches. The fat man took the wet cigar from between his lips and studied Brady above the pools of his eyes.

"Yes. Mr. Brady! Gut day, sir. Nice surprise." His German-accented words were slothful to match his appearance.

"I presume then you know what it is about," Brady replied curt-like. He wanted to set the right tone.

"Aboot? Aboot you give me no money."

The fat man worked the mush cigar back into his mouth before revealing a crooked grin.

Brady glowered. Years ago, he began storing daguerreotypes at this warehouse near his studio. Before and during the war, he continued to send glass negatives here and then to a second warehouse in Washington, where thousands more remained. The last couple years, Brady had been forced to surrender hundreds of his most famous images in lieu of legal action against debt. But there were many thousands still for Congress to purchase.

It was last year when ownership changed hands at this place that trouble began. This new owner, this crude man, probably had no idea who Brady was. And he would gladly recoup his money through whatever means necessary.

Brady remembered happening upon the studio of a Manhattan photographer who had died an untimely death last year. The men hired by the landlord to clean out the place callously cast so many glass plates into the back-alley way to shatter. Many years' work gone in an afternoon.

Brady heard too the stories of war photographers who had been forced to surrender negatives, only to watch them sold for scrap glass, to become sections in a gardener's greenhouse. The sun that burnt the chemicals to give them meaning now burned clear erasing all history from them.

Brady shuddered at the thought.

"You may be happy to know I come to make payment. Enough to keep them in safe keeping until I send for them this month or next month."

"You are moving them? Sorry to hear such a thing, Mr. Brady. But you pay now. Yes?"

Brady eyed him with disgust as he reached at his belt and unfastened his leather billfold, opened it and began thumbing out banknotes. The fat man's eyes widened.

"Gut, Mr. Brady. Gut idea. No more problems."

Brady stopped.

"First," Brady said, pushing the notes back into the leather fold as the man's sad eyes followed their retreat. "I should like to see them."

❧

The assistant led Brady by lantern through a door and down a long hall that opened into a cavernous room lined with rows of broad and cluttered shelving. The air turned cool by a number of degrees. All manner of crate and box littered the cut stone floor.

"This way, Mr. Brady."

He led Brady to a door among a series of doors along the nearby wall.

Brady watched the boy finger through a ponderous chain of keys, pitying the pale-skinned boy who looked as if he spent his waking life in this musty chamber.

The boy finally put a key to lock and opened it.

Matted cob webs stretched until breaking. The boy beat them back and pushed ahead. Brady followed him inside.

A high window, small and octagonal, lit the closet room from above. Upon shelves rested many dozen long and slender boxes.

Brady removed his hat, exchanging it on the shelf for a box he pulled forward with two hands. He blew across its lid. Dust bands whirled, suspending in the pale light above.

Brady felt a warm rush when he read the inscription, written in the hand of an assistant no doubt, upon a yellowed card pasted to the lid.

1855, it read.

He remembered '55 as the year he took his first glass negatives. A few years prior, Frederick Scott Archer had introduced the process whereby silver nitrate was fixed to a plate with a sticky collodion. The translucent glass captured a crisp negative from which innumerable positive prints could be produced on a gloss albumen paper. Brady was reluctant at first, but he saw times were changing and finally abandoned his beloved, one-of-its-kind daguerreotype.

Brady unlatched the lid and opened it, regarding the thin edges of plates, fifty to a row, and each snug in its slotted drawer. He took one glass negative by the corners and raised it to light.

Brady strained to see a group of individuals; their suits and dresses were pale, their skin dark, and light showing at the hair, eyes and lips, ghoulishly inverted. A man, wife, standing behind a young boy and an elderly woman center, seated. Brady must have posed thousands of family portraits, yet, remarkably, this photograph in his hands he recollected.

"Amazing, Mr. Brady," said the young man into dead air. "How did you come by it all?"

New York, 1850s

"I really cannot fathom the delay," snapped the old matriarch. "I do not care who he is," she continued. "Hire a portrait painter, he calls on us at our home."

Brady straightened his vest from behind the cracked door, listening.

He breathed in, doused his bemused laughter, and with a serious face strode into the sitting room.

A family of four gathered at the sofa. To the left sat the wife, a boy of eight or nine between her, and the old woman. The husband stood straight behind them. The suited man with a waxed moustache looked a great deal relieved to see Brady.

The matriarch's creased face scowled from beneath a black bonnet, her eyes fixed upon Brady.

"The very idea!" she huffed.

"Now mother, Mr. Brady is here," said the man, taking hands from his mother's shoulder to tug at his collar.

The camera operator made a final adjustment to the lens, then glanced at Brady. A smirk stole beneath the assistant's bearded lips.

Brady bowed his greetings, and they were at once a cheerful lot, save the matriarch. She would require some work.

He held his cane out and another attendant took it from him. Brady stared into the mother's coal-like eyes while he removed his kid gloves.

There Brady stood in doeskin trousers, his silk coat and merino vest tailored at Bellantoni's. He slapped his gloves against his palm, loosened his lavender scarf, and moved toward her.

He knelt and took her hand, wagering she would allow him that courtesy. He was right and Brady kissed the top of her aged and spotted hand.

"Dear Mrs. Winchester. It is my honor."

She folded her hands away.

"Were it such an honor you would have been here sooner. We've been here an eternity. Tell me, should I consider myself lucky to be put out so?"

"Mother, please!" said her son from over her shoulders. The man laughed a nervous laugh. "Forgive my mother, Mr. Brady."

"No, Mr. Winchester. Your mother, I can assure you, is correct."

Brady stood. He would play this out with care.

At this point in his career, he considered the old woman no significant challenge.

Brady opened this gallery in '53; his second, a mile up town at 359 Broadway. New York society had moved up Broadway and he followed. His photographs crowded a street display beneath a flowing banner announcing Brady's establishment to the city. The lavish gallery displayed imported damask carpets, chandeliers of cut crystal, gilded walls, and the finest furniture.

But none of this had managed to impress Mrs. Winchester. Neither did his gallery walls where framed portraits of every president since John Quincy Adams hung.

A few of Brady's early presidential daguerreotypes, James Polk and Zachary Taylor

Brady had persuaded Adams to sit in '47, months before his death. And it was President Polk who first allowed Brady and his camera into the Executive Mansion. Portraits of Clay, Calhoun, and Webster; of Washington Irving, James Fennimore Cooper and all the leading men of the day, too, were on display, as were the daguerreotypes that had won Brady every major contest he chose to enter, including those from London's Crystal Palace exhibition in the spring of '51, just after he and Julia were married.

"I am sorry, Mrs. Winchester," Brady began again. "I was attending to other aspects of the process necessary to secure the image for which we are all here today. These things are essential to a successful sitting. You see, I must insist upon perfection in these instances. For that, forgive me."

The old woman rolled her eyes.

Brady clasps hands behind his back and shook his head as if to disagree. "Madam, I shall risk the ignominy each and every time. Especially", he paused, "when it concerns the great mothers of our nation."

The woman looked at him for the first time with what he considered at least something less than hatred. It told Brady his tack was right.

"The Winchester Iron Works," Brady announced as if he were on a stage. "A tribute to American ingenuity and hard work. Your dear departed husband built it from the ground up. His able son now manages."

The standing man nodded with a proud smile.

"But I dare say a man can only achieve such things with the love, the unbending support of a strong woman at his side."

Brady now looked at the wife who blushed. "I will not be fooled into thinking otherwise."

Brady walked a few paces before turning to the matriarch. "I was so bold as to say the same to Mrs. Dolly Madison when she sat for me."

Brady's 1848 daguerreotype of Dolly Madison

And that was it. Brady watched the old woman's eyes light up.

"Yes. A few years ago now, the year before she left her nation to mourn her. I shall never forget it. And I must tell you, Mrs. Winchester, she did not take issue either with that idea."

The old woman was not yet ready to award Brady a smile.

"How much, I do say, you remind me of her. Yes. On that day, the weather was not as good as it is today. I required a lengthy exposure. I would characterize her mood as one of mild agitation, as I recall. But in the end, I assuaged her with much the same explanation that I now offer you: 'In certain instances, Mrs. Madison, I must insist upon perfection'."

The matriarch smiled for the first. The whites of her wooden teeth showed. Brady thought she must have been a lovely woman in her day.

Brady seized his opportunity. He posed each family member, coaching them each in posture and expression. Brady's man set into place the head-rests for each subject.

The operator removed the wooden slip, then lens cap, to let the process begin; a proud family and their matriarch, a fire in her old eyes.

Thursday afternoon

Brady returned the last plate to its box and closed the lid. The assistant, at first enamored by glimpses of each dusty plate, had since grown restless. Brady held his timepiece up to the window. Over forty minutes had passed in that crypt of a room. Perhaps the boy feared his boss' wrath for having been away so long.

"Very good," Brady said and started out the room. "You might leave that door open."

Brady paced across the corridor until he beat back into the main room where the fat man still sat behind his desk. The assistant hurried in at Brady's heels.

"Ten dollars I am in arrears. That you shall have." Brady pulled his billfold again and fingered past the notes, pulled out two coins and let them fall.

They gyrated on the desk below.

Less than an hour ago, Brady had arrived with the notion of paying sum enough to keep his plates safe for a year or longer. That was the plan.

"In addition," Brady said, adding three more coins, "three dollars against future bills. That should be enough until they transfer to the government at Washington. Very soon I should think."

"That money will not go so far, Mr. Brady. Is that gut idea?"

Brady did not reply. Then, he smiled. "One more thing. I will take two boxes with me now."

Brady boarded the night-bound train for Capitol City with an upgraded ticket purchased for the return trip.

He found a reclining chair inside the car with papered walls and gilded lamps. He set his cane aside and adjusted back the plush seat. He contemplated a visit to the washstand at the back of the car to douse his face, but comfort and exhaustion conspired to keep him rooted right where he was.

A young baggage agent appeared through the connecting door, wearing a black buttoned coat two sizes too large and wheeling a cart with a pair of wooden boxes stacked one upon the other. He caught sight of Brady and hurried forward.

"Sir, are you sure you wouldn't prefer that I collect a check for these and you can retrieve them in Washington?"

"No. Thank you. I should like to keep them close."

The agent unloaded the boxes.

Brady reached into his pocket and produced two dimes.

"Thank you, sir!" The agent took the coins and hurried off.

Thank you, Brady thought. With money in his pocket, it felt good to once more play the part of generous patron.

The train whistled.

It crept forward into night. The syncopated hiss of steam before she settled into a smooth roll, the hum and vibration of wheels on track soothing. Brady yawned.

Even he hadn't fully understood why he'd taken the boxes.

They might serve a purpose, were the committee interested in reviewing a sampling of what they were about to purchase. Perhaps he had done it simply for the added satisfaction of denying that slob of a man future payment for services that would never be rendered, once Congress acquired the collection. But Brady thought mostly he had done it because it felt right. A tangible act in that direction. *This was going to happen.*

The extra money he now had with him would ensure things went smoothly. *Leave nothing to chance.* No matter how many more letters it was necessary to pen, or how many drinks and meals he had to purchase at the Willard in the coming days.

Brady had much to do, but he had not forgot his noon engagement tomorrow with Truman Ash. He would not disappoint the young man who had been so eager to meet *the Mathew Brady*, no matter what obligations he might have. It did not hurt that Truman was so close to Wilson, whose attention he might yet need before the petition business was over. If only Brady had more time to attend to all that was needed.

Brady tucked the two wooden boxes beneath his seat and shut his heavy eyes.

He would need his rest.

V

G ardner watched from the gallery as the parson stepped upon the rostrum. Below, senators found their desks as the sergeant-at-arms chased visitors up the terraced floor. Congressmen, who previously sat unmolested at their desks, set down pens and papers and copies of the *Congressional Globe* that contained minutes of yesterday's proceedings.

When the commotion died, the preacher began. "O God we now ask for thy mercy as we convene on this day to do our just duty. Give us the wisdom, the strength-"

Gardner kept his eyes shut until the prayer concluded.

The galleries along the chamber walls held a modest crowd to send off the 40th Congress in its final days.

Patrons, whose fine clothing spoke of wealth, as well as those whose attire hinted a more modest existence, sat watching. The younger generation bantered, often laughing at the senators' barbs as if attending the playhouse. The elders, in general, were more respectful and solemn, some with ear trumpets pressed to their heads to hear above the din.

Gardner turned as a ruffian in checked trousers entered the row behind him. The man clutched the stained fur trim of a heavy coat draped over his shoulders, its threadbare sleeves swaying free. He took a seat, the smell of stale tobacco emanated from him. He met Gardner's eyes and a smile formed upon the man's whiskered face as he touched the brim of his tattered silk hat with two filthy fingers.

Gardner turned back round to focus on the morning's petitions.

Senator Sherman. For the Citizens of Ohio: "Praying for such an amendment to the Constitution of the United States as will fully acknowledge the obligations of the Christian religion."

"Referred to the Committee on the Judiciary," announced Ben Wade from his rostrum desk.

Senator Robinson. On behalf of one J.P.T. Camp: "Praying to be released from the payment of internal revenue tax assessed on certain whisky owned by him on the 7th Day of April, 1867."

Referred to the Committee on Finance.

So it went on, petitions from constituents who hoped the act would lead to deliverance through passage of a bill.

Gardner watched Pomeroy, seated below at his cluttered desk. He hoped Pomeroy would be next to rise and address the chamber on his behalf.

He felt a nudge at his back shoulder. He turned to the ruffian who stared back, a protrusion of skin below the lip. The man lowered his eyes to the floor past Gardner's shoes.

Gardner bent forward and passed the man up a brass spittoon by its handle and turned back around before the man rid himself of his vile condition.

Gardner shut his eyes a minute, listening. He knew sleep might have helped his present mood. He had little of it lately, fretting over his petition and, after disclosing his plan to Margaret, enduring not a harsh word, but her silence, always the worst of those two possible outcomes.

But when he opened his eyes again, Pomeroy's desk was empty. And the petitions continued on, unabated.

Referred to the Committee on Military Affairs.
Referred to the Committee on Foreign Relations.
Referred to the Committee on Judiciary.

Gardner scanned the chamber with no sign of the senator.

A couple minutes passed before the senator shuffled back through a side door to his seat. Perhaps Pomeroy was answering the written plea of another constituent in the reception room, or the call of a representative with message regarding a pending vote. Whatever the reason, it had the same deleterious result. Petitions had ended. The committees began to report out on yesterday's business. And a few minutes after that, Ben Wade charged into the discussion of bills.

Gardner's petition would not be heard today. He rose and started toward the aisle, past the roughshod man and his spittoon.

It was then that Gardner saw Brady, several rows left and up. Brady did not appear to see him; he seemed fixed on the proceedings.

Gardner wasted no time hurrying up the steps to the exit.

He left the Capitol for a damp, cold Pennsylvania Avenue and boarded the Washington and Georgetown car.

⌒⌒

At least the Committee on the Library did not report, Gardner assured himself. Brady's petition was still with them.

Perhaps they had not yet discussed it in their meeting room in the basement of the Capitol. Gardner preferred that notion to the thought of the committee having already begun the draft of a bill to appropriate funds for purchase of Brady's plates.

He brooded as the car rolled on.

Gardner needed to believe he still had time, else it seemed everything he'd worked for had been for naught.

The United Kingdom, 1850s

Gardner stood upon a chair and stared out upon the crowded Glasgow Green. He cleared his throat.

"Many of you know me," he began, holding up a leaflet in his hand.

A pudge-nosed man in a dirty cap elbowed his way among the crowd, shoving the same leaflet from his stack into hands of men who stared up at Gardner through breathed puffs of cool March air.

"For those of you who do not know me, my name is Alexander Gardner. I am proprietor of the Sentinel."

He held up a copy of the Saturday edition of the *Glasgow Sentinel* in his other hand.

"The Sentinel, as many of you know it, was founded on the principles of social reform and justice; a Christian duty to promote the rights of the working class men of Glasgow and of the world. It is for this that I come before you today."

Gardner took a few seconds' pause, taking pleasure in the sight of so many new faces examining the flyer in their hands, whether they could read its words or not.

"I have walked among you. Many of you have seen me with pad and paper, visiting your place of work, even your homes. So that the Sentinel may shed light on your situation. But it is a story that needs no telling to most of you. It is rather for those who would prefer to be blind to truth. The affluent man, safe at home by his fire after a meal to fill his belly, who may pick up the Sentinel for the first and find himself at once made aware of what is happening to the great numbers of Glasgow's working families. Their children. So that he may ask himself 'what is my Christian duty?'"

Indeed, Gardner had followed many of them home to the backlands, after long days toiling at the docks, or over hot blast furnaces, or in the mines. Home to dilapidated hovels, damp with rain and choked with coal smoke air of the foundries. He had watched their beggarly children play in trash-filled alleyways amongst the refuse and waste.

Gardner looked to a man in front. Pale and filthy, a poorly wrapped bandage around his head needed changing. A boy at his side, no more than eight or nine, wore too the dirty workman's clothes of his father.

Gardner thought of himself at that young age, about the same time that cholera took his father. The difference being Gardner's family had the means to provide him a good home and several years' schooling.

But for this boy and thousands more like him, there would be no escape. If he stayed in Glasgow, this was his life. This boy, Gardner reminded himself, is why I am here.

"Friends, we at the Sentinel believe there is another way, a path in which hard work can benefit everyone and I come here today to propose a solution. The Clydesdale Joint Stock Company."

Gardner lowered his copy of the Sentinel and raised the leaflet again.

"Over a year ago the first men and women left Scotland, I accompanying them, to form a cooperative community in Iowa, in the United States of America. My own brother and brother-in-law's family are there at this moment."

Gardner pointed a finger at the leaflet's written details.

"Each man afforded two acres, a homestead. Shares divided evenly among members, profits from time and labor divided and distributed back amongst the shareholders."

He tucked the paper away inside his coat pocket.

"Today I oversee their interests from Glasgow and stand ready to share its promise with any new persons wishing to retire to a more- civilized existence."

Gardner stepped down off his chair and took a step into the crowd. "I will be here to answer any questions you may have. God bless."

The crowd drew in. Before he knew it, Gardner was shaking hands like a politician. Answering the many questions asked of him.

∝⌾⌾

Gardner was nine when his father died, his brother James only two.

Jean Gardner, deep in despair, was left only hard choices when she abandoned the family grocery and ventured back across the river Clyde, from Paisley to Glasgow, to lean upon her own family. Taking this backward step meant her children would be fed and clothed and would receive an education.

And that they did. At fifteen Gardner completed studies and was apprenticed to a Glasgow jeweler. He learned the craft and developed some business acumen.

But after six years, the young man felt an itch. Intrigued by the world of finance, Gardner became clerk at the Glasgow Discount and Loan on Candleriggs Lane. Evenings, he attended lectures at the Glasgow Athenaeum. In the company of learned men, he devoured the latest scientific journals, feeding his passion for chemistry, conducting experiments and studying the latest scientific inventions.

He married Margaret Sinclair, a girl he had known since boyhood. She gave him a son, Lawrence, later that year. A few years passed before Gardner; husband, father, manager of finance, felt the itch once more.

Gardner grew up strong in faith; his mother's family contained more than one man of the Kirk. But it did not take a man of the cloth to see what the age of industry meant to the working men and women of Glasgow.

It had started long before Gardner. In his father's time, they began to close off the land, forcing farmers to the cities where they toiled in factories for a pittance.

The poet Robert Burns trumpeted attention to such injustices a half century earlier but, it seemed, his verses were to no avail. Conditions had only worsened since then.

Gardner saw it firsthand as he walked the slums where urchins begged for coins to buy necessities their mothers and fathers could still not afford after long, dangerous hours at work.

It seemed a bleak and desperate future awaited mankind.

Through the Athenaeum, Gardner heard of those who were doing something about it. Men like Robert Owen had carved a better life for such people in places like New Harmony in America.

Gardner was finally certain he knew his purpose.

Within months of purchasing the small newspaper, he and a handful of like-minded men chartered the colony in America, dividing parcels in Monona, Iowa a few miles west of the Mississippi River. Fifty dollars a share. Margaret's brother, Robertson Sinclair, with his soon to be wife, Jesse, was among the first to set sail. Gardner's brother James would go too. It was decided that, for a time, Gardner might best serve the fledging settlement from Glasgow where he could manage their affairs and, most importantly, recruit fellow Scots.

By that March of '51, fifteen families had settled in the Iowa colony.

Amongst its pages on social discourse, The *Glasgow Sentinel* espoused the benefits of the new settlement. Readership increased beyond what Gardner could have hoped. He began publishing a Saturday weekly, reporting national and world news as the larger syndications in Glasgow and London did.

It was in the spring of '51 that Queen Victoria opened the Crystal Palace in London.

The Sentinel gave Gardner the opportunity to pay visit as reporter the last week of May.

It was to be one of the most profound events of his life.

The Crystal Palace, a massive cathedral of iron and glass, stretched nearly a third of a mile across London's Hyde Park.

Gardner awaited entrance outside the gates, admiring the perfect specimen of angle and symmetry, flags from every nation snapped in the wind atop it. He doubted anything inside could match the marvel of its exterior.

He was wrong.

A great crystal fountain stood in the main avenue beneath the iron trusses and glass roof. Mature elms rooted throughout the park were enclosed within the building's open courts.

An interior view of the Crystal Palace in London, the 1st World's Fair
The exhibition ran from May 1st to October 11th 1851

From second-floor galleries, one could glimpse the grand displays of France, Belgium, Bavaria, India, and British colonies far and wide. Massive tapestries hung from rafters. Grand paintings, marble statues. Priceless jewels, a stuffed elephant from the Raj. The bronze-cast Bavarian

Lion fifteen feet in length. Displays of textiles, grand exhibits of machinery; reapers and ploughs and the latest agricultural implements, model ships, steam fired engines, and a locomotive that had been towed inside.

Grand clocks rang out the hours, competing with piano fortes and string quartets that played for the passing crowds.

Had Gardner another month, he could not see everything there was to see in the palace.

He took record of these many wonders, but with his pen he too made unambiguous his pessimism. Would these innovations alleviate the plight of the poor and disadvantaged, in Glasgow and London, and the civilized world over? Or would they only aggravate their condition?

On his third and final morning, Gardner visited the wing devoted to the United States.

The McCormick Reaper from Chicago, Colt firearms from Connecticut, textiles, light-weight coaches, ship ventilators from Boston. What the new nation might not yet possess in art and culture, it clearly made up for with its industriousness.

Gardner was drawn soon to the States' exhibit of photography, which seemed to surpass in size even that of Britain's. But ten years old this new art, photographers were turning out thousands of images in studios in Glasgow and every city in Britain.

He admired the daguerreotypes. J. Whipple of Boston, a photograph of the moon with all its surface imperfections in detail. Whitehurst of Baltimore, photographs of Niagara Falls among his collections. An eight-plate panorama of the waterfront at Cincinnati and so many others with placards bearing the artist's name. Also on display were the many new experiments with glass negatives from which paper positives could be produced, though they seemed not yet to possess the exquisiteness of the daguerreotype.

The largest collection occupied a spacious table and group of easels set aside in the bay. M.B. Brady, New York.

His *Gallery of Illustrious Americans* banner accompanied a series of framed portraits; Presidents Martin Van Buren and John Quincy Adams, Henry Clay, John C. Calhoun, General Winfield Scott. Among these were dozens more images; men, women, and children whom Gardner would never know. He would never pass them on a street. Yet they were here.

Clouds passed high above the glass roof and the sun's rays glided over the daguerreotypes, bringing every subject to life.

Gardner stood before one image, a girl holding proud her violin and bow, with ebullient eyes and a rather pensive smile.

"Her next song perhaps?"

Gardner turned suddenly.

Next to him stood a dapper man, an expensive suit and a pair of tinted spectacles low upon the bridge of his nose. He smiled at Gardner through a trim goatee, then nodded back at the girl and her violin on the table.

"You were wondering what she was thinking about."

Gardner looked to the man who sounded American, one of many well-to-dos who had crowded Gardner down every palace corridor.

Many such gentlemen no doubt considered themselves responsible for the exhibition, nay the Crystal Palace's very existence. Their push toward maximum profits the driving force behind many of the new industrial innovations; their money patronized the arts on display. They could afford the three guineas admission to spend their idle days perusing the queen's palace. Once admission lowered at the end of the summer, the working men of London might spare a shilling to glimpse these same wonders.

Gardner had endured his type the past three days, their whimsical remarks and put on airs.

He was not greatly interested in their opinions on art or any other matter. He did not wish to get to know them.

"Perhaps. We will never know," Gardner replied, turning his back to the man. "It is a wonderful piece."

"She loved that instrument." Gardner heard over his shoulder after a passing silence. "Her mother told me she carried it with her from morning's wake to evening."

Gardner turned once more upon the man.

"She played for me. Not an accomplished player by any measure I can assure you. But that tiny violin was everything she wanted for herself. One day, she told me, she would compose something beautiful for the world."

Gardner said nothing.

The man laughed and held out a hand.

"Mathew Brady. New York."

Gardner shook the hand after a moment. "Alexander Gardner."

"London Times, Mr. Gardner? I had hoped I might catch you."

Gardner was puzzled by the comment until he remembered the pad and pen in his hand.

"No. The Glasgow Sentinel."

"Oh, Glasgow. Splendid," said Brady. "My new bride and I are just beginning our tour of Europe. After London, I should like to visit the Trossachs, time permitting."

Gardner stared silently. Then "So you are the man behind all these images?"

"I am. Well, I am in the sense that I select the subjects, the composition, the lighting, but" Brady paused to tap his left lens, "rarely do I handle the camera myself these days. The finer details escape my eyes anymore. But the entire affair happens upon my direction. Should you be so inclined, Mr. Gardner, I could give you a review of my works on display."

Gardner pulled at his beard, contemplating.

"I haven't much space for my story, I'm afraid. I planned only to print something on the exhibit as a whole."

Then Gardner surprised himself. "But I do suppose I could take a few words."

The photographer did most of the talking. Gardner took a note here and there. For all his self-importance, this Brady was an artist of some renown. That much was clear.

Gardner closed his pad. He glanced to his pocket watch and knew he needed to move on if he were to see any more of the palace. The train left for Glasgow in a little under three hours' time.

"Thank you, Mr. Brady. Best of luck to you here and upon your return to America. It is truly a wonderful country."

"Yes. It is. Have you been to America, Mr. Gardner?" inquired Brady, still clutching Gardner's hand.

"Yes actually. I have business in America you might say."

Brady stepped back. "Do tell! Publishing interests of some sort?"

"Not at all. From Glasgow, I managed affairs of the Clydesdale community in Iowa. A cooperative shared equally among its shareholders."

Brady cocked his head and formed a crooked smile. "Oh. I see."

Gardner instantly regretted saying anything.

"Interesting indeed!" Brady continued. "I have heard a great deal about such experiments. I do believe America is the place for such a thing. A country large enough for all sorts of ideas."

Gardner put his pad and pencil into his coat. He forgot he was in a hurry and turned full to face Brady. He cleared his throat.

"Yes, Mr. Brady. You will be happy to know that it will provide, it is providing I should say, a better opportunity for former working-class men and women of Glasgow. Those left behind by the...progress of this New Age."

Brady scratched at his goatee as if he were considering Gardner's claim, then he smiled. "Well, I am sure it is in good hands, sir. I do wish you a greater success than others I have heard about. Your intentions are no doubt the best. But I might add that the industry and invention you see in this palace are the very makings of progress. And I suppose progress of any kind has always been inconvenient for some."

"The working poor find their condition terribly inconvenient I can assure you, Mr. Brady."

Brady held up a hand.

Gardner breathed; he could feel the blood simmering in his face, burning at the tips of his ears.

Brady, for his part, never stopped smiling.

"I understand. And it might pain you to know that I consider myself to be a charitable man. But men cannot simply abide without trying to outdo one another. It's how it has always been. Share everything? I simply do not believe, with all due respect, that it's in our makeup. I think you will find it no different in America. But I wish you the best, Mr. Gardner. I sincerely do."

Gardner started once more, then decided against it. He looked at the table. The girl and her violin staring back, mocking him in his agitated state.

"Thank you, Mr. Brady. I must be off."

"Thank you, Mr. Gardner." Brady took his hand. "I do hope you will have enough for your story."

Margaret blew out the candle on her nightstand. "Good night, dear."

"Good night."

He sat with his notepad in lap, lit by the light of a lone candle. Two days after his return from London, he reviewed the closing remarks of his editorial that would accompany the Sentinel's coverage of the Crystal Palace.

The scene was typical of world's condition. A vast assemblage of powers as yet unmeasured in their capacity but half reduced to order, armed force still watching to supply the defeat in the organization of society.

Society half-starved by its own toil, some rolling luxury, some weary and afoot, dusty, hungry, envying and dangerous.

Gardner's mind filled with the grand machinery, all the promise of invention. He recalled the works of art that graced the halls and, finally, the daguerreotypes by a man named Brady. He dipped his pen and wrote his closing sentence.

Yet in that crystal edifice was great work revealed.

~~~

The door to the outbuilding swung open on its hinge. Gardner turned to see Lawrence standing at the door. The sun's rays had grown dim in the yard at the boy's back.

"Mother says dinner is ready."

Gardner took a blackened rag in his hand and turned it over to wipe his hands. "Very good, son."

Gardner smiled, studying his boy in the faint light. So big. Eight years old now in that spring of '56. *Where had time gone?*

Lawrence ambled toward his father at the work table. The boy eyed the box camera turned up on its back, its oak legs lying flat beside it and a detached lens in its holder. Among these lay screws and Gardner's scattered tools; a brace, shank, and screwdriver with scalloped blade.

"Is it broken?"

Gardner laughed. "No. Just making a few adjustments."

"Can I watch?"

"After dinner. Let's get inside."

Father and son hurried into the house and to the table. After Gardner said Grace, they commenced to eat.

Gardner's mother, Jean Glenn, began to pick among the smaller cuts of beef on the plate. Lawrence piled meat onto a plate already heaped with potatoes. He just might finish it too, Gardner thought. Opposite Gardner at the head of the table, Margaret offered a plate to her mother Mary, who took the smallest of portions. Beside Margaret, Eliza bounced with all the energy the petite six-year-old girl could muster as she nibbled a potato from the tip of a fork.

Margaret's mother put her hands into the lap of her dark blue dress. There she sat, brooding eyes beneath a bonnet atop gray hair.

"Could I beg you to pass the rolls?" Margaret whispered to Gardner.

He nodded, thinking how he hated how tense his wife became when her widowed mother paid visit.

Gardner reached to center table and hoisted the basket.

He looked up at his mother-in-law and caught Mary Sinclair's ghastly stare. Margaret eyes widened too.

Gardner, puzzled, followed his wife's gaze to where his flannel shirt exposed his outstretched arm. It was nearly black to his wrist. Plate chemicals. He had been in haste washing his hands at the backyard pump.

Margaret seized the bread basket and Gardner lowered his arm.

The room held quiet. Lawrence started a second plate of cuts.

Gardner found he did not have much appetite.

Margaret's mother cleared her throat, putting the table on alert. "So, how is this photography business faring, Alexander?"

Gardner traded glances with Margaret. It was a conversation he hoped might be avoided.

He leaned away from the table.

"We are making due, I suppose."

Thankfully, the old woman offered no immediate reply. Gardner cut a piece of meat. He chewed it slowly.

When the Iowa colony failed in the spring of '52, it hit Gardner as hard as any.

Gardner's brother James had drafted the letter from Iowa, notifying him of the disbandment. Each family had agreed to farm their own plots along the banks of the Mississippi. Too many disagreements about their collected future to be reconciled. They decided they would be better off together, yet apart.

Gardner returned to America that spring. He spent three weeks in Iowa, returning not as shepherd to his flock, but as executer of last rights, undoing intertwined finances and settling accounts. The families, to a single one, assuaged Gardner that they had no regrets about settling in the new land. They would go on about their lives as farmers and neighbors. James Gardner decided America was his place too. Without wife or family, he became a produce agent, working on behalf of the Iowa farms in New York.

The *Glasgow Sentinel* continued with a healthy subscriber base. Gardner used it to satisfy his interests in other things, including the growing art of photography. Every month saw new studios open in Glasgow and along the river towns. He attended lectures and learned about Archer's new wet plate. Last year, he was able to review the prints of Londoner Roger Fenton, who had taken stunning images of the army in Crimea. He posted a glowing review in the Sentinel.

Photography was never far from Gardner's mind.

He confessed to Margaret that the itch had returned.

Gardner built his first camera with the help of pamphlets that circulated, encouraging newcomers to the art. His knowledge of chemistry gave him an advantage when learning the process involved in sensitizing and developing negatives.

He learned to love the work, the tuning of his instrument, the sweet smell of collodion poured exactly so upon the glass, and the search for the perfect composition, the balance of light and dark.

Wanting to dedicate himself fully to photography, he sold his interest in the Sentinel.

Gardner suspected his days with the newspaper would serve him well. The *London Times* had recently printed its first engravings based upon photographs, rendering life-like images in mass print, two mediums become one.

But there was no shortage of concern when Gardner opened his small studio in Dumbarton in that January of '56. Daily, Gardner made the long trek there, where the competition was not so great as in Glasgow where photographers such as John Urie had already established a strong reputation.

These past few months had been difficult, for everyone.

Margaret set down her fork.

"Yes. Well, mother," she started, flashing a nervous smile, "perhaps the studio is in want of some advertising. We were discussing that just this morning. Weren't we, dear? But business grows a little each week."

"Yes," Gardner added. He could not help but feel as if he were being interrogated for a crime. He resented it, yet he knew well his wife, with two children to care for, supported him. For that, he would endure.

"I know that it will, son," interjected Jean Gardner before she put fork to mouth. Strong as she was, Gardner would not ask his mother to fight her son's battle.

Margaret's mother nodded and sipped her tea. "And is it enough for a family of four?"

Gardner met her eyes. "Many a studio in Glasgow does a brisk business. It can be quite profitable."

Mary Sinclair shrugged. "Yes. But after how long? How many lean months, years even? And undoubtedly started by younger men without a family to look after. Isn't that so?"

Gardner breathed deep the air, suddenly thin and unsatisfying. Were there not the hint of hard truth in her words, they might not have stung him so.

Mary Sinclair had watched as her son Robertson left her for America, some grand social experiment that her son-in-law had dreamt up. Perhaps now she doubted that her daughter and grandchildren were in safe-keeping with the man. Gardner could understand her uneasiness but still he felt a rage swell. He felt himself ready to lash out from across the table.

"Father is going to teach me how to take a photograph!"

The adults at the table turned to Lawrence, who sat beaming.

His grandmother Mary formed a tight-lipped smile for her grandson. "Is that so?"

Margaret laughed and her mother did so too, turning to kiss the boy's head.

Gardner rose from his chair. "Excuse me."

Gardner watched Eliza off to sleep between the sheets. Too big now to sleep between them, he would soon carry her across the hall. For the moment, Margaret lay with her hand on her head, caressing her daughter's auburn locks, though not enough to wake her.

Gardner watched mother and child by moonlight from the window. The sight nearly chased away the worry that filled his heart.

Margaret looked up at him, a smirk upon her silhouetted face.

"What is it?" he asked.

She said nothing for what seemed an eternity.

"What?" he demanded in a whisper.

Then she said "America".

He lay there, stunned. He let the words sink in, careful not to get ahead of himself.

She continued. "Iowa sounds the place to raise a family. America has always been your dream. Your brother is there. And my brother. Your mother will go where we go. My mother has my sisters and-"

He thrust himself forward and pressed his lips to hers.

He pulled away to see Margaret, his hands cradling her face now. Overcome, he could only nod his acceptance. Gardner kissed her again with Eliza asleep between them, oblivious to the new fate which had just been cast her.

The United States, 1850s

Gardner took Lawrence starboard side that May morning when the *Glasgow* steamed into New York's harbor after a weeks' long journey.

Father and son squeezed their way along the crowded deck for a glimpse of the busy shoreline, the distant wharfs and buildings. Gulls circled the ship and sails as if to guide them safely to port, soaring then diving low to spread white wings broad against the water.

But once the steamer made land, all Gardner's plans seemed at once to vanish like sea mist into morning sun.

The telegram was brief but said enough.

Consumption had spread with ferocity among the Iowan farms. Margaret's brother Robertson was too ill to care for his infant daughter. His wife Jesse had succumbed the week before.

Gardner left by rail the next morning, leaving his brother James to watch over their mother, Margaret, and the children.

It was Gardner's third trip to Iowa since '49. And it occurred to him that each trip had been less happy than the one that preceded it.

He ferried across the Mississippi to McGregor's Landing, finding Robertson Sinclair in a serious state. His daughter had been taken in by a local magistrate; the man and his wife were childless, polite and God-fearing people. Gardner discussed the matter with his ailing brother-in-law just before he died. He exchanged telegrams with his Margaret, and it was settled. Gardner signed papers to leave his niece with her new parents.

On the mournful journey back to New York, Gardner felt the weight of decisions upon him as never before.

The room to which he returned to find his family was a place James rented when he came to the city on business, small and dank with but a plate-sized window too high to see out. The dilapidated building had two dozen more rooms just the same.

By light of a small fire, Gardner watched Margaret and kids gathered on the musty floor, playing draughts. *We'll make do here a while.* That is what Margaret had told Gardner that first night upon his return. But this was no way to live.

What else was to be done? Steam back to Scotland?

No. There was still time.

But as Gardner strolled along Broadway, he knew practicing as a photographer would not be so easy here as it might have were his studio situated on the west bank of the Mississippi. Dozens of photography establishments crowded the streets, more even than Glasgow. Another studio, even had he the funds for it, would easily go unnoticed.

He decided he would seek work in an established studio if he could yet find one that hired. And it was plain to see that one New York studio stood out above all others.

Gardner would not even consider it.

A week passed when Margaret turned in her bed, Eliza asleep between them. Beyond a green curtain lay the rest of the room, his son and brother snoring at intervals. His aging mother slept behind a similar cloth partition at the room's end, all of fifteen feet away.

Margaret nudged him and he looked to her.

"Go and see him."

"What?" Gardner whispered.

She smiled but said nothing more. She put her head to pillow.

He laid back, staring at the dark ceiling. "I won't do it."

He was ready to continue arguing his point but was left the remainder of the night thwarted by her silence.

The following morning, he passed the building, just as he had every morning.

For the first, Gardner went inside.

The young attendant rose from a desk in a space beside a narrow hall.

Gardner explained he had no appointment and was not here to sit, but that he knew the proprietor and wished to speak to him. The man told

Gardner he was in luck; the owner was in. Gardner followed him up three flights. The attendant slinked around a half-open door and shut it all but closed.

The door opened again. The attendant stepped out; his boss followed.

There he stood before Gardner. His dark goatee hiding a fuller face, but otherwise he was just as Gardner remembered five years ago.

The man smiled, studying Gardner with a cocked head.

"I beg pardon, have we met before?"

Mathew Brady did not seem to recall the man in his doorway.

So, it was Gardner who was forced to recount their meeting at the Crystal Palace years before, to which Brady then expressed some vague recollection.

Rather than disappointed, Gardner was buoyed by hopes that Brady would not recall the substance of their conversation.

If Brady did remember more of that long ago day than he let on, it did not show.

Gardner did not elaborate in detail his present situation. He explained in few words that he and his family were in the city, and he was looking for work. He expounded on his business credentials, then his experience behind the camera.

"I have been producing wet plate for over two years. You will find me a skilled operator. Single-lens, stereoscopic views. I would be happy to demonstrate any-"

Brady laughed and held out an open palm as if to concede. Gardner knew then that he had been racing his words. How desperate he must have sounded.

He sensed no small amount of magnanimity in Brady's next words, oh but how they put him at ease.

"Welcome to New York, Mr. Gardner. You may start tomorrow."

Gardner was managing the Manhattan studio after three months on the job, overseeing its many operators, like the young Tim O'Sullivan, and staff that worked in the developing and printing rooms.

Brady showed only for the most important clientele.

Gardner knew he enjoyed Brady's confidence that the studio was in good hands though their interactions were not always so agreeable.

"A word with you, Mathew," said Gardner one afternoon.

Brady looked up at Gardner, standing in the office doorway. "What is on your mind, Alex?"

For a time, Gardner had been singularly focused on photography, streamlining the process from appointments through delivery of the product for maximum efficiency and throughput. He had only recently turned his attention to business practices.

He was appalled by what he found.

"This past hour, I've watched your attendant accept payment from customers. I can tell you that many a note and coin exchanged hands without a single mark in a ledger."

"Not to worry. Charles is an honest man."

"I do not question it," replied Gardner. "But how then does your bookkeeper track payments and accrue expenses?"

"Ah. Book keeper you say? Well, if you would like to balance a book, I suppose that would do."

Gardner's mouth fell open, disbelieving. "Are you saying you have no accountant? There must be a thousand dollars a week that passes through this studio!"

"Yes. Yes, Alex, we are quite profitable."

"That is hardly the point!" Gardner said near a shout.

Brady ceased to smile.

Cautious, Gardner swallowed. He breathed in before continuing. "One cannot possibly run a business of this volume without recording each transaction. What of the issuance of customer receipts? Tracking payments due creditors and-"

Brady threw up a hand. His face flustered, the look he so often reserved for Gardner when he'd had his fill.

"Is that it then? Bookkeeper? Do as you see fit, Alex. Hire your man."

Gardner did hire his man. And he did almost whatever else he wanted. In the months that followed, the volume of daily appointments the studio could handle increased by a third, with every dime accounted for. Brady saw more money fill his coffers than ever before. Were Gardner a different kind of man, he might have pointed these facts out to Brady, and expected some hint of gratitude in return.

Brady had been slow to convert to the collodion negative. Other studios had abandoned daguerreotypes and the ambrotype, a glass positive backed in black felt, in favor of negatives that could be mass produced. Stereo cards, produced by two lens cameras, were in high demand to fill the popular three-dimensional stereoviewers. And the carte de viste trend had spread from Europe to America. A single glass negative could produce unlimited numbers of the one-by-three-inch calling cards on embossed paper stock. Brady soon regained any advantage lost to his rivals. Working men and women who might never had considered sitting for an expensive daguerreotype came and counted out pennies on the counter to pay for their likeness. Brady's high-profile photographs of notable statesmen, actors, and military heroes were being mass produced under Gardner's direction. Every respectable parlor album had them for display.

Brady's profits doubled.

Yet he lamented the new era and that, as he saw things, the art of it had given way.

And what was wrong with everyone having access to photography? Gardner would challenge him, on this as with so many other things.

More to Brady's liking was Gardner's introduction of the Imperial print; a life-size print touched in paint that could fetch up to three hundred dollars.

Brady too entered the world of illustrated media. As Gardner expected, American papers followed the lead of Europe where publications like the *Illustrated London News* used woodcut engravings to reproduce photographs. In '57, Brady's first illustration appeared in *Harper's Weekly*. Most fitting, it was of Brady's old friend Samuel Morse, whose telegraph had made him a rich man many times over.

✒

In the spring of '58, an opportunity presented itself to Gardner when Brady opened a studio in the heart of Washington, at 352 Pennsylvania Avenue, near the corner of 6th. Brady's studio occupied the top three floors over a banking establishment. The top floor had a grand skylight, thirty feet deep, installed by the previous photographers who found they could not compete with the city's more established artists. It showed a grand façade on the avenue, arched windows separated by iron colonettes. The rear C Street entrance's four bay windows displayed merchandise.

Brady needed someone capable to manage operations. After nearly two years, Gardner was sure of two things: that he was qualified for the job, and that it might be good for both he and Brady to have some distance between them.

Margaret agreed and Gardner moved his family to Washington. They settled into a spacious frame house on two acres, surrounded by poplars and fronted by a picket fence along Boundary Street at 7th.

The year before, Gardner had hired his brother at Brady's New York studio and James had become a skilled cameraman in that time. He now invited his brother to join him, in Washington, as his first operator.

Years before, Brady had operated a studio in Washington but found the competition too stiff, even for him. Things were different now. No need for discounts and gimmicks to attract clientele.

The name *Brady* was all the advertisement necessary.

Friday noon

Gardner turned to Truman Ash some forty-five minutes into their tour of the Smithsonian Castle.

The three men stood at the foot of stairs to the second floor, staring down the protracted hall where the crowd perused its many exhibits. It seemed Gardner's best chance to announce a polite withdrawal.

"I'm sorry, Truman. I must go, I'm afraid. Appointments at the studio. Thank you. I enjoyed it."

In truth, Gardner found it difficult to wait as long as he did. He had arrived to find Truman and Brady awaiting his arrival. Brady did not address him once as Truman led them among exhibits, then through the wings and labyrinth of castle rooms; laboratories and dust-filled spaces closed to the public. Brady, for his part, seemed to enjoy Truman's elucidation on one of Capitol City's great treasures, asking many a question. But Gardner knew well that, like himself, Brady had bigger things on his mind.

Truman thanked Gardner for coming. Gardner shook his hand, then Brady's, before starting across the floor.

"Alex," Gardner heard from over his shoulder. "Excuse me a moment, Truman."

Gardner turned and watched Brady step his way.

"A word with you, if I may?"

He eyed Brady as they stood in sunbeams that cascaded through the slender windows of the hall. Gardner scratched his arm beneath its sling.

At that moment, Gardner could still pretend he had not a clue as to what Brady might say.

"I had a conversation with Henry Wilson this morning, in the hall outside the Senate."

Gardner said nothing.

"He mentioned to me," Brady continued, "among other things, a conversation he had with Senator Pomeroy concerning you."

Brady formed a tight smile. "I'd say your timing of a petition is curious to say the least. Now where would you get such an idea, Alex?"

Condescension. Gardner had heard it enough through the years to recognize it. Brady had always thought himself the better of them, to that there was no question.

To step aside, now, and allow Congress to reward Brady, would be to allow him to eclipse all the important work Gardner had done in those years. It was not about the money. And though Brady's financial hardships since the war were well-known, Gardner knew it was about more than money to Brady too.

"Of course," Brady continued, "in a perfect world, they should purchase both our collections. Lord knows that is what should be done. But you and I know they would not be that foresighted."

"No. I should think not."

Brady stared, seeming to bait Gardner in further reply.

Gardner placed his hat upon his head and pulled tight his coat to button over his invalid arm. "Tell me, Mathew. What am I to do? Am I obliged to sit idly by while you assume the credit?"

Brady's face had reddened, his cheeks flush above his goatee. He looked ready to unleash a verbal tirade, though Gardner had never seen such a display. Brady was too composed for that. But he recognized the look of hatred in Brady's stare.

"No. I suppose you are not, Alex." Brady hesitated. "So, I guess there is only the wait and see."

Gardner nodded, agreeing on that. "If you will excuse me."

Gardner started away.

"Alex."

He turned to watch Brady draw close once more and reach into his pocket. "One more thing." Brady pulled an envelope out.

Gardner took it slowly into hand. Brady formed a wicked smile. "From Julia. An invitation to dinner. Tomorrow night."

VI

A glance at his timepiece and Gardner shot up, jarring the table. The cold remainder of his tea emptied over the front page of the *National Republican*. He grabbed the letters and envelopes with his free hand, saving them from the liquid's advance.

A stack of six letters to congressmen, written on heavy black bordered stationery with Gardner's studio seal.

Eliza entered the room and laughed at the sight of the drenched daily.

Emily followed from behind. "Let me take that, Mr. Gardner. I'll dry that paper for you if you weren't finished with it."

He held up his hands as if being put to gunpoint while Emily took the toppled cup and ran a rag across the brown pool. "Thank you, Emily. You can throw it out."

"I want to read the ads for parlor pianos," Eliza protested.

Emily turned to the whine from a kettle at the stove. She handed the paper to Eliza from beneath the sopping rag.

"Here you go, child. It's your mess now."

Margaret entered as Emily whisked past. She smiled, then turned back to Emily in the kitchen.

127

"Are you sure you won't come shopping with us?"

"No thank you." Emily reappeared. "But I will ride to the avenue with you if you give me a minute. I need to visit Center Market."

"I am helping with dinner tonight," Eliza said with pride.

Emily laughed. "Very good, ma'am!"

Margaret proceeded to the wall hanger and grabbed coat and shawl.

Eliza set the wet paper on an empty chair and followed, but not before kissing her father upon the cheek.

"Be more careful. Sure you won't come to town with us?"

Gardner watched his ladies dress for the winter's morning. "Sorry no. I have business I am afraid."

"Business," Margaret scoffed, casting a glance to the letters in his left hand. "Some business it is."

Margaret opened the door and Eliza stepped through it. Emily hurried past with her wool coat through the first arm.

Margaret adjusted her scarf and addressed Gardner once more, without looking his way. "Mind you not to let Saturday business keep you late. We have dinner plans this evening."

Dinner, he thought. As if there was a chance he could forget.

When Gardner returned home yesterday and reluctantly presented Brady's invitation to her, there was no surprise in it at all.

Julia Brady had paid a visit that same afternoon while he was away, perhaps to guard against the possibility that her husband might conveniently forget to deliver the invite. The ladies had tea and talked the better part of two hours like long lost friends before they bid farewell until tomorrow. Margaret talked it up greatly at last night's dinner.

She likely relished the thought of her husband and rival suffering through a meal together, whilst they plotted against one another professionally.

"Indeed." was all of Gardner's reply as she shut the door.

Gardner found Senator Edwin Morgan in the reception room at five minutes to nine, talking to a gentleman in a cut silk suit. The room was crowded with several such men.

Such overt persuasion; it was one of the reasons Gardner could not bring himself to set foot in places like the Willard, where he might find plenty of congressmen among the parlors being plied with French meals, imported brandies, and the best cigars while they discussed *business.*

But if Gardner could find at least one of his letters' recipients here before session, it might be worthwhile.

The room began to clear, congressmen headed for the floor. Gardner stepped to Morgan as he rifled over the envelopes that jutted from his coat pocket. He pulled one free.

"Senator Morgan."

The wealthy stockbroker turned senator stopped and stood, several inches above Gardner.

Morgan glanced at the gold watch chained at his waistcoat and pursed his lips beneath gray whiskers.

"Mr. Gardner." It sounded more like a question than statement.

"Yes. Hello, Senator."

Morgan let slip his watch into his waist pocket and shook Gardner's free hand.

He knew Morgan, if only professionally. In his four years in the Senate, Morgan had sat before his camera on at least two different occasions. Gardner remembered the senator as instrumental in the late war effort. What he knew of the man, he respected.

"What can I help you with? I was just on my way into session."

"Yes. Certainly. I have a letter that I mean to present to you."

The senator took it slowly, almost begrudgingly. He lowered it to his side.

"The fact is, Senator, I wanted to inform you that a petition will be presented today by Senator Pomeroy concerning the purchase of my war views upon recommendation of your committee. I expect you will soon hear of it and, well sir, I wanted the chance to express my reasons for it."

Morgan nodded. He lifted his watch once more.

Gardner stood there, silent. He regretted the imposition on a busy senator such as Morgan. Perhaps he was no better than the damned lobbyists. Yet he knew well that Brady was doing much the same, if not more, to draw attention to his own petition to ensure action was taken.

Morgan cleared his throat. "I see." His feet were already moving toward the door as he took hold of Gardner's hand. "I will read your letter, sir. I always like to be prepared. Thank you."

"Very well, Senator. Good day and thank you."

Gardner watched the senator hurry out.

He decided then and there that he would summon a page to deliver the remaining letters.

The gallery quieted and the session began with prayer. Gardner slipped into his usual spot on the bench seats.

He was relieved at once to see Pomeroy below at his desk, in the first row to the right of the rostrum.

Across the aisle Morgan had reached his desk in the last row, with old Senator Fessenden seated in the row ahead. Fessenden would soon receive his own letter from the youthful page now in possession of Gardner's notes. In the same row as Fessenden, a desk between them, sat Senator Henry Wilson.

Gardner scanned his section of gallery; a good crowd.

In the row behind sat the ruffian from yesterday, the tobacco chewer. His coat spread over him and the tall and tattered hat down over his eyes, he breathed heavily in his nap.

He did not see Brady and did not know what to make of that.

Gardner turned his attention to the first of business.

He focused his mind, preparing himself. Gardner thought about the petition bearing his name that would soon echo aloud in the chamber below, and all the reasons it mattered so.

July 1862

Gardner choked on the bitter taste of beer.

Across the table they had a good laugh at his expense. He set down his mug and wiped a bit of foam from his bearded lip. Over his shoulder, the tavern door creaked opened atop the stairs.

Firecrackers echoed loudly from the capital streets above them, popping at random intervals until the heavy door was pulled shut once more.

Gardner took out his pocket watch. Nearly eleven. In an hour it would be Independence Day. *July 4th, 1862.*

A plump barmaid set down four shots on the table.

O'Sullivan smiled at Gardner; his curly head of hair pressed back against the high-backed booth. He took up the first whisky, tipped it in Gardner's direction, and drained it with a wince.

"That's alright, boss. Let's get you a lemonade."

The barmaid looked down at Gardner as if to confirm the order.

"No. Nothing thank you," corrected Gardner before coughing from the smoke.

Gibson laughed so that the cigar between his teeth glowed bright beneath the wide brim of his hat, enough to light a face flushed and eyes glazed from drink.

"What's the matter, Mr. Gardner?" asked Jay Sneed, sitting between O'Sullivan and Gibson and showing an impish grin, "I guess where you come from the beer tastes like gingersnaps."

Jay Sneed was with the *New York Herald*. Gardner's men knew him well. They had crossed paths with him often in the field and camps as he chewed his cigar, taking furious notes, wearing the same brown stitch back coat and plug hat he wore now.

"Well, it's about time," Sneed said over Gardner's shoulder.

Gardner turned to see the group of reporters approach. They slid a table beside the booth and proceeded to draw up chairs, screeching legs to the attention of other patrons.

"Girl. A round of the brown and beer for my men and another for these *photo-graph-ers.*"

The barmaid set down a mug and started away when Sneed smacked her ample hind quarters to which she giggled in reply.

They sat, cross-legged, slouching, or with their mud boots stretched out before them. They lit pipes and cigars as they received their drinks.

Just as with Sneed, Gardner had come to know each of them over the course of a year; Horace White of the *Chicago Tribune*, Henry Flint with the *New York Herald*, Uriah Painter; *Philadelphia Enquirer*, and Whitelaw Reid of the *Cincinnati Gazette*.

Members of the so-called *Bohemian Brigade*.

Gruff men with unkempt beards, slouch hats and slop coats; they looked more like mule drivers than the educated men they were. They chased stories at the front, far removed from the city presses. They drove hard for bits of information to wire in telegraph dispatches, hoping they would not be censored. In former lives, they were small town reporters, some schoolteachers. The war, for better or worse, gave them purpose; they chose the harsh conditions and dangers of an unpredictable war to a cramped desk along Pennsylvania Avenue's *Newspaper Row*.

That evening they drank, laughed, and shared stories. O'Sullivan matched the newsmen, joke for joke and insult for insult. Gibson, in his own quiet and mercurial way, joined in with a few jabs of his own.

As for Gardner, he sat, listening without judgment passed, even among the bawdier tales. By twos and threes, more reporters showed.

They sat and stood about the booth and nearby tables; the size of the party producing many splintered conversations.

Gardner's brother James arrived after closing the studio.

More of Gardner's men arrived as well, John Wood and David Woodbury. A blade of grass, no doubt pulled from the Virginia countryside hours before, still rested in the corner of young Woodbury's mouth and against the tufts of his beard.

They ordered whiskeys and lit smokes and enjoyed the company.

A few minutes before midnight, Alfred Waud trailed in, clean by comparison to his fellow newsmen, a kempt beard and white shirt beneath suspenders. The famed illustrator for *Harper's Weekly* caught sight of Gardner and leaned across to shake his hand.

A cheer went up from across the smoke-filled bar as someone had taken note by their timepiece that the day had passed to next.

"To Independence," David Woodbury announced, extending his glass, eyelids already heavy from drink.

The lot of them leaned to one another in turn, clanking with force to test their mugs' durability.

"Independence!"

"Independence. Yes, sir."

Gardner smiled. "To Independence."

With Brady's consent, Gardner had granted his men a reprieve from the field that night and following day, to rest and reload supplies.

Tonight, Gardner wanted his home and family, his bed, and nothing more. But when O'Sullivan asked him to a drink to celebrate, he acquiesced. He knew he owed them that much.

It had been a rough spring. For them. For the Union.

Early that year, Brady sent more men to join Gardner at General McClellan's headquarters.

They anticipated *Little Mac's* long-awaited thrust to Richmond.

In turn, Gardner dispatched them in pairs to the field.

Word came of bloody Shiloh in Tennessee. And then came the offensive in Virginia. Each fight bloodier than the one before it. Gardner's men trailed the army, capturing troops on glass plate when granted permission. They photographed them on the move, the cavalry and artillery positions, and at camp.

That spring, Barnard and Gibson ventured to Manassas. In late May, Gibson and Wood accompanied the army at the Battle of Fair Oaks.

Since December of '61, O'Sullivan had kept on the heels of General Thomas Sherman's forces during his South Carolina campaign, photographing Beaufort and Port Royal and the ruins of Forts Pulaski and Walker after Union assaults. He had since come north to join Gardner's ever-increasing team in Virginia.

Captain John Tidball (beard, center) and company, June 1862, J. Gibson

With each month's passing, field operations became more efficient in the production of quality photographs.

The diligent and soft-spoken Gibson became as skilled a field camer-aman as any Gardner knew. O'Sullivan had spent months on his own making great quantities of negatives. John Wood and George Barnard, a dapper man who kept his tailored suits clean even in the field, joined the team from Brady's New York studio. David Woodbury, the thin blue-eyed young man, gave himself to work so completely that he would die a year after the war of consumption. Gardner always regretted not forcing him from the cold and damp Virginia fields sooner.

George A. Custer (front right) with staff of General Porter, May 1862, J. Gibson

At night, the lot of them sat round fires, swatting away the mosqui-toes. At times the scent of wood smoke from Confederate Army camps wafted from just across a narrow river or forested stream.

They learned to bear the sweat and grime, the insect bites, cold nights, and the ever-present danger of war.

They made do with one another's company and visited the soldiers' camps when permitted, clowning and commiserating.

Show me how to work that camera.

Give me your gun. You can have it straight up.

Better get a picture, Tim. We might not come back tomorrow.

Alright then. Get the boys together.

Tell Charlie. He'll want in on this.

Crossing the Chickahominy, June 1862, D. Woodbury

Battery near Fair Oaks, Virginia, June 1862, J. Gibson

By the first of July, it was clear to all of them that McClellan's Peninsula Campaign would not bring Union victory. New to his command, Robert Lee had fought them well.

Gardner's men covered the counter assaults that pushed McClellan's forces back to the James River, always on the edge of it, waiting their chance.

But it seemed for all the spring and summer's casualties, there was nothing to show.

One half of a stereoview, Union Field Hospital, Savage Station, J.Gibson
A rare glimpse at the awfulness of war before September 1862

The tavern had emptied by half.

The boisterous evening beginning to draw in on itself as several of the newsmen left for whatever bed awaited them that evening.

Gardner's four men remained, as did a half dozen reporters.

Gardner scanned his watch face, awaiting the opportunity to make an exit, content in feeling he had been there for his men.

Sneed took a drink of beer. He formed a crooked smile, then reached into his worn coat to pull out a folded copy of the latest *Harper's Weekly*. He let it fall to the table. The creased front page had an illustration, *Photo by Brady* appeared below it.

Sneed puffed his cigar. "I swear that Brady is everywhere."

"He may get the credit, but I got the sores on my ass, and I share them with no one," said O'Sullivan.

They laughed. O'Sullivan lifted his mug and took a drink and, as he did, stole a fleeting glance at Gardner.

With his men in the field, Brady held court with the rich and famous, currying favor with those who influenced the war effort. Every general that passed through his studio had their likeness gracing thousands of calling cards.

Gardner had supposed all these things, too, were essential aspects of the operation.

But it did not make it easier to accept.

Gardner's men were rarely afforded a night's sleep indoors. Gardner went weeks without seeing Margaret and the kids. When at home, he found he could not sleep; concerned for his family while away from them, worried about his men in the field otherwise.

Since the war began, hundreds of images produced by Gardner and his men had appeared in *Harper's*, competing for space with the sketch artist's renderings and the written word.

"Well, I say you cameramen have a long way before you take our jobs," Horace White said, and was awarded a nod from Sneed. "But I suppose you're off to a good start."

Sneed raised his glass. "Or should I say Brady is?"

This time neither O'Sullivan, nor the others, laughed, so Sneed pressed on. "They may like the pictures but they will always want the finer points. Something you can't give them. That goes for you too, Waud."

The quiet illustrator tipped his hat and smiled.

"Un bon croquis vaut mieux qu'un long discours," said Gardner.

They quieted. Gardner had barely put two words together to that point and that fact had clearly been noticed.

Sneed looked at him with a puzzled stare.

Waud let go a small laugh. "A good sketch is better than a long speech." he added as translation.

Sneed snickered before lifting his glass. "You don't say."

"Napoleon Bonaparte said, to be exact," added Waud.

"He knew a thing or two about war," Horace White quipped.

"You boys may yet put old Waud here out of a job," Sneed grumbled. "I suppose that's one good thing to come of it."

"Well, friends," began Waud, unfolding his legs and putting boots to the ground, "I will, for the time being, consider my position safe. There seems to be more than enough carnage to go around these days."

Even Sneed turned solemn at this.

"I do hope our boys can pull it out this fall," Sneed finally said.

"Hear, hear."

"Yes, sir."

"They just might."

"But tonight," Waud said, rising to his feet "I just want to go to bed."

Waud left them.

Discussion turned again to lighter things; soldiers' vulgarities, stories of camp ladies, and other things which Gardner would have rather avoided hearing.

There was talk of slipping off to another tavern, even some paying visit to a bawdy house south of the avenue.

With the war on and legions of men far from home, sin had flourished in the capital. So many establishments with women and drink for sale, it put the free and easies of Glasgow to shame.

With some new destinations decided upon, the lot of them rose to depart, to Gardner's relief.

The Bohemian Brigade offered to pay the photographers' tab in full; an offer accepted.

❦

Gardner rode his horse north and east to home where he woke his wife and children to kiss them and talk for a few minutes' time before he slipped down into bed.

But sleep did not come easy.

He lay awake, thinking about the war, about his men, about Brady, and about Roger Fenton of all people. He thought about the opportunity both he and Brady agreed this war would be, over a year ago, in the summer of '61. Something much more than what Fenton had managed with his crude van and cameras in the Crimea.

Gardner thought too about his visit to the studio earlier that afternoon, first thing after arriving back in the city.

He walked the gallery floor. He watched them, in fine suits and stylish dress, gathered upon the silk rugs and beneath the glass chandeliers where they admired the latest photographs; framed prints, sanitized views of troops and officers, grand displays of cavalry and artillery. They stood before outsized Imperials touched in India ink, of McClellan and generals who peered back at them with the confidence of Achilles.

They might purchase one of the expensive Imperials for their lavish parlors; they might acquire several war views and cartes de visite to fill their albums. It was their way of supporting the war.

But most would never understand it. It would not touch them as they attended plays on the avenue and dined upon extravagant meals, all the while growing rich through military contracts or from investments in companies flush with cash from government war coffers. None except a few of their bravest sons would ever serve.

Neither was Gardner soldiering for the cause. That fact was not lost on him.

He wanted to believe he played an important part in bringing home the war. But as he watched them on the gallery floor, Gardner knew he had failed in that charge thus far. This was not the war. *Not the whole war.*

What was needed was a Union victory, something far too rare thus far. The army would not be forced to retreat from the field, and neither would Gardner's men.

That would give him what he needed.

VII

G ardner pinched at his beard and listened to the thunder of war. Gibson leaned against the old elm tree opposite him, chewing his unlit cigar.

Together, they watched the pair of officers that rode up the path on tired horses, handing reins to orderlies as they quickened to the house that stood upon the hill's crest. A local farmer's pride no doubt, the two-story brick and stone, with its wide double windows, steep roof and paired chimneys, now served as McClellan's battle quarters.

The officers entered as a colonel exited the door. He climbed his horse and rode away at full gallop down the same farm road. Reports from the front had been coming in all morning and now into afternoon.

But whatever the news, it was not being shared with Gardner.

After the second defeat at Manassas in late August, Lee had surprised them; he turned north and crossed the Potomac into Maryland. With the Army of the Potomac pushed back near to Washington, McClellan set off in pursuit. Gardner and Gibson reached the general's headquarters in Rockville on the 9th, but things moved fast. No time to stop and photo-graph an army that forged ahead at such a clip. A stiff fight at South

143

Mountain followed, then a struggle at Harper's Ferry. Lee finally drew up across Antietam Creek with his back at the Potomac, spread out along Hagerstown Pike.

Last night, September 16th, Hooker's I Corps skirmished to the left and a great cannonade followed. Gardner laid his head down to his cot, supposing, as did the tens of thousands of soldiers along that creek, that the morning would bring fierce battle.

Now hell's fury had come, the ceaseless crash of artillery and the musketry exchanges that began before daybreak. The acrid smell of powder wafted up and swept over the distant hillside.

Gardner and Gibson looked out over the valley and creek below, but the gray veil of smoke revealed little of the beast, the flash of guns like thousands of fireflies against a shrouded sky. Gardner awaited any urgent orders, copies of field maps or otherwise.

None came.

Little Mac himself came out of doors at intervals, blanketed by staff officers who provided him with a field glass. The cocksure general bit incessantly at his mustached lip in a manner Gardner had never seen before. Perhaps the general could discern something of the battle from the direction of smoke and noise; the firing of the ten-pound Parrot guns, the pop and roll of rifle-muskets.

The cornfield and the Iron Brigade, Dunker Church, the sunken road, and stone bridge where Burnside waged his bloody campaign to cross; names and places that would soon pass into lore. But by evening's draw on September 17th, they were as yet unknown to Gardner.

The night visited rumors of a Confederate assault at dawn. And so on into the next morning, as more officers raced through the double front doors of the farm house.

By noon on the 18th, recommencement of hostilities had still not come. *Stand by for further orders*, Gardner had been told.

Gardner and Gibson had to satisfy themselves with but a few images from the high vantage at headquarters, Union batteries in wait across the fields west. Temporary truces were being called to retrieve the wounded. The Union army commanded the field; burial parties would set out, if they had not already.

Quarter to four by Gardner's watch piece, he bounded to his feet from a camp chair, quick enough that Gibson took note.

"What's the plan, boss?" asked Gibson, chewing the last bit of his cigar and trailing Gardner to the steps of the house.

Gardner strode into quarters, entered the quaint parlor and waited there to be recognized. He stated simply his case, asking permission to take the field. After conference with a colonel, the captain returned.

"Permission granted."

Lee's forces were still out there. Any Rebel attack, once commenced, it was made clear by the prim captain, would leave them at God's mercy.

Two vans and full stock between them, Gardner and Gibson set out on the farm road to where it turned on the Boonsboro Pike.

They moved south along the road where they crossed the nearest bridge over Antietam Creek. Gardner led on until they reached the town of Sharpsburg, and they turned northward on the Hagerstown Turnpike.

They would now need to wait for a new day's sun to take their images. But they could survey the field. And plan for it.

They encountered little at first, abandoned wagons and debris. Many a Union camp and the soldiers who directed them to continue north. The road began its ascent and soon appeared dead horses in the fields at road-side.

Gardner and Gibson came upon a line of canvas tents. Union stretcher bearers scuttled across the road, delivering wounded men and hauling away corpses. Gardner observed the arms and legs, tangled in great heaps behind many a tent. More of these makeshift hospitals dotted the opposite side of the road further ahead, the late day sun casting long shadows of their pitched roofs. The land began a yet steeper rise and became littered with ordinance, spilled caissons, crippled and abandoned wagons. There too, Gardner saw the first dead men. Many more soon followed.

They continued, the turnpike there lined by a split rail fence. A break in the fence was wide enough to navigate through and they tied off to a tree beside a cart path that ran adjacent to the road. Without a word the pair of them set out on foot, scarcely believing what their eyes showed them.

Hundreds if not a thousand dead upon the field; men, pieces of men. They moved up the road guided by the tall fence, splintered and broken. A white church stood on a rise west, it too riddled with shot.

Along the road and fence lay the fallen covered in dried blood, beside arms and accouterments; tin cups, canteens, discolored rags in clenched fingers.

Crimson-stained and sullen faces. Ghastly, contorted shapes of every manner. Many dead over a day now; the rigors of death had gone to work on man and beast alike. Limbs suspended in air. Innards exposed and the smell of feces, a final ignominious act of these dead men.

Gardner felt his stomach turn out. He held his kerchief to his face and did all he could to keep from retching, for if he started upon that course, he felt he might not be able to stop.

Beyond the fenced road and opposite the wood stretched a wide field and the remnants of a corn crop. A hundred or more tents for the dying. Straw hut hospitals lined the horizon where the land fell away toward the creek. Everywhere among the surrounding lands, the burial parties were out in force.

Night fell on the 18th. Gardner and Gibson sat fireside beneath the wagon, perhaps fifty yards from the closest tent camps. They did as best they could to ignore the stench of death the wood smoke could not mask, and the cries of pain that chloroform or laudanum would not take away.

"Whisky, boss?"

"No."

"Where do we start come morning?"

"Over there, if possible."

"Fine. I've got some bacon to go with the bread if you want to fry some. Damned mosquitoes. Damn don't they bite!"

"No. I can't say that I have much an appetite."

"Me neither. No. I guess me neither."

<hr/>

They languished and died in great numbers in makeshift hospitals that night, but there was no Rebel action.

At daylight, Gibson fried the bacon and cut the bread. Gardner stopped a passing cavalryman who told him the rumors that Lee and his army were already across the Potomac into Virginia.

Gardner managed to eat a few mouthfuls as he reviewed their equipment one last time.

High clouds thinned and a cool morning gave way to a warming sun. It was just past eight.

Gardner stood. He dumped the last of his coffee gone cold into the fire that hissed in reply. "Now, Mr. Gibson."

<hr/>

They started along the shattered fence they had visited the day before.

Gardner set up his stereo camera at the first cluster of dead. He had noticed the regiment etchings upon knapsacks the day before. Louisiana men, they met the Union troops just across the pike, hoping, no doubt, the slender rails might be enough to shield them from the withering fire that cut short their lives.

The burial parties; teams of Negro men and groups of soldiers in shirt sleeves, were already busy at a grisly day's work.

It was rare that they began photographing before nine at the studio. It was no exception in the field. Without sufficient light, the images would not be successful. But with the hour fast approaching, they sensitized a batch of plates in advance and stored them in their light-proof wooden slips.

They discussed their strategy once more. Gardner at the camera, Gibson would shuttle him sensitized plates and take the exposed negatives back to his van, set up to develop and fix the images beneath its dark canopy.

If execution was flawless, they might complete the entire process for a plate in less than ten minutes. With so much ground to cover, they had one chance to get it right.

Gardner studied the skies and decided it was time. He slipped beneath the cloak and brought the lens to focus. With each turn of thumb and finger, the subjects drew sharp and clear before him.

With Gibson's first plate, he exposed the negative to the group of dead soldiers.

Five more exposures followed in succession.

Flies dotted the corpses and swarmed about Gardner's ears. He kept his kerchief in his pocket for when the stench became too much to bear. He envied Gibson, who had the strong, sweet smell of collodion whilst inside the van to help him through.

All the while the diggers pushed closer toward the road.

Troops and wagons passed along the pike. Souvenir hunters scavenged the field for morbid keepsakes; they claimed canteens, knapsacks, and bedrolls near the bodies or in the clearings at the edge of wood where troops had unburdened themselves before the fray with thoughts of retrieving them later.

Gardner and Gibson worked with efficiency for the next two hours, stopping at places where the dead lay in clusters.

Two of Gardner's negatives along the Hagerstown Pike, September 19ᵗʰ, 1862

They drew up across the road in the direction of the church belonging to the German Baptists, its white walls battered from canister, minie ball, and shell. Horses lay strewn about the land before Christ's temple, fallen men heaped across the slow rise of ground that led to its doorstep.

Along the rise to Dunker Church, A. Gardner

It was half past one when they drove south, arriving upon the sunken farm road that ran across the field, deep and furrowed from years of wagon traffic.

Gardner climbed down and walked out to where he could look down and across the road.

Hundreds lay dead in the rutted earth.

Wooden planks ran across the hollow in places for men to cross over. The smell of so much rotting flesh heavy in the air.

Between shovelfuls, a burial detail of soldiers, some twenty yards down the path, studied Gardner and Gibson and the black-cloaked wagon. A haggard bunch in muddied shirtsleeves with sweat-streaked faces and hair, they drank from canteens and cursed their lot for all to hear. They were moving, corpse by corpse, up the road, clearing the heaped dead into shallow roadside graves.

"What you got there?" a tall one called out. "Hardly a time for my photograph, fellar! I need to wash up first!"

This generated some laughter and snide remarks from the others who rested upon their shovels.

"What in the hell you doing?"

Gibson only nodded in return. "Afternoon, gentlemen."

"Cap'n says I's ta shoot any man who tries to pick these boys clean," said another of the soldiers. "Best not try it. I'm in some awful mood".

"Nothing of the sort," Gibson said, tipping the brim of his hat.

"We'll not disturb these men," added Gardner.

The soldiers traded stares, then turned away.

One took his knapsack from the ground and retrieved some hardtack which he passed about.

A few broke pieces and began chewing. How they could eat in the midst of that, Gardner did not know.

One of the older diggers, his gray beard streaked with mud, stepped closer. He bent over his spade and continued to watch the photographers.

Gardner moved his tripod to the high ground on the south bank of the road.

He fixed the stereo camera box to the legs. The grayed soldier announced they were soldiers of the 130th Pennsylvania and proceeded to tell Gardner of the fallen.

Mostly Alabama and North Carolina men, a number of whom had also been taken prisoner. Entrenched in the sunken road, they repulsed the Union assault until New Yorkers got into the road and delivered a lethal fire down the length of the thoroughfare, cutting them to pieces in the earthen trap.

Gibson retrieved the first plate. Gardner focused on what the lens took in.

Men three deep in places.

Rebel or not, Gardner could only imagine the horror; the fallen, many perhaps only wounded, suffocating beneath those who fell atop them.

Gardner took Gibson's wooden slip, slid it into the camera, and returned his head beneath the black cloth.

"Jesus almighty," said the old private, as if he had not discerned Gardner's true intent until now.

Gardner took the image.

Several more images followed.

The digging soldiers had moved close up on them. They had been content to slow their progress for a time but were growing restless by the delays.

A passing sergeant heard the complaints and told Gardner and Gibson, matter-of-factly, that the next photograph would be their last.

Gardner took a final image, a large format of the sunken road. He reappeared from beneath the sheet and handed the spent plate, snug in its holder, to Gibson.

Gibson looked once more upon the road where the soldiers had resumed pulling up the corpses from the wooden planks. He spat. "Roger Fenton never did this."

Gardner thought of that London photographer atop his bulky wagon, bouncing across the Crimean countryside in search of subjects. He cast a sidelong glance up the road. "No he did not."

Views of the Sunken Road, or 'Bloody Lane', September 19, 1862, A. Gardner

✑

They made camp early that evening near a burned-out farmhouse where they ate a small meal of biscuits and dried ham.

Gibson added copious amounts of whisky to his water. He smoked and drank and stared at the fire with heavy eyelids.

Gardner forced himself up on tired and sore feet to take stock of a day's work, stereoviews and a few large formats. Twenty-nine plates in all.

He mounted one of the horses.

"We need more supplies. I'm going back to headquarters and wire Knox at the studio." He took pause. "Is there anything you need?"

Gibson stared blankly for a moment then shook no.

Gardner rode off. Upon his return, the fire was low, and Gibson was fast asleep beneath the stars.

✑

Three more days they continued, more or less unmolested.

McClellan shifted his headquarters closer to the field but gave no indication that he would pursue the Confederates.

After the dead had been buried, Gardner captured all the surrounding area near the creek and woods.

He photographed the Reel barn, roofless and its right wall crumbled, where they were told a Union shell set it ablaze, burning hundreds of wounded southerners alive. The town of Sharpsburg, its shattered windows, damaged homes and shops. They photographed Rohrbach's Bridge, and its crossing to a high wooded bluff scattered with quarry boulders where Confederates rained fire down upon Burnside's New Hampshire and Connecticut men. And the Antietam Bridge on the road to Boonsboro, where Lee's guns owned the high points only days before.

*Devastation at Antietam (previous page), and a tranquil view of
Rorhbach's Bridge ('Burnside Bridge'), A. Gardner*

By the 23rd of September, they had seventy exposures. Gardner sent Gibson to Washington with the negatives. He returned to field headquarters, satisfied with their efforts.

Gardner heard about it later. When Gibson arrived at the studio and rushed the first box of plates to Brady's office.

Brady shut the door behind them and pulled the first of the negatives from the box and held it to the light.

It was not certain whether, in the gallery below, the patrons heard the shattering of glass as Brady, in his astonishment of what he saw, let it slip from his hands and crash to the floor.

McClellan seemed in no mood to break his Maryland camp.

Brady sent Gibson back to Gardner in late September with fresh supplies.

He sent news too.

Lincoln was soon to pay a visit to General McClellan's camp. And Gardner would photograph them.

⌘

The president's caravan did not arrive at headquarters until the night of October 2nd.

Gardner watched Lincoln exit his coach, tipping his tall hat as he stepped among soldiers and officers in the growing dusk. Too late in the day for camera work.

President Lincoln was accompanied by a handful of men, officers and civilian friends, and Marshal Lamon.

To Gardner, the president looked grossly thin and his tall felt hat made him look two rail ties high, especially when beside the compact McClellan. He wondered if the president would remember him from those early sittings in Brady's studio, before the war began, when Gardner operated the camera.

After his greeting the men, the Second Cavalry Band serenaded Lincoln to the tune of *Yankee Doodle*. He thanked them and rose from his camp chair. He started toward the large tent reserved for him beside McClellan's where two privates stood at the flap doors with bayonets. Marshal Lamon followed close behind.

Gardner stood with the others as they drew in around the president to bid him a good night.

At the tent's lip, the president stopped.

He turned and looked directly at Gardner.

Gardner watched, stunned silent, as the President of the United States closed the gap between them with great strides from his long legs.

"Mr. Gardner. It is mighty good to see you again."

"Mr. President. A pleasure."

Lincoln's large and bony hand kept Gardner's hand tight in its grip. The marshal now stood beside and studied Gardner with near a look of suspicion.

"Ward, I nearly forgot. Gardner here will photograph me tomorrow. What do you think of that task? General McClellan and myself. I must have seven inches on the good general."

Lamon snickered. "At least."

"Now," Lincoln continued, "if only that counted for something."

"Not to worry, Mr. President. I'll manage," was all Gardner could think to say.

"Yes. Yes. I'm sure we'll make a go of it. Now, I must get to write Mary before the courier leaves. She'll get to worry."

❧

Gardner took his first images of Lincoln the following morning. Gibson assisted with the plates.

Gardner was soon excused by a colonel and the president said nothing and returned to his tent.

An hour passed. Gardner began to worry that he had taken all the images to which he was entitled that day.

The colonel who had earlier dismissed him then approached at a fast clip.

"Have your man bring up your wagon at rear. You may ride in the third ambulance there. We're off to see General Porter."

Gibson readied the horse and van. Gardner was escorted to a covered ambulance parked in the shade of two elms. He settled into a spot on the cushioned bench seat.

He heard men approaching. A hand reached in and took hold.

Gardner watched Lamon Hill swing his body aboard. An officer whom Gardner did not recognize followed, then two more civilian gentlemen in black suits who had arrived with the president the night before. The marshal slid up his bench, nudging Gardner further in front. He smiled at Gardner; his breath smelled like cabbage.

"You again?"

Gardner said nothing. He tried to smile.

"Oh, I am only making fun." Lamon slapped Gardner's knee. "Good man," he added.

General John McClernand climbed aboard followed by Captain Rives, the thin, clean-cut aide to McClellan whom Gardner knew from headquarters. The once spacious compartment was crowded.

In the commotion, Gardner did not even see him approach.

But he watched now as the president stepped up and into the elevated frame of the car, his long pant legs seemed to hardly bend at all. He moved into a spot at the center of the bench, snug between two officers, directly across from Gardner.

General McClellan and other members of the party could be heard boarding the other two ambulance wagons in quick fashion and soon the wagon train started out.

Lincoln smiled at Gardner. "I've had fancier rides to be sure, but we'll make do, won't we? I thought you might like to take a few pictures at General Porter's camp."

"Thank you, Mr. President."

The president nodded and the wagon rolled on. Lincoln held back the canvas to study the fields they passed; he asked questions of Captain Rives beside him.

The captain recited the key facts of battle; troop positions, commanding generals, some of which the president surely had been made aware through official reports.

The president listened, studying the land. He interrupted at intervals to ask about casualties of a particular regiment or brigade.

The captain communicated those facts, rattling off numbers in the hundreds and thousands, without flourish, as might a quartermaster's agent tallying receipt of army brogans. Gardner watched the president as he listened; he watched Lincoln turn increasingly somber as his heavy eyes trained the countryside.

The president let the canvas fall. He turned and sat forward in the shadowy silence.

There, thought Gardner, was the same face, thinner now by measure but the same, of the burdened president-elect he first photographed in February of '61, with the prospect of the war upon him the instant he stepped off the train. Gardner imagined that between the war and the president's well-known troubles, namely the death of his eleven-year-old son Willie earlier that year from typhoid, there was not another man alive with such a weight upon him.

The wagon passed along the rutted road, every man silent, taking his mood from the president.

"Lamon," began Lincoln a sudden, "sing one of your little sad songs."

The marshal nodded his consent.

Marshal Lamon, a brute by reputation, removed his brimmed hat and ran a hand through his damp brow. He placed the hat upon his chest and began to sing a verse of *Twenty Years Ago*. A soft tenor voice belied everything visible about the man.

I've wandered to the village, Tom;
I've sat beneath the tree upon the schoolhouse play-ground
That sheltered you and me
But none were left to greet me, Tom,
And few were left to know
Who played with us upon the green
Some twenty years ago

The president formed a sad smile as he listened with his head now upon his breast.

I visited the old churchyard
And took some flowers to strew
Upon the graves of those we loved
Some twenty years ago

The marshal finished his song.

Quiet. Only now the creak and roll of the wheels, two blackbirds singing in some not-so-distant tree.

The corners of the president's lips turned down toward the edges of his beard. His eyes, black and hollow shells, told Gardner he was somewhere far away.

This continued a minute or more before Lincoln lifted his chin, his eyes now focused. He smiled, then leaned forward to slap the palm of his right hand upon the marshal's knee. Lamon smiled, himself buoyed at the president's new demeanor.

Marshal Lamon rolled back his shoulders. He took a deep breath and launched into comical verses of a Negro minstrel.

Picayune Butler's comin', comin',
Picayune Butler's come to town.

Lincoln gave a quiet little laugh.

By the second verse, he had a wide smile upon his face and the officers too. Gardner too could not help but find something comical in the marshal's offhand delivery.

Soon they arrived at Porter's headquarters. Gardner took his images.

Among them, he exposed a large format amongst field tents outside the brick schoolhouse that served as hospital.

The president rested a hand on a field chair facing McClellan who gazed up at the commander in chief, among his officers and generals; Porter, Morrell, Humphrey.

The president, McClellan and officers (George A. Custer appears on far right), Taken Oct.3rd, 1862, A. Gardner

Gibson developed the plate.

Later, when Gardner was taking the final inventory, a far corner of it broke in his hands. This of all plates, Gardner thought. Luckily, Gibson would successfully mend and mask it at the studio, making it good.

But if Gardner were given to fortune telling, the fractured plate of McClellan and President Lincoln was surely a sign of things to come.

༺༒༻

The following morning on the 4th of October, back at McClellan's camp, Gardner was granted his opportunity to photograph the president numerous times; a portrait with Pinkerton, with General McClernand, and others.

President Lincoln and General McClellan gathered inside the general's tent. Gardner had the flap turned open and received permission to adorn a table and a second smaller table with instruments, a map, and a draped American flag.

Gardner was allowed a stereoview and a large format of the pair before they settled into official business.

Glass negative, Lincoln's last day at Antietam, in McClellan's tent, A. Gardner

Three weeks later, Knox arrived with supplies and joined Gardner and the others who took a late sup at their headquarter camp.

Knox brought a copy of the *New York Times*, printed three days before. October 20th, 1862. He tossed the paper on the wooden table beside Gardner and took up a plate and began heaping stew upon it.

"Another write up of our photographs in Manhattan. Big to do at the studio I hear. Haven't read it yet myself. You go ahead, boss."

"Thank you, David."

Gibson ate, never once looking at the paper.

Gardner tried not to seem that interested. He slid the paper beneath his plate and finished his stew. He ate slowly.

In time, Gardner rose from his empty plate, stepped out to the campfire and took a chair. Before he even opened the paper, he felt uneasy.

He recalled *Harper's Weekly* issues he had read the past month. The first on October 4th contained only vague details of Antietam, alongside President Lincoln's Emancipation Proclamation. The 11th issue had more specifics of the battle and included a number of Alfred Waud's sketches.

In the October 18th issue, however, Gardner's images appeared. A collage of destruction; ravaged fields, dead horses and debris. Dead men spread across the land and deep in a sunken road. Beneath the photograph renderings, the caption read:

SCENES ON THE BATTLE-FIELD OF ANTIETAM
From photographs by Mr. M.B. Brady

It did not surprise him. Gardner had witnessed what had happened to the images that Brady was selling by the thousands across the country.

Photo by Brady. The stamp appeared on the back of every calling card and photograph that left the studios in New York and Washington. As if Brady had been there, in the field, standing behind the camera.

But when Gardner learned that Brady was to exhibit the Antietam series on October 10th in New York, he did feel satisfaction.

He knew the people would come to see them. They expected, no doubt, to find photographs of generals and infantry gathered in the fields, along the rivers, and stationed at battery posts. But they would get something else. They would get carnage, death. The real war.

Gardner unfolded the paper. He read the title of the article on the printed page:

Brady's Photographs
Pictures of the Dead at Antietam

The fire crackled at Gardner's feet. He began reading by the light of it.

Mr. Brady has done something to bring home to us the terrible reality and ear-
nestness of war. If he has not brought home bodies and laid them in our door-
yards and along the streets. He has done something very much like it.

Gardner studied the fire for a moment, then read on.

When finished, he folded the paper on his lap. He sat quiet. Gibson and Knox joined him fireside for a time but it was not long before they turned in.

Gardner soon decided to do the same and he rose.

Before he put out the fire, he put the paper to it.

VIII

The large wooden placard hung above the Broadway entrance:
The Dead of Antietam
    Two weeks since the exhibit opened at Brady's studio. Men and women crowded the front street windows, gawking, disbelieving the images just back from Antietam that were on display behind the glass.

    Word spread quickly. Advertisements in the papers were not needed. Traffic between the studio and A.T. Stewart's department store slowed to a crawl to accommodate the sea of pedestrians that drew daily upon Brady's.

    Brady watched them from a top-floor window, gathered in the cool autumn morning on his Broadway walk just before doors opened at nine.

    In they came; the wealthy in their elegant clothes, the workmen in double-breasted wool and sack coats. They climbed steps to the reception hall in unison, moving through the open cut-glass doors toward the exhibit. And crowds were steady into evening when attendants lit the row of ornate gas fixtures upon the walls.

Amongst plush easy sofas, dozens of pedestals held framed photographs of Antietam. More adorned the long walls where portraits of presidents and the famous temporarily made way.

They viewed the images in awe. Twisted shapes, once active, virile men. Ashen faces, gone from this world.

Brady took interest in their reactions; men silent and grave, women reduced to tears, their white gloved hands covering parted lips.

After their tour, many parties left for home. Others gathered in corners, where men comforted wives upon sofas as if taking a moment's respite in the parlor of a loved one's funeral.

A city reporter had paid a visit and heralded the scene to his readers.

Of all the objects of horror, one would think the battle-field stand preeminent, that it should bear away the palm of repulsiveness. But on the contrary, there is a terrible fascination about it that draws one near these pictures, and makes him loath to leave them. You will see hushed, revered groups standing around these weird copies of carnage, bending down to look in the pale faces of the dead, chained by the strange spell that dwells in the dead men's eyes.

At the glass counter, they purchased cards and larger prints of the macabre as if compelled to do so, by patriotism or some other enigmatic motive.

Brady wondered where they might decide to keep the ghostly prints, surely not amongst their collection of photographs of stately politicians and generals. He imagined the places for this new assortment, in the bottom of a cedar chest or in a box tucked away beneath a bed stand, to be retrieved behind closed doors in some secret and cathartic ritual, or prayer of remembrance for the dead.

Whatever their intentions, they bought the images with fervor and in great numbers. Anthonys added the cards to their *Brady's Album Gallery* collection. They had to double the number they printed after the second day.

The number doubled again two days later.

Brady's hard work had paid off. Since the early days of war, he had worked every angle, gaining the ear of congressmen and military men as he summoned them before his camera. So many strings he had pulled. A constant race between his Manhattan and Washington studios. He called on them in their home parlors, or at desks on the Capitol floor. He spent great sums of money in restaurants and smoke-filled bars, at the Willard and Brown and the others, in hopes these politicians and officers would remain accommodating to Brady's men. Those teams, in nearly every theater of the war, sent back dozens of new images each week. It was Gardner's team at McClellan's headquarters who had brought him the dead of Antietam.

It required vision. It required a great deal of investment. And it had paid off.

But not all Brady's partners were so easy to convince.

Edward Anthony showed a polite smile beneath his trim beard; his curled black hair matched his silk suit.

"Mathew, let's just say we have our concerns."

Brady listened from a chair across a cherry wood desk, the largest desk he had ever seen. Edward's younger brother Henry stood behind the desk, a crooked arm upon a shelf of brandies, twiddling a gold watch pulled from his waist coat.

Brady cleared his throat. "Would you be so kind as to share them? These concerns."

"Nothing to be alarmed about," Edward said. "You and I, we've been business partners a long time. Friends longer."

"We have, Edward."

Brady crossed his legs and looked about the large office, with its crystal fixtures and polished furniture, papered walls filled with oils and photographs in gilded frames. "And from appearances, I'd say our current partnership is serving you quite well these days."

The Anthony's massive American and Foreign Stereoscopic Emporium at 501 Broadway, with its iron façade of pillars and capitals, was a testament to just how big the two brothers had become. Edward Anthony had first studied, like Brady, under Morse and become a daguerreotypist. A shrewd businessman, Edward sensed an opportunity in '47 and converted his business into one that sold equipment and supplies to the ever-expanding group of photographers. His first supply store was at 205 Broadway, a building shared by Brady, one of his first customers. When the wet plate negative took hold, the brothers Anthony sensed another opportunity and launched printing houses that now dotted the city, where employees printed, fixed, and cut thousands of cards a day.

Customers made selections from long, uncut sheets and for a few dollars, came away with a dozen images for their parlor books. Of all their collected photographers' works, it was Brady's war views that generated, by far, the most demand.

Brady's royalties from Anthony's had totaled twelve thousand dollars since the fall of Sumter. God only knows how much the Anthony's had profited since then.

Edward smiled. "We do alright, Mathew. As I suppose do you."

Brady laughed. "Yes. Well, I'm sure you didn't invite me here to reminisce about the old days so let's get to it. I do hope you haven't called me here to press the terms of our deal or something otherwise, which might force me to rethink our business relationship, if not our friendship."

Edward Anthony straightened in his chair.

"It's a question of volume, Mr. Brady," said Henry, stepping forward behind his brother. "The pace at which our partnership has accelerated. It concerns me quite frankly. It's my job to be concerned, for my brother and this company."

Edward must have seen Brady's frustration. He looked ready to speak but Henry continued.

"We have, Mr. Brady, as of the end of October, over eight hundred of your plates on consignment to us. In the last six months alone, we supplied your field teams with nearly five thousand dollars in supplies and material. Cameras, glass plate, chemicals. Each month, the sale of your prints increase, but not at the pace at which your need for supplies grows."

Brady folded his arms. He said nothing.

Edward Anthony cleared his throat from behind his desk. "Yes. As Henry said, it's a question of pace. The sum of money here is considerable. As long as your images continue to sell-"

"They will," Brady said. "And you won't get a better deal than the one you already have."

Brady knew the Anthony's had begun to send their own teams to the field, contracting photographers on far less generous terms to feed their hungry war printing machine. All the while, they happily profited from Brady's inventory.

They had become greedy.

No matter.

It was Mathew Brady who delivered. It was his repute that enabled him to secure the most sought-after views. The Antietam series demonstrated this beyond any doubt.

"At present, we are satisfied with the deal, Mr. Brady," Henry said calmly, a crooked smile upon his round white face. "But I do wish to remind you of the terms. As per our agreement, the negatives you submit to us, upon which we pay you so handsome a royalty, provide us collateral against unforeseen liabilities. The plates themselves carry great value no doubt, should circumstances change."

Brady let those last words settle.

Was the man suggesting Brady's venture might do them financial harm, as profitable as their card business was?

He felt his temperature rise.

"Edward, you listen–"

"Hold on a moment, Mathew," Edward Anthony said with a raised hand. "These things must be managed closely by us, and we are doing so. After all, we are a business. Same as you. That's all."

Brady took a breath to regain his composure. He sat silent a moment. "Very well."

There seemed little point in continuing. He rose.

"Edward, you are lucky to have such a brother to look after your interests. And I dare say we men need to mind our pennies. Consider me aware. And, by all means, should you have any more concerns, please do not hesitate."

Edward rose from his desk, sweat beaded on his forehead. He extended a hand to Brady.

Business men. That they were. Even now, with the war, it was dollars and cents to the Brothers Anthony. And yes, Brady thought, profits be damned in times like these. This was about more than money. He had no time for men with such lack of vision. He had other options, but Brady also knew none could match the production and distribution capabilities of the E. & H.T. Anthony & Co.

For now, he guessed they would all have to make do.

Word came on Saturday evening, the first week of November. Brady was surprised as anyone to hear.

"Have you not heard?" whispered the old man in a claw hammer suit, taking hold of Brady's arm. "McClellan is relieved of command."

The impish man grinned, sharp points of small teeth showed beneath a crooked smile. Bushy brows hid his beady eyes. Brady seemed to recollect him as a manufacturer of guns.

"I had not. From whom did you hear this?"

The man laughed. He scanned for eavesdroppers.

"Why, Mr. Brady, you shame me. I hear things. Same as you I suppose. Men like us, we hear things. Let's leave it at that for the evening, shall we? But it is true."

The man led Brady toward the group of men and women gathered nearby, Julia among them. Brady rejoined his wife, locking arms.

"Did you hear about McClellan?" asked a brunette lady of Brady, her ringed fingers tight around a champagne flute.

The small man turned pale.

"I told you that in confidence, Mr. Watkins!"

"Oh nonsense, Fielding," said a tall man. "Half the world knows by now. You are not the only one to *hear things.*"

This produced a great deal of laughter. The little man Fielding raised his thick brows and drank his champagne, wearing a smile of his own.

Julia did not laugh.

Brady could see that a polite smile was all his wife could afford these people. He couldn't blame her.

Nouveau riche. They crowded the rooms of every soiree in Capitol City these days. You never saw their faces before the war. Now, they were everywhere. They hosted parties of their own in great mansions on the northern outskirts of the city.

For most, wealth came courtesy of fat government war contracts. Enough money could buy acceptance into high society, even if they incurred the occasional sneer from the older aristocrats of Lafayette Square. Of course, the old money did their share of reveling as well. They were not to be outdone. During the height of the social season, with Congress in session, one had to choose between parties. There were not enough nights to go around. Dancing. Drinking the finest wines and champagne. Feasts of gamecock and turkey and mutton, pies and sweetbreads. And, of course, gossip and hearsay.

"Yes. Lincoln made it so this very afternoon," added the thin-faced Mr. Watkins between sips of champagne. "McClellan has been removed as general. They say the command is Burnside's to lose now."

A plump woman in a blue gown aside Fielding scoffed. "What will the country do without Little Mac? It seems foolish to me. Then again, you never know with this president."

"Come now, my dear," Fielding said with a laugh. "These are complex matters. I do believe he is doing the best he can. After all, he's not splitting logs anymore!"

They laughed, and soon continued to their next gay topic, sipping from glass flutes. More than a few of them flush from the effects of spirits. Brady slipped to the next room with Julia at his arm, where under crystal chandelier many more gathered, ladies in crinoline dresses and bejeweled necks, men in silk suits with white kid gloves. Politics and war oft the topic of their conversations.

It soon reached time he promised her they would leave.

Their carriage started back toward the National just after midnight.

Brady sat quietly in the dark cab, mulling over the implications of McClellan's exit. He had been an ally; it was the general and his man Pinkerton who employed Gardner and delivered unto Brady's teams their elevated status with the Army of the Potomac. Now, things would be different.

How exactly, Brady could not say.

He looked across to Julia in the passing glow of the gaslights along the avenue. She looked exhausted. Despondent.

She had accompanied him through yet another evening, making conversation, biding with the ladies in the parlor while Brady joined men for brandy and cigars, playing her part dutifully.

She did it for him. For all her shyness and humility, Julia was capable of a radiance and charm that impressed upon the greatest of men. She made Brady proud. And though she never was one to enjoy these events, it was a different matter of late. The frequency of social obligations had worn on her.

Brady knew all this. He could see it plain, yet he could not help asking the question.

"What is the matter, dear?"

Julia turned her eyes away. She removed her gloves and pulled her shawl tight against the crisp evening air that had filled their cab. It was quiet.

He attempted a few jokes about some of the more foolish guests, their outlandish garb and phony gestures.

She said nothing for a time, then "It tires me so to attend these spectacles. I rarely get to see you and when I do, we must rush to these parties. I never want to attend another."

The words stung Brady.

Before there existed the possibility that he was wrong, that the social obligations he imposed upon her were not so painful.

Not now.

These past months, Brady knew too that there was more that weighed upon her. She saw the mail that arrived daily at their home at the National. A year ago, such letters of business would have come only to the studio. There was no concealing the steady stream of bills; equipment, clothing, meals, cognac, imported wines as gifts to congressmen and officers. The costs of studio alterations. Letters from creditors and hostile contractors who did not mince words. She now insisted on reading every one of them herself.

But Brady feared, above all this, what might be the greatest source of her unhappy days.

Over these years, he had tried to make a happy home for his wife. It seemed he had failed. He was away long hours with no one there to keep her company. Her only role in life to sit at home and wait. Abandoned. And the one thing she had wanted most, he could not give, nor could anyone help, not countless doctors to whom they paid visit for her to endure their probing and tests. By the mid 50's, Julia was already well into her thirties. She began fearing time. All of their consultations and elixirs, it was all the same and no use. There were to be no children in their future. Now, at nearly forty years of age, the topic had died a slow death. But such a pain never goes, Brady knew. And he wondered how much of it was still there, every day. A heart-to-heart talk might have put the matter to rest, but he feared that conversation more than anything in this world.

"You were splendid as ever, my dear. Thank you for putting up with such nonsense," Brady said, hoping to mollify her discontent. But it was soon clear he could not.

"It is more than nonsense. Those people and their noses in everyone's affairs. Please announce me sick at the next. I won't be there."

Brady studied her dark eyes. Part of him wanted to console his wife, as he did so often, but another part wished not to be bothered by this. He did not need it, not with everything else on his mind.

"I will do so, if you wish. I do not want to force these things upon you," he said calmly. "But my work demands it of me. I need to keep pulse on things. These people, like them or not, are useful to me. This is something I must do."

"For what? For the money?"

"No."

"Fame then?"

Brady said nothing, then "No."

"No?"

"Covering this war, it is my duty. And it's far more important than money. It's an opportunity to-"

She let go scoffing laughter. "Oh, spare me the *opportunity* speech. I've had my fill. What is happening to this nation is terrible. I can see it. Anyone can. But what drives you to all this? Why must it be you? Always you?"

Brady crashed his fist against the carriage door. "Because I will be remembered for this!" The carriage slowed its roll. "And nothing else before or after matters. Everything I've worked for, my whole life, has led me here."

He breathed, unclenching his tight fist.

He could see the fear in her wide eyes.

"This is what I do. It's who I am. Of all people in this world, I hoped you could see that."

Brady leaned back now. He realized now the carriage had fully stopped. He rapped a knuckle against the inside wall and the driver rolled onward again.

Across him, Julia had gone from shock to tears.

"I am sorry, my dear."

But she turned full toward the window. The lights showed the moist glow of her tears upon her profiled face. "I never wanted any of this," she whispered. "I never wanted to be *Mrs. Mathew Brady*. I only wanted to be your wife."

He did not attempt another word. He sat quietly, as did she, until they mercifully reached their destination.

Gardner sat across Brady's desk.

"Please sit, Alex. I got your note. Yes. We should talk."

Gardner sat, he removed his wide-brimmed hat and placed it into the lap folds of his mangy coat.

"How are you holding up?" Brady asked.

It was their first meeting in nearly a month, the first since news of McClellan had rippled through the capital.

Gardner and his men remained in the field. But it was little surprise when Brady received word that Gardner's official role with the army would end. Still, there were other avenues being pursued, to regain their advantage with the armies in the field. Brady would find a way.

"As to be expected I guess," Gardner said, adding nothing more.

"Good. I am glad to hear it."

He smiled at Gardner. The Scot's beard ran unkempt over a thinner face; he had dark rings for eyes. Brady was wont to admit he had not noticed the change by such degrees until now, as Gardner sat there in his office room. He wished that Gardner was more forthcoming. If he needed something to improve his condition, Brady would make every effort to see to it.

"Rest assured, Alex, I am looking for ways to keep you in your position now that McClellan is gone. It has been difficult, but I am certain I can manage passes for the team and things can continue much the same. It may take a few days more-"

"Mathew," Gardner began.

He looked at Gardner across the table who stared at the floorboards a moment, then met Brady's eyes. "That's not why I came to speak to you."

"Oh?"

Gardner shook his head no and said "You needn't worry about any of that."

IX

Margaret reassured him it was the right thing to do.
They had sat at that same table an evening ago, before Gardner paid a visit to his former boss.

Now it was done.

From their vantage at the front window, the sun crept behind distant oaks, a fire orange seeping through the naked limbs of mid-November.

They watched Eliza and a neighbor girl in their sweaters, playing Games of Grace in the yard; taking turns catching hoops, beribboned in reds and blues, with their thin wooden wands, laughing as young girls do in their own company.

Margaret tugged at her shawl, laughing at the sight.

Gardner warmed his hands against the cup of tea and sipped it with thoughts of fetching wood from the back to start a fire in the hearth.

She turned to him, her eyes serious now. "I trust it is all for the best."

"I hope you are right."

Margaret smiled, taking his hand across the table. "Have faith," she said. "Iowa is not so far."

❧

Brady had seemed neither hurt nor shocked by news that Gardner would be leaving his employ.

He shifted in his desk chair, then smiled. "I am sorry to hear it."

Gardner thanked Brady, for everything he had done.

Brady asked not the reason why. He did not offer terms to stay.

Gardner was grateful he would not have to elaborate. It was better this way.

Instead, the two embarked upon a pleasant, and unexpected, conversation of the years they had spent together. *Six years.* Gardner could hardly believe that time had passed since he entered Brady's studio, desperate for work.

"It goes by quickly. Doesn't it, Alex?"

They shared a laugh.

It felt good to Gardner. It occurred to him that there had been far too few light-hearted conversations and laughter between the two of them in those years.

But there was one issue of business that Gardner still had to broach.

"Mathew, I would like to discuss compensation." He cleared his throat. "It has been near two months now since I've received pay. You should know the men have mentioned the same to me."

Brady looked surprised by this, as if he had no idea.

Gardner half-expected such difficulties when he left the studio for the field over a year ago. It was not lost on anyone, least of all Gardner, that Brady was not one to manage these types of things with care.

"I see. Well, I do apologize for the oversight. Things have been moving fast these days," Brady said before slipping off into silence. Then "I will make it right at once, for everyone."

With this Gardner understood that despite whatever good intentions Brady had, back pay would never be received.

For months now, Gardner had a dreading thought about the state of Brady's finances. He was no longer managing them to be sure. He knew the war views sold well. He saw the gallery full with patrons every time he returned. Yet he was not blind to the immense cost of field operations. It was in Gardner's nature to pay attention and he could not help but keep a crude tally in his head of the expenditures that passed before his eyes, and speculate on the costs that went on unseen by him.

Once Gardner and his brother James were gone, Brady would have O'Sullivan and Gibson, Wood, Woodbury, and scores of others still in his employ. Even if Gardner managed to get them some of what was owed, what about after he was gone? He was not hopeful.

Over the past days, Gardner had forged something in his mind, a plan to remedy the situation.

"Mathew," he began, pulling up in his chair and placing his elbows on his knees, "perhaps there's another way."

Maybe she was right. Iowa was not so far. But it would not be easy on anyone. Gardner squeezed her hand and sipped his tea, watching the window as the girls continued to play.

He was still ill at ease about the plan. He would return to the field, he and his brother. For how long, he could not say. He believed he could stay close enough to the Army of the Potomac. The officers with whom he had worked so closely would support him, not perhaps with an official post or even a tent and soldier's mess, but with access to troops, and most importantly, the field of battle.

In that time, they would work to lease space for their own studio and see about hiring a few men.

In the near term only one thing was certain; Gardner would be away a great deal. It was too much to live in constant worry about the safety of his family.

That spring, Gardner had sent Lawrence to board at school. Working out of Brady's studio, James had been able to look after their mother, Margaret, and the kids with Gardner away. But Gardner would need him in the field now.

The city had been manic in the days before Antietam when Lee drove his army north of Washington. Tensions had since eased. Still, with soldiers and every sort of man, honest or otherwise, roaming the streets of a crowded, distracted city at all hours, it was no longer a place for three women.

They would go to stay with friends in Iowa, at least for the time being. There they would be safe.

Margaret let go his hand.

Gardner wished she had not let go, that she would never let go. He felt a lump in his throat and a wave of emotion overtaking his senses. He rose up from his seat.

"Getting cold. I should get that fire going."

⦆⦆

Gardner packed their belongings the next day and the following morning he called upon a coach to drive his family and their three cases of belongings to the New Jersey Avenue depot.

The Friday morning train would take them, via a circuitous route, west to the Mississippi. From there, they would ferry across to McGregor's Landing in Iowa. Gardner had arranged, via letter and wire, for John Craig and his family, old friends from Glasgow, to take them in for a time. Margaret would have a chance to visit her late brother's daughter there.

It was for the best. It was temporary.

These were the thoughts that raced through Gardner's mind, standing there on the depot planks, his arms tight around his weepy thirteen-year-old girl.

He kissed his mother, then his wife and watched them board through tears that welled in his eyes.

❦

The silver candelabra, an ostentatious piece from Margaret's mother that had been gathering dust in the back of the dining cabinet, held six flickering candles. It lit a table swathed in maps and newspapers between James and him. They seemed to Gardner a couple of generals brooding over battle plans.

Empty tea cups on saucers. Beside James, a glass of whisky stood beside a tray of ash and two cigar nubs; the habits of Gardner's former team had left their influence on his younger brother.

The fire in the hearth warmed the room on that crisp November night.

Gardner's home, once vibrant and tidy with Margaret's attention, resembled something of a crypt. Beyond the fire and their table, white cloth covered the sofa and chairs pushed close to the wall, leaving open a barren wooden floor.

Housekeeping, and everything else, could wait. Gardner had much to consider these days but he and James both knew that getting back to the field of operation was paramount.

In the end, Brady had done right by Gardner. He agreed, most willingly, to the proposal that Gardner take with him a number of the negatives he had taken over the last year and a half, from the Peninsula Campaign to Antietam. Earlier that year, Gardner had encouraged his men to begin to copyright their images. He believed they would benefit from it someday, somehow.

Brady took no issue. As their employer, it was his name still stamped upon the thousands of cards. The caption *Photo by Brady* had accompanied the images in the newspapers. To most, they would always be Brady photographs.

Now, Gardner would present an option to O'Sullivan, Gibson, Woodbury, and the others still with Brady that would allow him to market the images, beside his own. The proceeds from sales would serve as their back pay.

It was the least Gardner could do.

After a time, they folded the maps away. James lay before the fire to smoke a cigar. Gardner poured another cup of tea at the table as he copied a series of numbers onto a fresh sheet of paper. He double-checked his figures; the costs of supplies, salaries for a few more men, and the lease of a studio near the avenue.

It was then he heard a horse neigh in the yard.

James rose to his feet. He set the cigar on the stone mantle above the hearth. He reached inside his coat folded over the chair for his revolver.

Gardner lowered his pen and slid past the table to the window. He peeled back the curtain to glimpse a figure in the black of night approach his door.

James stepped to the side. Gardner took a candle from the candelabra. He turned the knob and opened.

O'Sullivan stood there, arm extended and ready to knock. Behind him, Gardner watched as Gibson finished tying off his horse to a porch rail.

O'Sullivan said nothing for a moment, then cocked his head back and spat off the edge of the porch. Gibson stepped up beside him.

"So what's the plan?" asked O'Sullivan before showing a crooked grin. "Boss."

❦

James shared the bottle of whisky. Gardner kept his tea kettle going.

They sat round the fire on the floorboards, their backs propped against a sofa and the chairs draped in ghostly white.

"I have passes," Gardner said, as he rose to toss another log onto the fire that hissed in reply.

James tipped the whisky bottle into O'Sullivan's, then Gibson' glass. He poured his own.

"I think we'll have no trouble accessing Burnside's quarters at Warrenton," Gardner continued, settling once more on the floor. "I'm leaving day after next. James thinks he has a place for a studio across the *National Intelligencer* at Seventh Street. It will take a few months to get things set up."

The studio space Gardner mentioned was but a few hundred yards from Brady's in fact. Until spring, however, they would not have a base in Washington.

Both O'Sullivan and Gibson nodded as Gardner shared the plan that, only minutes before, included only James and him.

"Meanwhile, we need to stay as close as we can to the army. I'll find a channel to get the photographs distributed and sold. If Anthony's won't meet us on terms, we have other options. I'll advertise the images under my label, each man receiving credit and fair compensation."

"They'll break for winter camp here before long I suspect," O'Sullivan said, returning the topic of conversation to more immediate concerns. "The others; Knox, maybe Wood. I suspect some of them will come knocking too. Those boys would welcome a steady paycheck."

"Get yourself a new coat and blankets," Gardner told them.

They agreed to do so.

Things sounded to Gardner as if they just might work. They talked, and joked, by the fire for another half hour before Gardner rose.

"I'll get some linens."

James won a coin toss with O'Sullivan and took the sofa.

Gardner surprised O'Sullivan with the offer of his bed. The Irishman declined for his lack of bathing, which gave rise to a few laughs. Gardner took the comforter and sheets from his bed. He distributed the pillows and spread quilts upon the floor. There they all lay, the smell of wood smoke in the room. Save the sofa and a fire within four walls, it was as if they were in the field again.

Gardner tossed long after the others lay sleeping. His mind churned with the unsettling thought that he was responsible for all of them now, even more so than before. They were putting their faith in him.

He only hoped to God he was up to the task.

Perhaps the war would end with next spring's offensive.

It seemed unlikely. Lee waited across the Potomac. With McClellan gone, it seemed as if the war was about to start a new chapter.

His family safe, Gardner was at least freed from worries that the war would reach his loved ones. He lay there, drifting toward sleep with pleasant thoughts of what his mother and wife and daughter were doing that night in Iowa, gathered in a warm home, surrounded by old friends.

Then he thought of Lawrence, his son boarding away at school while so many boys, just slightly older than he, were fighting and dying in the field or in a thousand army hospitals.

Selfish or not, what mattered to Gardner was that his son was safe, far removed from war's wrath. *Thank God.* Out of harm's way at St. Mary's in Emmitsburg, Maryland. Gardner had no reason to count the few short miles from this haven across the state line to Gettysburg, Pennsylvania.

X

General Burnside peered up from his dispatches, a gnawed and wet cigar between his teeth.

Brady stepped forward to offer his hand to the general who sat on a folding camp chair. Dying leaves from a maple fell down around them, littering the nearby ground, announcing that fall's best days were behind them.

Ambrose Burnside handed the papers to an assistant and rose. Over six feet tall, he towered over Brady. Unlike the lanky President Lincoln, Burnside was stout, his shoulders wide. He smiled and the corners of his mouth turned up beneath the long whiskers that trailed down to his thick moustache.

He shook Brady's hand with a solid grip.

"Mathew. Good to see you."

The general nodded and his two aides excused themselves. Burnside then ambled away, and Brady moved with him.

"Likewise, General. Thank you for seeing me. The Union will want photographs of its new general. I myself was thrilled to hear of your new role."

187

The general stopped in a clearing amongst slender pines that whistled with the chill breeze.

He turned and pulled the stump of his cigar from his lips. He smiled no longer; he looked as if he were nauseous. The general cast a glance around to spy anyone else in earshot.

"I think you'll not be rewarded for espousing such a vote of confidence in many circles. I have been promoted out of necessity. Perhaps not desperation. Not yet. But necessity."

Burnside, for all his physical prowess, had none of the swagger of McClellan or Pope in him. Brady had known him years and considered him as good a friend as any in the army.

"And I do not blame them," the general added.

He did not want the job, he went on to reveal. Brady was not surprised by the candor in which Ambrose Burnside spoke. Such candor was refreshing, yet for someone with his charge, to hold himself in such low esteem?

Looking back, Brady should have known how Burnside's tenure at the top would go.

But at that moment, standing beside the commander of the largest army in the nation, Brady could only feel good about his first return to the field in more than a year.

Alex Gardner's departure two weeks earlier made him realize what he had been missing. The Scot was an able man and had managed Brady's team well. But even Gardner did not enjoy the advantages that Brady could expect in the field.

As Brady's liaison in the field, Gardner had established himself, gaining confidences that would no doubt allow him to continue to enjoy access to the army on some level. But it had always been he and he alone who could summon an audience with top commanders with a note or wired request, just as he had done with General Burnside. The Anthony brothers, pained as they were to admit it, knew this. Gardner would soon realize this too.

Carte de visite of Burnside in Brady's studio, circa 1861

Julia had begged Brady not to go that November. The nation's capital awoke each morning to frosted rooftops. There were the afternoon snow squalls; a taste of the winter to come. But Brady knew Gardner, at present, was again with the army at Warrenton. Brady needed to be certain the most sought after photographs of the newly appointed general of the Army of the Potomac would be his.

"I believe you will do your country proud, General. There is no one better to win this war now, yet this year, than you."

"Well, I thank you, Mathew," he replied, then after a moment "I suppose we all have a job to do."

Burnside tossed his cigar in the dirt, smashing it beneath his giant boot heel. "Now, I have a rather busy day so let's get on with yours so I can get back to mine. What do you say?"

"Yes. Right over here. My man is setting up."

He called over Woodbury from the van, then directed the general into the clearing for two exposures. Brady then posed Burnside, surrounded by his officers, for Woodbury's large format camera.

Brady would need more David Woodburys, more men to assist him as he took a greater role in the field, to take the images that Brady's weak eyes would not allow him to take.

He would hire them, as many as he could.

Brady did not waste any more of the general's time that afternoon. He wished him luck and, keeping his promise to Julia, left for Washington.

On the front page of the Saturday, November 29th issue of *Harper's Weekly*, Burnside received his proper introductions.

The portrait of General BURNSIDE, which accompanies these lines, will introduce the reader to the face and figure of one of the most gallant of our soldiers-the Commander of the Army of the Potomac. It is from a photograph by Brady.

The following week, ships began to arrive at the docks. The army had expelled its wounded from camp at Warrenton. Brady watched the supply boats, loaded to the point of sinking, steam off in the opposite direction to the army base at Aquia Creek. Burnside was on the move, crossing the Rappahannock to meet Lee and his Confederate Army.

Early December meant long and tiring days as Brady tended to his studio and readied new teams of photographers for the field. Nights belonged to the Willard.

Every night they crowded tables and booths, the shoulder straps and politicians, feasting and drinking courtesy of men, like Brady, whose fortunes depended on the shifting winds of war. They knotted at the bar, sipping aged scotch and filling the place with cigar and pipe smoke. Brady spent a fair sum on meals and drink rounds. Every once in a while, he learned something not entirely useless to him.

Like most, Brady chewed over any morsel of news from the front. But no news arrived for many days. The wait was agonizing.

Then, it came.

The night of December 13th, Brady bought second brandies for Senator Henry Wilson and himself.

Whispers of a battle near Fredericksburg. Tensions were high, every man trying to wrestle bits of information from one another, like sending bucket after empty bucket down a well long since dry. Even Wilson knew not.

The tired senator finished his drink. He shook Brady's hand and put on his coat, ready to quit the game for the evening when Henry Villard came through the doors.

Wilson's heavy eyes lit when he saw him. "By God, now there he is," he whispered Brady's way.

Villard, field correspondent with Greely's *New York Tribune*, lumbered in the doorway to but a few turned heads.

Wilson hurried over to pull Villard aside. Brady stepped a few paces behind.

"What do you know, Henry? Have we won the fight?" Wilson asked in an excited hush.

Villard, barely inside the hotel, turned to Wilson, but said nothing. He removed the hat from his balding head. He looked at Brady, running fingers down a thick moustache.

"Hello, Mathew," Villard said in his German accent, ignoring Wilson, perhaps repulsed by the senator's go-ahead manner.

The reporter looked exhausted. His gray suit spattered in mud, just as Brady remembered when they last crossed paths at Bull Run in July of last.

"Hello, Henry."

Brady realized now, as Wilson surely already knew, that Villard had just come from Virginia.

Villard looked upon the senator's excited face once more then started for an empty table in the restaurant.

Wilson had no choice but to follow on his heels. Brady would have been a fool not to do so as well.

Villard sat, finally meeting Wilson's eyes. "I will not tell you what it took to get back to the city. They shut down all roads leading out. I risked my life crossing the Potomac in the black of night," he said in his halting accent. His face screwed tight and reddened. "And now they will not let me wire it! War Department orders. Ach! What a waste!"

Wilson sat. Brady too. Then, as if telling someone was better than no one, Villard broke down a review of what he knew for fact, keeping quiet so as not to alert the crowd.

He spoke of disaster at Fredericksburg. Untold numbers of dead Union, the result of Burnside's miscalculations. In Henry Villard's mind, it could not have gone worse.

Brady listened and felt his heart sink inside him. He watched the pallor that fell upon Wilson's face. The senator mumbled a string of semi-coherent words and put his hand to his forehead.

"Go. Go and tell the president if he still does not know," said Villard with a wave of the hand. "I am going to eat a hot meal for God's sake."

Wilson stood up. He fastened the top buttons on his overcoat and dashed for the exit into the chill night.

Brady rose. He could see that the disheveled reporter wanted peace and quiet. He had to respect that. A few more words and he left him at the table.

Brady returned to the bar, downed the last swallow of his drink that remained and started home. He later learned that, no sooner had Villard finished his meal and returned to the Tribune office across the street, Wilson called upon him there. This time, he took the reporter directly to the Executive Mansion to tell President Lincoln, first-hand, what had happened.

The world learned the full details a few days later, when Villard's report, and others, appeared in the papers: *Disaster at Fredericksburg.*

Waves of men slaughtered upon the heights beyond the town in one senseless charge after another. Meagher's Irish Brigade, along with scores of others. Torn to pieces in the tall grass set ablaze by shot and shell. Wounded burned alive. Others left to freeze to death on the hillside under a clear December moon.

In the hotels and bars along the avenue, Brady heard men boast over their whiskies they knew all along that Burnside was not fit for command.

The papers began printing the long list of casualties on the 16th. But for the residents of the nation's capital, accounts from the newspaper extras were unnecessary. Days before, apocryphal waves of boats carrying wounded began arriving at the 6th Street landing. Brady rode down more than once to see for himself. They transferred the poor, wretched souls to ambulances. He heard their cries at every hole in the road. Those able to walk limped through the cold and damp streets, slung and bandaged, bloody rags upon their heads. The stench, emanating from hospitals that dotted the hills and every vacant lot in the city, was noxious.

Brady took long walks those December days and nights, along streets and through the chaotic hospitals where they anguished and died daily by the hundreds. Something compelled him to witness the destruction and misery first-hand, to stare into the gaunt, pale faces marked with pain and sorrow.

He needed to understand what it had all been for.

The city homes were scarce with Christmas decorations. Even the elites, at least for a few days' time, were in no mood to dine and soiree.

Never before or since did Brady remember feeling as low as he did in those early December days of '62.

❧

The sun set upon Saturday, December 19th, hastening the day's cold and dreary end. Brady excused himself from the crowded parlor, intent on heading home to Julia, whom he had excused as not feeling up to that afternoon's social.

His cab rolled forward on Lafayette Square, past the stately gas-lit homes that lined both sides of the street.

Brady breathed into cold hands and looked out across the gated green of the park to the outline of the Executive Mansion with its portico and stone corner piers lit, its grand columns glowed a soft white through the evening dark.

"Stop."

The cab halted abruptly followed by the whinny of its mare.

It waited at the edge of the park where it met Pennsylvania Avenue.

"Sir, I've changed my mind. I should like to walk a bit."

Brady exited and paid.

A long walk back to the National, but he wanted time to think. If he got cold, he'd stop another passing driver once he made his way down the avenue. He might even stop by the Willard for a late brandy.

Brady breathed deeply of the cold air. He looked up, searching dark clouds for the nascent moon. A fine mist brushed his skyward face. There would be few stars tonight. He buttoned his coat to his neck and turned up its collar and slid on his doeskin gloves.

He stepped across the paved street and stood there before the north lawn of the mansion.

Brady had recently upgraded to newer, thicker lenses. He put them to test, casting a stare across the gated garden, the bronze statue of Thomas Jefferson halfway between the president's mansion and where he stood.

Past the ornamental wrought iron fence and naked-limbed trees at the garden's southernmost edge, two bluecoats met on the portico steps to confer with one another a moment, then disappeared.

From Brady's collections, Executive Mansion, 1860s

There Brady stood, listening to the horses and wagons click along the cobblestones at his back. Down the avenue, two lamplighters were busy on their ladders. Brady knew that on his way back home, he would still find plenty of men and women about the walks, slipping in and out of shops to purchase Christmas gifts. Many would pay visit to his studio, which stayed open late, to purchase prepackaged bundles of calling cards.

As he looked upon the quiet mansion, he thought of Lincoln.

Brady knew the president spent summer evenings at a cottage out Seventh Street to escape the heat. But this time of year, he was likely inside the house before him, and being pressed upon greatly with matters large and small. Lincoln had failed to visit Brady's studio even once this year, having cancelled numerous appointments with his apologies courtesy of

Secretary Hay. The war had consumed him, just as it had the nation. Brady was disappointed, but he understood.

He considered these things and more as he watched the great house, its balustrades and gleaming white pilasters. A cold wind blew past him and down the avenue.

He sensed it was time to go.

And Brady was about to turn away when a figure appeared.

The door of the great house opened ever so slightly. Brady would not have noticed were it not for the flash of light that poured out a brief moment. No sooner did the person slip through that the door was shut at his back.

Brady watched the man step quickly down the east steps of the portico. A man tall and thin, who carried something in his right hand. Brady no longer saw the two sentries that earlier manned the portico and the man's gait continued unabated as he stepped out of reach of the gaslight.

Brady began walking east along the avenue, the gated park between him and the fellow as he kept pace. Brady watched him proceed down the wide stone walk along the wide gravel drive until he reached the avenue himself some thirty paces ahead.

Brady felt a rush of blood to his head, a tingling in his gloved fingers. He tried to contain his excitement as he followed.

He knew, as many did, that the president was oft to slip past his guard and walk the grounds alone, venturing to the War Department for news from the front. Rumor was that he could be seen many a night, unaccompanied, riding north from the city to his summer cottage.

Whoever this might be, Brady was bound to discover.

Brady followed him onto New York Avenue, across 15th, then 14th Street under a black sky.

The man continued on, finally crossing the muddied street where he slipped into a shop front.

Brady caught up to the place. He stopped on the walk, recognizing the slender two-story brick building painted white with red double-doors and green shutters. Above the door and display window hung a bright, red-lettered banner.

1207 Stuntz 1207

He and Julia had passed the Stuntz toy and candy store many times to gaze into its large front window. But never once did they enter, nor did they speak of a day when perhaps they might go inside to purchase toys for one of their own.

They would stand for some minutes, watching parent and child at the penny counter, buying pieces of wrapped taffy, licorice, and chewing gum. Children would sift through bins and carts of smaller toys; tin whistles, bean shooters, and more. Upon the shelves rested the finer items; china dolls and small doll houses, wooden soldiers with appendages that moved on hinges.

Now as Brady peered through the steamed glass, he knew certain that it was the President of the United States he now saw perched upon a stool at the glass counter.

It was his face in profile; his prominent nose, his pale cheeks against a trim beard. The tall beaver hat that he had carried in his hand now rested bottom up on that counter.

The shop owner Stuntz, a little rotund man of later years with thin gray hair combed over, stood behind the counter, waiting as the president's long fingers examined something tiny by comparison. Brady had seen the old toymaker through the window and on the nearby streets many times over the years, yet they had never shared a word.

Brady breathed deeply. Before he could gather his thoughts and make a rational decision as to how to proceed, he had opened the door and stepped inside.

Joseph Stuntz straightened. The smile vanished from his round face.

"May I help you?" The hurried words sounded of alarm, as if caught in the act of a crime.

Lincoln then turned round from his stool. His dark eyes fixed upon Brady a moment, then brightened.

"Why, Mr. Brady. This is a surprise." The president let out a quiet laugh. "Come have a word with Mr. Stuntz and me."

The president stood bent forward, long enough to shift to an adjacent stool. He rapped the seat he had just vacated.

Brady removed his hat and held it, its lip wet with cold mist.

"Hello, Mr. President. I saw you on the street and I-" Brady stammered as he cast a glance over his shoulder to the dark street. "I feel a bit embarrassed now for the intrusion."

"Nonsense. Come now. You can help me decide on a Christmas gift for Tad."

A smile returned to Stuntz's face. The owner reached under the counter, snagged several small toys between his chubby fingers and fanned them out, each clanking the glass to sound their arrival.

Brady finally sat on the stool next. Inside the president's turned up hat, Brady saw a bound volume that had been placed inside for safe keeping. *Scott's Poetical Works by Sir Walter Scott.*

"Mr. Brady, this is Joseph Stuntz if you have not made one another's acquaintance."

Stuntz laughed and held out his thick hand. Brady took it. "I know you by reputation, Mr. Brady. A pleasure indeed."

Stuntz offered the men something from the jars of penny candies. Brady declined. Stuntz set out a few pieces of black licorice for the president on a sheet of wax paper.

There in the lit room they sat and talked, the black of night staring back at them through the front window.

The president explained his wife had gone to Philadelphia and son Tad, at present, was asleep at the mansion.

"Mary and I will spend Christmas Day at the hospitals. She has purchased enough baskets to fill several wagons. This is the first time, and likely only time, to purchase Tad a gift myself."

Stuntz stood up from his counter. He held up a fat index finger. "I think I have something he will like, Mr. President."

The toymaker hobbled down the length of the counter and slipped through an opening to a backroom behind the shelved wall. The president stared, a coy smile upon his lips, until Stuntz reappeared seconds later and took up his former position.

"I wanted to add a little more paint. A little touch, but I think they are good enough."

Stuntz opened his cupped hands and let several toy soldiers fall to the glass counter.

Five in all, each perhaps one and a half inches in height. Three of the soldiers wore deep Union blue, with matching kepis for their heads. The final two were Navy men in white issue trousers.

Lincoln smiled down upon them. He took the two Navy men, one then the other, and turned them upright on their round bases painted green.

"Ah, yes. Here we are." Lincoln cocked his head toward Brady a moment. "Mr. Stuntz here is a veteran of the Napoleonic Wars, you know. He knows a thing or two about soldiering."

The president stood up the remaining three so that all five were uniform, a few inches apart.

Brady could not help but admire such intricate detail. Light rose colored cheeks and two were mustachioed. Three held rifles of dark brown across their breasts. At their sides, beneath dark blue coats dotted with gold, a miniature pistol appeared against powder blue pants with white piping. Two of the soldiers were musicians, one with a drum strapped round his front and the other a gold trumpet to his lips.

"Now, Mr. Stuntz," the president started, then paused. Brady saw sadness in dark eyes that ran dully over the tiny wooden men. "If only I could trade these for each one of my own lost."

Neither Brady nor the shop keep knew what to say.

It was their good fortune that the president brightened no sooner than he had gone glum. He tapped the counter top.

"I will take them! All of them. They are the best I have yet to see from you, I do believe."

"Very well, Mr. President. Thank you, Mr. President."

Stuntz fetched wrapping materials and began to cover the soldiers individually and place them in a paper bag. He refused payment but the president eventually won that contest; he took coins from his pocket and fished out five dimes from his opened palm and placed them on the counter where Stuntz collected them.

Then, the president picked out two half dimes and slid them across the counter before he returned his hand to his pocket.

"If you will please, Mr. Stuntz, a bag of candy. The licorice and taffies are Tad's favorite."

President Lincoln turned to Brady. "Help yourself, Mr. Brady. Tad will not notice a few pieces missing."

"Oh, no thank you, Mr. President."

"Very well. I do indulge I suppose, but as I tell Mr. Stuntz," said the president, his eyes focused upon Stuntz's scoop working the candy jar, "I want Tad to have all the toys I didn't have, and all the toys I'd have given the boy who went away."

The words caught Brady by surprise.

Willie Lincoln had been gone ten months now by Brady's quick math.

The president's beloved nine-year-old son had died of fever in February of the present year. Now in but a few days, that year would vanish into history.

Lincoln kept silent for a moment. Brady and Stuntz could only wait for Lincoln's return to them, which he soon did with a kind smile.

"Mr. Stuntz," began the president, a bag of soldiers and a bag of candy filled far more amply than ten cent's worth now on the counter before him, "You have been too generous."

Brady heard the sudden rush of footsteps. A great whoosh and the loud clang of the door's bells filled the room. Brady shot up from his stool.

"Mr. President!"

The lean young man with a thin moustache stood red-faced and breathless, his wide eyes fixed upon the president. He showed a captain's stripes on the arm of his blue coat.

"You really must not slip away-" the captain began before halting his words, his eyes flitted toward the floor as if to admonish himself for his harsh tone. There he stood in the open door, one boot in and the other still on the brick walk.

Brady turned to Lincoln and watched a wry grin take form above his beard.

"It seems, gentlemen, Captain Derickson would like me back."

The president maneuvered his long legs from the stool and rose up with a grunt. He placed the bags inside his tall hat, beside the Scott book, and took hold of it.

The captain, still panting, removed his kepi and ran a hand over his sweaty brow and hair. He held wide the door and the president started toward it.

President Lincoln paused. He turned toward Stuntz and Brady, and with the flick of his wrist tipped his bottoms up silk hat their way, the top of the bags poking out its rim.

"Merry Christmas, gentlemen. Pray for the new year of 1863."

The president left, he and his guardian captain into the black night.

Brady watched as two more soldiers in blue overcoats fell in some distance behind them. Brady returned to the stool and sat for a time with his new friend Stuntz.

A young couple entered the store, completely unaware of the chance encounter they had so nearly missed.

Brady watched them for a while. He felt the inexplicable urge to make his first purchase with Stuntz that evening. He ordered half a dozen bags filled with small toys and several more bags of candy.

He paid in full and walked the three blocks to the Washington City Orphan Asylum at H Street between 9th and 10th where he made fast friends.

Early 1863

Brady ventured to Fredericksburg in early February when the weather let up.

He and two assistants photographed the town and still shattered heights.

The disaster at Fredericksburg, then the attempt to launch a winter offensive a few weeks ago, only to be halted by a deluge of rain and mud, had doomed Brady's old friend General Burnside.

Lincoln had placed General Joseph Hooker in command.

Hooker, a muscular man with steely eyes and sharp features who had posed for Brady on more than one occasion, seemed an able choice.

Gen'l Joseph Hooker

Entered according to the act of Congress, in the year 1863 by M. B. Brady, in the Clerk's Office of the District Court of the District of Columbia.

A Brady carte de visite, General Hooker in '62

The bearish Burnside took it in stride. He seemed in good spirits when Brady met him at camp, perhaps it was relief from a charge he never wanted.

Within days, Burnside would be transferred out. Yet a new era in the war was to unfold.

⚬⚭⚬

Lincoln sat once more in Brady's chair the morning of April 17th.

The shock of his Emancipation Proclamation had ebbed, a winter's night of riots and throwing stones in the Washington streets seemed a distant memory. The country had time to wrestle with it; both the abolitionists who complained it had not done enough and those who feared the war would now become a war of liberation rather than one to save the Union.

Brady watched spring arrive with its warmer skies and blooming dogwoods. It seemed to temper the mood in Washington.

Across the Potomac at Arlington, thousands of contraband, former slaves, set up their makeshift camps in the Freedman's Village, their northward exodus one to rival the biblical tales of old.

Many came forward to fill the ranks of colored regiments. Those left behind waited for the Union to deliver their friends and families from bondage.

The country waited too, expecting General Hooker's grand overture to commence any day; a resumption of war.

XI

Summer 1863

Two riders approached at a distance.

Gardner watched from his front porch. Through the morning mist, he could see they donned civilian clothes; one wore a wide-brimmed straw hat. They were not soldiers. Nevertheless, O'Sullivan rode out into the center of the Seventh Street Road and flagged them down.

O'Sullivan had staked out the road before sunrise on that July 3rd, hoping to catch any news that might trickle down it. For days, the road was busy with the comings and goings of commissary and ambulance wagons. But it had been some time since a southbound rider carried any news from far north of the capital.

Gardner watched O'Sullivan turn away from the pair and start his horse toward the house at a full gallop.

"Pennsylvania," O'Sullivan said. He pulled up, climbed down and led the horse by its lashings to the porch. He tied off, his eyes set to the ground before he looked up to meet Gardner. "Gettysburg."

Gardner had agonized much of the past week. Now, with O'Sullivan's single word delivery, his greatest fear was brought to bear.

Gardner understood the movement of the Confederate Army northward two weeks back. Scant on supplies of plate and chemical, he left Hooker's army on the 26th of June, two days before Meade replaced Hooker at the head of the Army of the Potomac.

He had hoped to rejoin the army within the week.

Upon his return home, Gardner found a letter dated the 18th of June awaiting him. Lawrence wrote to his father of some account of hysteria near Mount Saint Mary's in Emmitsburg.

Two weeks back we saw the first of the army. Michigan 6th rode past The Mountain in early morning. The boys and I watched them from the fences. They must have come a long way in a hurry, the greater of them half asleep at the necks of their horses.

Then fire at Guthrie and Beam's stable couple days ago. Burned through Main Street and the town. Many of us came in relief and formed the Bucket Brigade all night. Talk is the Rebs are up in this country now and that they started it though I doubt it some.

The letter went on to describe a hurried and early commencement so a few boys could start home ahead of what was now feared to come. Lawrence expressed hope that they made it, for it seemed that every soldier and wagon in the Union army was now pushing its way northward along every road past *The Mountain*, as the boys referred to their school.

It may be the last letter for some time. No worries from me and none from you either, if you please.

Gardner and his team had already prepared, stocking two wagons in anticipation of the battle that Lee sought north of the Potomac; the second time in ten months the general had taken such bold action. Jeb Stuart had briefly touched Emmitsburg the preceding year, but it seemed safe. Gardner had enrolled his son at the school for that reason.

But he knew there was always a chance.

Roughly seventy-five miles now separated his team from Gettysburg and a battle whose outcome was still a mystery, if it was not still being fought. It would take all but ten of those miles to reach Emmitsburg, and Lawrence.

Gardner now regretted not racing north for his son in late June. He told O'Sullivan so that morning.

"Old enough and smart enough," O'Sullivan reassured him after Gibson arrived and their vans started north. "He'll be fine."

With Lee's target unknown, wealthy families had abandoned their country estates and rode down Seventh Street to hotels deep within the heart of Washington. Were the Confederates to target the city's northern defenses, Gardner's home lay directly in their path. To race into Maryland, O'Sullivan had argued, fighting might commence. They would have to hole up somewhere, pinned by the advancing armies. They would not only put themselves in danger, but without having replenished their supplies, they would be in no position to photograph the coming battle.

Gardner knew it made sense.

Father McCaffrey would see to the boys' well-being. Lawrence was a young man of sixteen. He had his senses and he had refuge at Mount St. Mary's.

⁂

The wagons crossed north into the Maryland countryside before noon on the 3rd. O'Sullivan's outfit held in its bed the bulk of chemicals and plates. Gibson followed in a second wagon with three cameras and the development baths. Gardner had saddled Bess and led her from the barn. He rode her separately. The bay mare would give him flexibility to maneuver. He could scout terrain without harassing the wagon teams.

He could do other things, if need be.

They pushed north all day and into night. Some thirty-three miles south, the beginnings of Independence Day fireworks were no doubt being set off in the Washington streets and on its neighboring hilltops.

The road stayed quiet at first light. Further north, traces of the army began to appear, abandoned wagons roadside. Signs of an army pushing northward, converging fast. When they crossed over the rail line connecting Baltimore to Frederick, there were a half dozen wrecked cars before a station house left smoldering in ruin, an ominous sign.

Hopes they could maintain their quick pace faded when an early drizzle turned torrential by afternoon. Sheets of rain deluged them and mired the road, puddled deep in ruts made by wagon traffic. It worsened with each mile.

They passed a detachment of cavalry. O'Sullivan managed to slow a few of them in the muddy road, long enough for them to announce that Lee had been beaten back to the Potomac. A Union victory. As encouraging as the news was, there was no time to waste on gathering details, even had the soldiers been able to provide them.

Flies drew about in the humid spells between downpours. The skies flashed and thunder grew deafening at times.

It was dusk. By Gardner's calculation, he had perhaps nine more miles to the school. But Bess, with head low and the occasional misplaced step, told him she could not make it even that far. Gardner knew the horses, everyone, needed rest.

❧

They made camp on the night of the 4th, wet and exhausted.

They set the horses out to water and feed. They scavenged for dry wood then took the ax to wet wood, enough to set a fire. O'Sullivan cooked biscuits with beans. The three of them ducked beneath bedrolls and shut their eyes to a fire pestered by a light and steady drizzle.

It quit raining sometime after midnight. Lying there, Gardner heard plodding hooves out on the road as a wind shook trees that still rained from saturated leaves. Above, skies broke clear, and stars showed between passing clouds. The world was cool and damp.

At three Gardner prodded O'Sullivan awake.

O'Sullivan sat up on elbows from his bedroll.

"Time to break, boss?"

"No," Gardner said, now standing across camp, the glowing ruins of a fire between them. "I am riding ahead."

He climbed atop Bess and turned her round. Gibson lay sound asleep. "Set out by dawn. I'll meet you along the road sometime tomorrow morning."

O'Sullivan, still squinting across the dark, looked ready to speak but only nodded. Gardner knew he understood.

"Roads will get worse here on," Gardner said. "Stay alert. Take what time you need to get the equipment to the field."

He told O'Sullivan he was taking a canteen and one of two maps. He was leaving Gibson and O'Sullivan both pistol and rifle. He took the reins and brought the brim of his damp hat down close over his eyes.

"And if you don't find me, get to the business of it. Don't wait."

⤛⤜

An hour up the road at first dawn, the roadside pines and thatch began to take form. Gardner vaguely recalled the bends in the road from his prior journey to the school with his son. He knew he was getting close.

Bess side-stepped the deepest pools. The road was so quiet. But Gardner thought little of it.

He would give the mare a few minutes more at this pace before he pushed her on toward the destination. He lowered his bearded chin against his chest and flirted with sleep as he rode on through the morning fog.

Had Gardner been more alert, he could have taken cover in the trees. They might not have seen him.

At first the voices came a distant murmur, indiscernible enough that seconds passed before his tired mind paid closer attention. One of them laughed. A man's laugh.

Gardner brought his eyes up to two horseback figures thirty yards ahead, shrouded in mist just as the road trailed left.

His mind locked shut. And Bess drew closer with each slow hoof.

Gardner was close enough now he could see their butternut coats and hats.

He felt his fingers on the leather reins and he pulled up. But Bess saw them or had picked up their scent. She stopped, and whinnied.

The taller of the two men in the saddle turned his head. Gardner grabbed the pommel of his saddle with white knuckles.

"You there! Stop!"

The Rebel pointed a finger. The second spun round on his mount and began to unholster.

Gardner kicked Bess, turning her left toward a partial clearing in the roadside trees and went in. He lowered his head and felt branches beat against the crown of his head. A stiff branch met his chest and pulled him up and back before snapping clean.

A shot sounded. Gardner had no idea what direction or where he was going. He lifted his head at intervals, fearful the next branch might knock him clear from the horse, but the morning sun had yet to light the dusky wood.

A second shot sounded, louder than the first.

Gardner looked up to see a break in the trees. Light of day.

He steered up a small rise toward the clearing. There he stopped and tried to grapple with his fear.

He was in the road again.

Gardner turned his horse. There stood the riders upon their taller geldings, watching him not twelve paces away.

The shorter of the two held his revolver in the air.

The taller one had his carbine pointed at the ground. At first, he looked nearly as startled as Gardner, then his thin face drew tight. He swung down from his saddle and stepped to Gardner. His stony eyes narrowed as he swung the barrel up to Gardner's head and thumbed the cap.

Gardner realized he led the mare round in a circle back to them.

"You don't hear or somethin?" barked the tall one.

The short one pulled his horse up and when he reached out for Bess' reins, Gardner saw a captain's straps on his arm.

"Come on you. Get down," said the short captain.

Gardner dismounted. The taller patted down Gardner's coat, then pant legs. He stank of days, if not weeks, of grunge and summer sweat. Gardner was glad he had not brought a weapon.

The Rebel captain asked Gardner his business.

Gardner explained he was a civilian photographer, but he was unsure if the captain was listening, for he offered nothing in response. Finally, the captain turned his horse and started up the road at a slow trot in the direction Gardner had been headed.

The tall one then prodded Gardner back onto Bess and remounted his own horse and fell in behind him.

At intervals, the soldier would pull up beside Gardner and smirk at him through yellowed teeth, only to fall back again.

"Now that is one beat down animal."

Gardner did not trust something in his eyes. The hotspur passed and circled him. "He's a spy in plain clothes. We ought to shoot him. You one of Kilpatrick's lookouts, ain't you, fella? Yes sir. Let's shoot him."

The tall one spat and directed his next words to the captain. "Suppose a whole spell of 'em come riding full down this road again like yesterday, how you think we'd fare?"

"Shut up, Harrow. That's an order. Now ride. You," he started at Gardner, "pick up the pace."

And that the three of them did, Gardner and his Rebel captors.

Their horses pushed up the mud road. Somewhere a woodpecker worked an old oak as the day took hold with morning's light.

To the left, Gardner caught the first glimpse of the seminary cupola at Mt. Saint Mary's, its copper dome tall above the trees, green hills steep behind her.

He had almost made it.

If the Confederates had taken hold in Emmitsburg, what had become of the Mount and the boys there?

When Gardner turned his gaze back to the road, this elicited a cackle from Harrow, as if he was aware of Gardner's situation and reveled in his state of helplessness.

They rode on past until they reached the town, many of the buildings in a state of ruin from a recent fire.

They came to a two-story inn where two muddy roads met. Three Confederates stared down from its second story porch, following Gardner's entrance into a dirt yard where dozens of Union soldiers sat in a circle. A third that many southern soldiers surrounded them on horseback or stood about the yard puffing rolled smokes. At the edge of the plot, four Union men lay dead, uncovered, shoulder against shoulder. There had been a sharp skirmish that was clear, and not long ago.

Harrow nudged Gardner to dismount. The captain took Bess by her reins.

Harrow prodded Gardner forward. Most of the captive soldiers did not look up. The flags affixed to their low hats told Gardner most were members of the Signal Corps. On narrow wood planks at the inn's entrance lay a scattering of men upon stretchers and spread sheets, no doubt convalescent Union soldiers rousted from their beds to make room.

Gardner knew that every house within five miles now likely served as hospital and ward, for one side or the other.

The captain and Harrow tied their horses and Bess with the band of sorrels and bays hitched at posts along the length of the porch. With the flat of his palm, Harrow pushed Gardner up the porch and on through the door.

He was led down the small corridor and seated at a chair beside an oak table. Harrow peered down at him. He grinned and chew juice trickled down his chin before he spat on the floorboards at Gardner's feet. The tall Rebel soldier rocked on boot heels as he strained his neck to glimpse comings and goings down the hall. He said nothing for minutes.

"I'll be back but I'm a watchin'," Harrow said. "I'll shoot you too. Think they'll care? Don't you move."

He disappeared round the corner.

From the light shown above the wwindowsillpast the stove, Gardner guessed it almost seven now. He tried to lean a few inches and peer down the hall. He saw a parlor door, about two feet ajar. A glimpse of gray coat officers gathered at a table, their arms and hands running over papers upon it, probably maps. A man with a light brown beard stood bent and still.

Distant words, difficult to discern save for the word *Kilpatrick* Gardner was sure he heard. With Lee's army in retreat, they were being pursued. They were looking for a way out.

Gardner heard footsteps creak upon the floor. He snapped back and saw a man looking down on him with hands fisted at his hips.

The officer wore a soft felt hat; he was thin with narrow, coal-colored eyes. His goatee was brown and tinged with gray. He could have been considered handsome were it not for a scar that jutted down his left cheek from ear to mouth, above the two gold stars on his dull collar.

"Photographer?" said the lieutenant colonel in a soft yet direct tone.

"Yes."

"All by yourself? Way out here? Where's your equipment?"

It occurred to Gardner that there was nothing whatsoever to suggest that he was a photographer. A lone rider on horseback, certainly not a soldier, but a photographer? There were not nearly as many photographers among the ranks of the Confederate armies due to scarcity of supplies, but Gardner would be shocked if a southern officer had never seen a photography van or the cache of supplies, plates, and most of all, the camera, it required.

He stayed quiet until the officer pushed air through his nose and crossed his arms. His eyes fixed.

"Perhaps you are on a military assignment? A courier or even a-"

"My son."

The officer stopped mid-sentence. He scratched at his goatee. The pushing of chairs and the creaking of a door briefly drew the officer's attention down the hall.

"My son is at the school a mile from here. I rode ahead. There are two more in my team, each driving a wagon with cameras and equipment. They will be up this road in a few hours."

The sound of hurried boots filled the silence between them, and Gardner heard voices down the hall.

The officer looked down at his mud-splattered boots, then again to Gardner.

"Wait here."

The officer left the room.

And he never came back.

Fifteen minutes and the sound of boots and horses and scuttle that had become less frequent stopped altogether.

Gardner got the nerve to rise from his seat. He stepped down the quiet hall. Nothing remained save the disarray of chairs and cups on saucers on the parlor table where maps had been studied only minutes before.

He went out the front door. The mud yard was empty. The only soldiers to be counted were the four dead and two lying comatose upon porch stretchers. He saw no tied horses. They were gone, including Bess.

Gardner walked back into the vacant inn. A woman appeared from around a corner, a stout middle-aged woman wearing her gray hair tight in a bun, an apron around her hips.

She glanced at him but said nothing and gave him no clue as to her thoughts. She brushed past, across the foyer and into the parlor. As if nothing was amiss, she began to straighten the chairs and collect the dishes.

Gardner started out, crossing a field and through woods thick with undergrowth and dark except for a morning sun that split through the trees. He met the pike and set out at a jog to the south until the entrance to the Mount came in view. He ran up the dirt road that led to the fenced yard, across its mall and climbed the steps to the stone building's terrace where three boys watched him come. Others could be seen from the rows of narrow windows. They had, no doubt, seen many a stranger come and go of late.

The three boys began their questioning when he reached the terrace.

"Can we help you, sir? Pies, bread, fresh water."

"We got it at good prices. Are you a Union man or a Rebel?"

"Or maybe neither. How do? I'm Charles."

Gardner shook Charles' offered hand, and then explained who he was. Charles led him inside.

Lawrence looked astonished to see his father, unkempt and standing in the corridor.

They went to a small table where one of the three boys brought coffee and slices of bread. Lawrence told his father to eat and then began to tell his story. How they had watched the army pour through every road north; the men, wagons, and artillery. So many soldiers their dark coats turned the road black at a distant. They camped at Emmitsburg, their campfires lighting the night sky like a thousand stars. Nearly everyone; students, seminarians, and faculty had spent the better part of three days atop Indian Lookout behind the school to watch the battle, twelve miles distant, through scopes and opera glasses. They had not known who won until last evening when a Union officer showed up to tell them to ready clean beds for the wounded.

"Of course we were safe. I said I would be."

Of course, Gardner thought. A hasty retreat down the Emmitsburg Road, a wayward shell or misdirected cannonade could have changed everything in an instant. Gardner knew that, even if those boys did not.

"Pack your things. You're coming to Washington, at least for now." Gardner stood and put on his hat. "When I return."

Gardner left his son with a gentleman's handshake. As Gardner stepped from the school, an ambulance road up the yard, bandaged soldiers laid out and others propped up against its bed walls.

He moved at a quick gait back to the road and started on foot north.

Fifteen minutes later, as if events of that morning had been of no account, O'Sullivan's wagon rounded the bend.

"Where's your horse?" Gibson asked.

Gardner shook his head then, with a glance to the next bend in the road, said "Nine more miles." He climbed aboard beside Gibson. "Let's get going."

⤙⤚

The bandaged man leaned upon the split rail that ran several yards before it broke down in places then disappeared entirely. The ragged solder waved to them, as if he might to neighbors on their way to market as he mended his pasture fence. The road had taken its toll on the horses. The wheels needed inspecting. Besides, Gardner was not sure exactly what lay ahead. He told O'Sullivan to stop.

O'Sullivan lowered his canteen to the man whose tourniquet was in need of changing, his sunbaked face stained with mud. He gulped water that ran down his whiskered chin and streaked his dirty skin.

"You seekin' out kin? Maybe I can help. What regiment he from?"

"Nothing like that," Gardner replied, then began asking questions of his own; about the terrain, the course of battle.

Gibson leapt down to stretch his legs.

"Good Lord. Fightin' all over no need to go lookin'. In the fields up ahead this road they gave us a hell of a fight. Boys gettin' to bury 'em all. Course the rebs will have to wait their turn."

Gardner pushed for further details.

"No."

"That's right."

"Just beyond them trees," responded the man in turn to the questions except for when his mouth was full of the tepid water and he could only shake his head in sweeping gestures.

The man laughed and wiped his mouth.

"Course my unit was north up the road a ways toward town. Fine little town. They caught some of it but not too bad, I suspect. Yes, I suppose it wasn't too bad for most folk there. Not good times for solderin' though."

A violent cough overtook the man. When he settled, a wide grin formed upon his bristly cheeks.

"But we whooped ol' Lee good. The boys done it. Now if they catch him before he crosses back over the river, we all go home. Not that there's goin' to be any harvest needs tending to at this point but-"

They waited for the man to continue but he never did. He scratched at his head and his face screwed tight. Lost in some train of thought.

Gardner, then Gibson climbed the wagon once more.

O'Sullivan told the soldier to keep the canteen.

Gardner took the reins and tipped his hat. "Thank you. You should have someone tend to that bandage."

⁓

They came through a wood that opened upon a trampled field. A pair of Napoleons still pointed toward distant hills where halved and shattered trees showed against the rising land.

They soon led the wagons from the road to the first of the dead. The fallen lay in clusters east of the road. Some ravaged and dismembered by close shelling; others in loose rows having succumbed to volleys of minie ball. The diamonds of the 3rd Corps upon many a Union corpse; they were bloated, shoeless, many a pocket turned inside out from looting. There were many dead horses among them. The humid air was putrid with the stench of rot and feces.

To the east where the earth began to rise to forested hills, Gardner could see the bands of soldiers and Negro diggers along the edge of woods, toiling beneath gray skies that appeared still more than capable of unleashing a thunderous rain. Buzzards circled on high, with no shortage of targets.

They drove further across a field so reminiscent of Antietam, past six Union soldiers tied together by their bare feet. Face down, their bare asses partially exposed from where gas released from their bodies had forced open their trousers. Two Negro men pulled rope, dragging the corpses toward a fresh hole. Gardner knew their process well, how they would use the dirt from the first ditch to cover the next, just deep enough under shallow patches of earth to keep them from the feral hogs who would otherwise root them up at night to feed.

Horses and small hacks were parked at battle-scared trees; souvenir hunters engaged in spirited pursuits, and the forlorn, already searching the land for a familiar face.

Gardner chose a spot, and they parked the wagons. They set to work. It was just after eleven in the morning.

The three would alternate between the stereo camera, and the large format that produced eight by ten negatives. Gardner and Gibson would share duties sensitizing and developing at the wagons. Gardner guessed the drab weather conditions called for nearly ten seconds per exposure.

In this heat and humidity, he knew they had perhaps five hours of good light, at most, to produce quality images. The diggers would not be constrained by such limitations; their work would continue into night.

The three pushed on to their limits. Not a plate ruined in haste as they considered their compositions; the many subjects, the angles.

"A Harvest of Death", July 5th, 1863, by Timothy O'Sullivan

Union dead, ½ of a Gibson stereoview, burial party is waiting

They beseeched the burial parties to give them time, allowing the extra minutes needed to capture the tragedy upon glass.

Confederate dead, by A. Gardner, one of his vans is in the background

"The Horrors of War", negative by Gardner of a mutilated soldier

They secured twenty plates by late afternoon when Gardner called off the work.

O'Sullivan made camp. Gardner and Gibson rode out to scout the next day's work, along a farm road toward the ridge running north. They moved south and east until they came upon the rock outcroppings where fallen soldiers dotted the quiet crevices and overhangs. Across the boulder strewn land and a ravine that had no doubt ran with the blood of battle in recent rains, to the hills that loomed over the grisly spectacle.

They returned to camp for a few hours' sleep and with a plan for morning.

A quarter past nine the sun gained sufficient strength. They began photographing the rocky landscape, over grassy slopes and amongst the boulders where the bodies of soldiers still awaited their hasty burials.

Bands of diggers, soldiers with bandannas wrapped about their faces to mask the stench, operated like workmen in some macabre factory line. They seemed no longer in a mood to wait on the photographers, and some commenced digging right alongside without a word otherwise.

Men young and old alike appeared upon the battlefield, many filling the quiet air with sobs as they mounted a desperate search, perhaps having received word from soldiers where their beloved might lie in rest. Most often they found nothing. Sometimes they found the fresh mound graves that rains had already washed away, exposing hands and feet.

Gardner once commanded the attention of a weeping private who stepped between his camera and a fallen soldier.

The bereaved red-haired boy removed his kepi. "Please sir. Don't take that picture. I don't want his pa to see that."

And Gardner, moved by his tears, felt compelled to honor the request.

They soon found Alfred Waud in the field and O'Sullivan took a photograph of the *Harper's Weekly* illustrator atop a rock overlooking the morbid site.

Alfred Waud, Harper's artist in Devil's Den, July 6th, T. O'Sullivan
Newsmen, sketch artists, and photographers were often side by side in the field

Gardner photographed bodies of soldiers that lay scattered up the rise among the oak and pine.

The photographers took pause as a light rain fell and risked ruining their work, but it did not last long, and they took their cameras all the way to the top of the north most hill to photograph the abandoned Union breastworks.

Gardner negative, Confederate dead at base of Big Round Top, July 6th, 1863

Gardner's caption: "All over now – Confederate sharpshooter at foot of Round Top"

It was after three when the three of them worked their way back over the rock outcroppings to make sure they had covered every vantage sufficiently.

They came across a Rebel boy on a slope where diggers had yet to discover him. O'Sullivan took the image.

Just a boy. Seventeen or eighteen Gardner thought, staring at his ashen and stilled face. One more life lost in a misguided cause. He had died alone, hundreds of miles from home.

And for what?

It was then Gardner remembered a stone wall he'd seen nearby, forty yards away perhaps. A narrow, cavernous place between larger rocks, its gap closed by a pile of stones.

He found his way back to the place.

Perhaps a sharpshooter, this soldier or another, had taken up position there, killing Union men before suffering a mortal wound. Or he had succeeded, and escaped with his army.

The wall was an unnatural construct of war, a contrivance for killing indiscriminately.

It would have been a lonely place to die.

Maybe nothing of the sort had occurred at that stone wall. Gardner began to doubt the propriety of his idea. But he was angry. And tired. So tired. He wanted to tell that story. If it was not this soldier's story, then the story of others just like him.

Gardner hurried back to the wagon and retrieved a blanket.

With O'Sullivan's help, they rolled the boy's corpse onto it and dragged it down the hill and into the vacant sharpshooter's pit. Gardner laid a rifle beside him.

At Gardner's request, O'Sullivan brought the camera in and faced the interior of the stone wall where the Rebel soldier now lay.

"Good. This is good, Tim."

Gibson arrived with a plate in its wooden slip. O'Sullivan looked at Gardner, then focused the camera and took the image.

O'Sullivan reappeared from the black cloak of the camera. He removed the plate and handed its holder to Gibson.

"Well," Gibson began, then spat his chew as he eyed the dead boy among the rocks, "Fenton never did this."

Photo at bottom: "Home of a Rebel Sharpshooter, Gettysburg." July 6th
This second photo is believed to be a fabrication, same soldier appears in both views

The dead were buried by late day on the 6th. To the south, they began the burning of some five thousand dead horses, the stench of it adding to the misery at Gettysburg.

Gardner led his team north along the ascending road to photograph General Meade's quarters and they camped at the gates of a cemetery.

They photographed the outskirts of its broken yard; shelling about the headstones had chewed the shrubbery and much of its border fence. Near the old cemetery's gateway, O'Sullivan could not help but shake his head as they read the wooden sign's dire warning.

All persons found using firearms on these grounds will be prosecuted with the utmost rigor of the law.

Evergreen Cemetery Gateway, Gettysburg, T. O'Sullivan

They ventured to the town itself and photographed it.

Shell had done its work upon a number of the buildings.

The spared homes and churches now served as hospitals, attended by doctors and local women alike.

They set up camp on a green near town and Gardner took stock. He and Gibson would start back to Washington in the morning. O'Sullivan volunteered to stay, and they left him the stereo camera and most of the remaining supplies.

∽✎∾

Just south of town, Gardner passed Woodbury and Berger. They told him Brady had already left his Manhattan studio and was to join them there in a few days' time. Berger, the German-born painter who had joined Brady in Manhattan years ago, had been summoned to the capital in the wake of Gardner's departure. Gardner admired Berger and his skill with the camera. Standing there in a white duster and wide hat, and with his goatee, Berger reminded him of Brady at Bull Run.

Gardner told the pair of them what he knew of Gettysburg, and where they might find Tim O'Sullivan. And he and Gibson moved on.

Heading south, Gibson insisted they first return to the farmer's inn where Gardner had his adventure a few mornings ago.

Gibson negative from July 7th, entitled "Emmitsburg, Maryland. Farmer's Inn and Hotel where our special artist was captured, July 5 1863"

From there they drove the wagon to Mount Saint Mary's, the roads south of Gettysburg toward Washington now heavy with the doings of the Union army.

Lawrence loaded his belongings, and they began to beat the slow course back toward the capital.

❧

Lincoln smiled and relaxed into Gardner's high-backed chair.

"I do not think I budged a bit on that one."

It was August 9th. A little more than a month had passed since Gettysburg. Lincoln had finally accepted Gardner's invitation to his new studio, not far from Brady's.

The president and his secretary, Hay, arrived at 7th and D. A large white banner across its brick façade read *Gardner's Portrait Gallery*.

The studio was not the grand spectacle to rival Brady's, but business had been strong since its May opening.

Congressmen and officers, who had posed for Gardner at Brady's, had already accepted invitations to sit. Word of Lincoln's visit could only help attract clientele.

In recent weeks, crowds drew to the new studio to glimpse the views of Gettysburg. Sales of prints were strong.

If the president had seen the images, he made no mention. Lincoln's eyes were heavy and his face pale and weathered, but the man seemed in brighter spirits.

"Fine place, Mr. G. I suppose this means twice as many visits for me between you and Mr. Brady then?"

Gardner's expression must have conveyed his surprise for the president let out a slight laugh.

"I hope it is not asking too much," Gardner replied.

"Not at all. I shall consider it one more place to escape."

President Lincoln in Gardner's new studio, August 9th, 1863

A week after the president's August visit to Gardner's, *Harper's Weekly* featured several views of Gettysburg, all of them by Brady.

By the time Brady arrived at Gettysburg, a full week after Gardner had left the battlefield, the dead had long been buried. Gone were the shocking remnants of battle. But Brady had the advantage of pleasant weather and guides who were now there and able to detail the exact course of the three-day battle.

MR. BRADY, the photographer, to whose industry and energy we are indebted for many of the most reliable pictures of the war, has been to the Gettysburg battle-field, and executed a number of photographs of what he saw there.

Harper's displayed captioned images of the battlefield.

The names now common place upon the lips of the nation; *The Round Tops, Devil's Den, the Wheat-Field.*

Gardner had been eclipsed by Brady once again.

Late 1863

"I do believe there's not much that can be done, Alex," Walt Whitman said as he sat before the camera that October.

"If you seek answers from me, you will find only disappointment."

Gardner had settled into his city studio as the war dragged on that year. He had watched the gray beard poet on so many days, straggling about the capital streets in his slouch hat and mangy coat, coming to and from the taverns. Stranger to no one it seemed.

Walt Whitman in Gardner's studio, 1863
Whitman would one day publish a eulogy to Gardner

Gardner had even once accompanied his friend, across the Seventh Street Bridge to Armory Square with its thousand convalescent beds inside white-washed pavilions, to look upon the wounded and dying.

Long rows of iron beds filled with the most pitiful of God's creatures; those anguishing between doses of calomel and morphine, those feverish and in stupor. The smell of gangrene, so much sickness and death.

The poet had made their care his true vocation.

"We do what we can I suppose, and we should be satisfied with that."

Whitman rose from the chair and his blue eyes lit. He took hold of both Gardner's hands.

"And I have seen your gallery walls. You are doing just that, friend."

❧

President Lincoln visited Gardner's studio yet again on November 8th.

President Lincoln at Gardner's, Nov. 8th, 1863
Considered by many to be Lincoln's finest portrait

Then, on December 2nd, Freedom was finally set atop her dome and the scaffolding removed to reveal a completed Capitol.

Great cheers and a cannonade announced the event to the city.

Gardner looked distant upon the magnificent bronze statue many a morning thereafter from the top floor of his studio at Seventh, convinced her rising was a hopeful sign.

XII

The short winter days kept Brady busy at his studio; none so much as the morning of February 9th.

"Now, Tad. Behave yourself."

The president watched as his son made mischief about Brady's sitting room; kicking prop columns, punching at the canvas backdrops, and crawling beneath chairs along floorboards that dusted up his navy blue suit. On occasion, Tad would stop at his father's plea, his dark eyes wide and full of innocence. Father would admonish his boy, but end with a laugh, voiding the reproach's affect. And Tad would bound into new antics.

Brady only hoped his equipment would survive the sitting without permanent damage.

Lincoln had arrived at the studio twenty minutes earlier with Tad at his side. Secretary Hay parked the wagon in the back lot and, with the escort of four blue coats, they made their way inside. The boy raced into Brady's gallery, staring wide-eyed at the gilded chandeliers and framed pictures.

"Look at all the pictures, papa. Look at 'em," said Tad, a thick lisp that drew out the *s* on the word *pictures.*

The ebullient boy leapt upon a fine damask settee with his muddy boots before Brady could escort the party through the door and up two flights to the top floor sitting room.

Tad did not settle there. President Lincoln in his chair, Berger waited patiently at the camera, as did Brady, while Tad had his run about the room. Brady had heard the stories of Tad kicking in the doors of cabinet meetings, even locking staff in closets. Brady also had heard the president did little to quash the mischievousness.

Following his latest reprimand, Tad pulled on the camera's tripod. Berger caught the camera and steadied the legs, breathing a sigh of relief.

"Tad. Come here!"

The president's tone was different than before. Hard and unyielding. It startled Brady even to hear him speak so.

Tad stopped. He turned to his father.

Something of the devil gleamed in those round eyes. Brady thought perhaps the father might scold. Instead, Lincoln wrapped his long arm around him and pulled him in. The president stooped down and whispered words into Tad's ear. The boy nodded, smiling.

Brady saw the two were inseparable. Two years now since Tad's older brother had died. Brady watched father and son, embracing. Never before had two souls needed one another more.

"Tad, perhaps you would like to have a look through one of our stereoscopes?" Brady interjected. "We have new images just in. The Falls of Niagara."

Brady knew he had to risk his gallery below in order to buy peace enough to take the photographs he desired.

Tad pulled free of the president's arm. "Let's go!"

"Very good," said Lincoln.

"George," Brady said to his young attendant who stepped forward, "Why don't you take Tad down for a few minutes."

Lincoln smiled. "Tad, be a good soldier and listen to your captain."

The boy turned to his father. "Yes, sir. Sir."

He clicked his boots together and gave a sharp soldier's salute.

Just then, something fell from Tad's pocket.

Brady looked to the floor. It was one of the painted soldiers Brady remembered from December last at Stuntz' toy counter, now nicked rough and specked with the underlying tin in places. Brady could not help but smile.

"My soldier!" Tad said and stabbed at the floor to pick up the toy man and return it to his pocket.

Tad turned and rushed out the door and into the stairwell. Brady's attendant was close at his heels, hurrying to keep pace.

Berger took out the first wooden plate slip and moved it into place atop the large format camera.

"Thank you again for accepting my invitation today, Mr. President," said Brady following the second exposure.

"Thank Mr. Hay. He persuaded me a break from official duties might do some good. It's not that I don't enjoy seeing you, but they do keep me awfully busy these days."

Hay, seated on a chair nearby, smiled at his boss for a moment then resumed his stoic, statue-like air.

"Thank you, John," Brady said to Hay with a laugh, as he studied Lincoln's position. "Perhaps your chin a bit higher, Mr. President, if you please."

The president complied. Brady turned to Berger, who made one final adjustment to the lens.

The president stared at the camera with a calming gaze, his dark eyes softening at just the right moment. Always the consummate professional when it came to the camera.

Brady lamented the fact that he had been unable to photograph Lincoln even once in the year of '63.

But he intended to make up for it.

It was just last month, on the 8th of January, that Lincoln had paid his last visit to Brady's studio.

Brady was delighted to see his next invitation accepted so soon.

The president seemed to understand the camera's power like few did. Not a vain man, and surely not one who thought himself handsome, the president knew he had a face that was expressive, emotive, and altogether perfect for the medium. It was the best tool by which a nation might come to know their leader, to look upon his face with the intimacy allowed by a photograph in their hands, and know that he was with them.

Brady gave little advice to his sitter through the series of exposures that followed. An assistant adjusted the immobilizer behind Lincoln's head as it required.

"Let us do one more just like so, Mr. President."

One of many Lincoln negatives taken Feb. 9th, 1864, A. Berger photographer

"I was at Gardner's place just a few months ago. Perhaps November?" the president said as he followed Brady's lead in turning full to the right for a profile portrait.

"November, Mr. President," Hay interjected from his corner chair.

"Yes. He has a fine studio. You and Mr. G have parted ways, I know. But you remain on good terms I trust?"

Brady said nothing a moment. He was aware the president sat for Gardner, whose studio was now closer to the Executive Mansion than his own, twice in 1863; in August, then again in November. Gardner too enjoyed a rapport with the president, having operated the camera so many times when Lincoln sat in Brady's chair. Despite any resentment Brady felt entitled to over Gardner's departure, magnanimity was what was called for now.

"Yes, Mr. President. And I have no doubt that Alex Gardner will do very well indeed. I wish him the best."

"Good. Good. I am glad to hear it. As I have said before, the better part of a man's life consists of his friendships. And I have found that to be true, over and again." He smiled. "How are we doing on time, Mr. Hay?"

"Just a few minutes longer, Mr. President."

Berger removed a plate from the camera, snug in its light-proof box. He traded it for a new sensitized plate from the assistant who turned and headed for the dark room.

The sound of hurried boots echoed outside the door. Tad bounded into the room and sat upon the arm of Lincoln's chair. Brady watched them for a moment. It occurred to Brady only then what should have been so easy to see.

"Ah, I am so happy you have returned, Tad. Mr. President, might I suggest a couple of quick portraits of father and son?"

Lincoln's eyes lit.

"I was hoping you might suggest that."

The president smiled before nudging Tad's arm.

"What do you think, Tad? Would you like to make a photograph? Will you sit long enough for that?"

"Oh Yes!"

Even Hay laughed heartily at that.

Famous print of father and son, photograph taken February 9ᵗʰ, 1864 at Brady's

In March, Secretary of War Stanton escorted the gruff general to Brady's studio.

Lincoln had just promoted Ulysses S. Grant, the first three-star general since Washington.

The sun clouded over during the sitting that afternoon and Brady asked his man to climb the roof to remove the mats and allow more light.

The assistant slipped.

His right leg came through the glass, sending jagged pieces showering all around the general on his podium, the back of his head fixed inside the metal prongs of the immobilizer.

Grant never budged.

He glanced skyward after a moment and grinned at the boot sole that dangled above him.

Stanton, on the other hand, was pale white. Breathless.

He took Brady by the arm.

"For God's sake don't let this get out to the papers. It would look like a design to kill the general."

General Ulysses S. Grant in Brady's studio

Brady agreed to keep it to himself, giving some comfort to the Secretary of War.

Later that afternoon, Brady thought over the event and Grant's reaction. He smiled to himself. *Here is a man not easily shaken.*

And that, he hoped, portended good things for the Union.

XIII

Brady took Grant's hand for the second time that year.

"Thank you, General. I will try to be quick about things."

But the general offered no immediate reply. He stood straight from his wooden chair, no taller than Brady himself. The compact Grant, whose beard was in need of combing, watched Brady with his dark eyes. He pulled the mush end of his cigar from his lips and nodded.

"Here, Mr. Berger," Brady said over his shoulder.

Berger set up the pair of cameras among a grove of thin pines beyond a row of white tents. The heat of June had settled in upon the day. Brady removed his straw hat to wipe his wet brow and the nape of his neck.

"General Grant, how about by that tree there? Yes. That will do. We will bring your chair along."

"Alright, Mr. Brady," Grant said, almost pained. "Let's do that."

The general had been no great conversationalist at Brady's studio earlier that spring. He was even surlier that afternoon. With good reason, Brady guessed.

The year had started so promising. Then Grant met Lee in the wilderness, then at Spotsylvania. The casualties so horrendous nearly everyone

241

in Washington expected the battered Army of the Potomac would slink back across the Rapidan, to regroup and spend the summer months licking its wounds and plan its next move.

But they misunderstood their new general.

Grant pushed on. The bloodbath at Cold Harbor the latest result, when Grant had ordered the 2nd, 6th, and 18th Corps to move on Lee's entrenchments with disastrous results. *The butcher,* Brady began to hear in the same circles where *Unconditional Surrender Grant* was once held in such esteem.

Standing before the camera now, Grant seemed unfazed.

Whatever hell might lay between him and General Robert Lee, he seemed only ready to be done with Brady's camera so he could get on with it.

Grant at his headquarters after Cold Harbor, 1864

Brady had twenty minutes and the camera had just exposed a fourth plate when he heard "Mr. Brady, I hope that will be all." Grant lowered his elbow from the pine tree it rested upon, no sooner than Berger capped the lens.

Brady knew better than to press his advantage.

"Yes, General. I believe it will be."

⤸⤹

The old waiter finished pouring Brady's tea in their room at the National.

"Thank you, Abel. That will be all. Good night."

The man nodded, leaving a small tray of cakes on the table.

"Good night to you, Mr. Brady. Mrs. Brady."

Brady followed him to their door and shut it behind him.

Julia slid off her shoes. Holding back the seat of her dress, she sat on the sofa, a moan to mark the close of their tiring evening.

Brady untied his cravat and removed his jacket. He sat back and exhaled. Gas-lit orbs on the gold fixture above him brightened the wide room; the furniture, paintings and photographs upon blue papered walls. In the walkway to the adjoining room, the grand clock chimed a quarter to midnight.

Brady leaned forward and took a ginger cake from its plate on the table. He took a bite, its sweet taste was delightful.

"Have some, dear." He took a sip of tea.

"None for me."

He let out a laugh. It was plain that she was spent.

After dining, they had taken in a play at Grover's, followed by a long ride in their barouche down Pennsylvania Avenue and along a circuitous route back to the National, admiring their city at night; from the illuminated pillars of the Treasury to the Capitol aglow with Freedom now atop her.

It had been a wonderful evening. Just the two of them. But he too would welcome its end. He needed to get up early as it were.

Brady finished his cake, picking the crumbs from his pant leg and vest. Another sip of tea and he set the saucer on the table. He yawned. He turned back to Julia and caught her stare.

"Tell me one thing," she finally said.

Brady said nothing but waited for her to continue. She wore a new and serious expression.

"Are we in trouble?"

Brady let the words sink in before he met the question with a laugh that was meant to reassure. He could tell by her stare, it did not. Brady knew, too, exactly to which she referred.

The letters. Those damned letters. The latest arrived yesterday to the National. Julia received it in the lobby after a trip to the market. A disgruntled carpenter, demanding immediate payment for his work at the studio in Manhattan.

In these hectic times, Brady would explain, an overlooked invoice was unavoidable. With such a breakneck pace, payments might be delayed. The same thing happened with the government and its myriad of contractors, did it not? Did every baker, who enriched himself like never before producing hard tack for tens of thousands of troops, complain so every time his payment was a bit late in arriving? Perhaps a few but not the majority, Brady thought. Most understood.

He could not stop what he was doing to placate every immediate need of his creditors, whom he was keeping quite busy with work these days. They would have to be patient.

"We are fine. You'll see."

"I wish I could believe that, but I have eyes of my own. Isn't it possible things have gotten away from you? Perhaps you need to slow down."

He did not reply, and she added "Mathew, I'm scared."

Brady smiled. They had shared a lovely evening together. No shouting tonight.

"No worries, dear. And believe me, I cannot wait for the day to be able to slow down," he said, taking her hand. He could see her eyes soften in the dim light. "When the war is over, when it's behind us and I've done my part."

She looked down at her dress.

He squeezed her hand. "I need you to understand. I need to know you're behind me."

She turned her eyes up to him. Her lips quivered as tears welled beneath her dark eyes.

"After all these years, you still have to ask?"

He took her in. Brady kissed a single tear that ran down her cheek. He kissed her lips.

They lay their heads down on the sofa pillows, tight in each other's arms until sometime deep in the night.

⌘

Brady arrived at the Petersburg defenses on the 21st of July.

Three days ago, Grant's offensive had stalled on the eastern outskirts of the Virginia town. The push that began on the 9th of June ended in a standoff.

A hundred thousand Union soldiers now faced a line of defenses ten miles long. The *Dimmock Line*, as history would remember the series of Rebel forts and batteries, connecting trenches that kept the enemy below ground like burrowed animals. As Brady's van rolled along, skirting the massive troop positions. He wondered if the world would ever see anything like it again.

Brady spent the warm summer days photographing the artillery units that faced the beleaguered city; Cowan's 1st NY battery, McKnight's NY battery, and the famed Cooper's Battery that fired at the Confederate lines six hundred yards distant.

But no action was forthcoming.

Battery at Petersburg, Brady placed himself in many of his images
He wears his white hat in the right foreground, June 1864

Brady had promised Julia a speedy return and so he left his team in position at the lines and started back toward the city on the 22nd.

❧

Under siege, Lee refused to budge, unwilling to surrender his lifeline to Richmond.

The summer dragged on. For a time in July, Washington was a buzz when Jubal Early appeared just north of the city's defenses, battling the guard that rushed up the Seventh Street Road to meet him. But after the action at Fort Stevens, Early slipped across the Potomac to the city's great relief.

Brady learned Gardner had suspended field operations, abandoning the stalled lines at Petersburg.

But he would not follow suit.

If a break were to come, the Confederate capital lay open and, with its taking, the war would come to a swift end. His cameramen would follow the Union all the way to Richmond.

He would not stop. Brady even hired James Gibson away from Gardner with the promise that Gibson would manage his Washington studio. He relished the idea of plucking one of Gardner's men away, just as the Scot had so often done to him.

But since Grant's appointment in March, it seemed the war had gone from bad to worse. Worst of all, it looked as if President Lincoln would lose the coming fall election. Many no longer shared Brady's view that Lincoln could win the war. Would the new president make terms with the south, willing to offer up everything that had been sacrificed these long and hard years? A truce would establish the Confederacy. *Everything for naught.*

Brady did not want to believe it could happen.

But as the summer of '64 waned, he had problems of his own.

༃

Edward Anthony looked up from behind his desk as Brady charged into the room.

Anthony's elderly bookkeeper must have read much from Brady's angry face for he gathered papers and scurried out. Brady tossed the creased letter upon the desk.

"What is the meaning of this?"

Brady asked the question, though its message was clear from the first sentence: *Extension of credit has been denied.*

Yesterday, Brady's man had wired from the Manhattan studio that an order to Anthony's store for additional supplies had been rejected.

Brady boarded the late train for New York, fidgeting sleep all the way. He would not cancel appointments because of some foolishness from the Anthony brothers. Soon, no doubt, his Washington studio would too be idled by the action.

"For God's sake, Mathew, shut the door."

"I gave you a start in this business. Remember that, Edward?"

Anthony brushed away the letter Brady had cast in front of him. He apparently did not need to read it. He sat up straight.

"You are careless. Did you really not see this coming?"

"What a short-sighted fool your brother has made you."

Brady watched Edward's face redden. He had never seen Edward Anthony like this. Good, he thought.

"Stop this nonsense," Brady appealed. "You know better."

"Good God!" said Anthony, throwing his hands up. His eyes narrowed upon Brady then and he leaned forward, thrusting out his long index finger at Brady. "Do you have any idea how much credit you have with me?" He paused. "Any idea?"

Outside the still open door, heads turned up from their desks at the shouting, before they returned to business.

"There is a war on. You know what I am about," Brady replied.

"I told you this couldn't continue. And now here we are."

Brady said nothing in reply.

Edward huffed. He tugged at his suit lapels and stared back at Brady.

"What would you propose, Mathew?" Edward Anthony began again. "I already assume all your royalties for sales of prints. You are in arrears by tens of thousands of dollars. More so with each passing month. My God, whom else do you owe? No," he caught himself, "I don't want to know."

Brady's mind raced. A fear took hold for the first time, that in the final act of this national play, at the moment the Union would claim victory in its hard-fought struggle, he would not be there to record it.

The doors, so long open to him, were now closing shut.

Edward Anthony looked out his 5th story window and spoke.

"As a businessman I need to look after my business, but as a friend, Mathew, I tell you I am worried for you."

He turned back to Brady. "The army has not moved in months yet how many teams do you have in the field? Five? Ten? The truth is I know how many you have in the field. Not as many as you once did. I hear things.

The ones who quit you. Woodbury. David Knox. Quit because they haven't been supplied in weeks or received pay in months. It's a small community, these photographers. I am quite frankly surprised you still find men to come and work for you."

Brady paced a minute, before stopping. He took deep breaths. Calm and rational thinking was needed. Yes. Mistakes had been made. Perhaps he had not been as conscientious as he could have been. But he could fix it.

He sat on the corner of Edward's desk. He pinched his goatee. "Very well then. What will it take? New terms? I suppose that is what we are talking around. Yes?"

Edward Anthony's eyes grew sullen. The corners of his mouth turned down. The man looked genuinely hurt.

"You are not to be believed, Mathew." Then he shook his head and laughed. "It's as if you've heard nothing I've said."

Anthony released orders for the flow of supplies to Brady once more that afternoon. But not after he called in his brother and the three sat round the desk and discussed new terms, and not generous ones.

Brady had to sign over a great deal of his claim to future profits from his photographs.

A bitter pill to swallow, but for the first time, he felt he had no choice.

Brady recalled the size of his fortune, his estate in the years before this war. One would have scarcely believed it. Perhaps a hundred thousand dollars. More. *What of it now?*

News early that September came like a jolt of lightning. Atlanta had fallen to Sherman.

National sentiment turned again for Old Abe. Brady was sure the president would be reelected.

Lincoln would stay the course. And so would he.

XIV

Gardner hoisted the last box into the back of the wagon. That, the second day of the New Year.

He locked eyes with O'Sullivan and asked, "How does he do it?"

Gardner had posed the question about Mathew Brady so many times, it seemed rhetorical in nature.

But he really wanted to know.

O'Sullivan grinned. He took a seat on a wooden crate there in the alleyway. He pulled a flask from the pocket of his denims. A light but cold rain fell from dreary skies.

"It's still eating at you, boss. That so?"

Gardner said nothing. *Yes, it is.*

In the last week, Gardner had decided to make the investment in O'Sullivan's journey south to cover the coastal campaigns. Fort Fisher in North Carolina, where action seemed most likely.

It was the first time he had sent a man to the field in months.

With the war a stalemate in Virginia, good news had since come from other corners. Sherman had taken Atlanta in September. Sheridan had delivered a crushing blow to Jubal Early's raiders, who had so recently

251

harassed the capital. Hood's Rebel forces were routed in Tennessee. Then, Sherman captured Savannah at Christmas.

And above all, soldiers voted in overwhelming numbers to re-elect their commander in chief in the November elections.

President Lincoln would press forward. The war would resume in Virginia at some point.

It was too expensive for Gardner to equip idle teams in the field. But Brady's men had somehow kept with the Army of the Potomac. If the winds of war were to abruptly shift, they would be there for it.

"Well," the Irishman started slowly, "short answer is I don't rightly know."

Gardner watched O'Sullivan take a swig and shake away its sting.

"I suppose," O'Sullivan continued, "it would bother me too if I were you."

The photographer shook his bottle, studying the swirling brown in the last inch of it. "I myself take no issue with it. His men do good work. The more cameras out there, the better. That's how I see things anyway."

Gardner nodded. Then said, "That's right, Tim."

The two of them now quiet, they stared toward the light of the street where a sliver of traffic passed by. Gardner ran a hand over his beard and glanced skyward. He was starting to get wet.

"With things the way they are now," O'Sullivan began again, "it would take deep pockets to do what Brady does. And deep pockets he has. Or had. You know the men have been quitting him pretty regular of late. Hell, he may be losing a fortune."

O'Sullivan then drained the flask with a long drink. Finally, he shrugged. "And it just may be he doesn't care about any of that."

Gardner nodded and let go a small laugh. He lifted the rear lip of the van and latched it shut and rapped it once with his open palm.

"Let's get you on your way."

≈

President Lincoln waved his hand.

"Now come over here, Tad," he said. "Mr. Gardner wants your picture too."

Gardner pulled the last exposed plate from the camera by its wooden slip. He handed it to John Reekie who started away.

At first Tad seemed not to hear.

Gardner watched the boy who knelt, coloring paper on a chair at the wall. Beside the chair sat Presidential Secretary John Hay, who looked down at Tad and his drawing of bright blues and greens, suggesting some outdoor scape conjured from the boy's mind.

Gardner had requested that the president bring Tad along if possible. It was no secret Lincoln rarely left the boy's side these days and Gardner thought the president would appreciate the gesture. Brady's photograph of the pair from the year previous had sold handsomely. They made for a touching portrait.

Whatever the motive, and if Brady's father-son coup had played its part, Gardner was determined not to put much thought into it. Lincoln was all too happy to comply with the request.

But Gardner had expected the mischievous boy he heard so much about. And he saw none of that on this morning of February 5th, 1865.

Finally, the boy lifted his head and turned round to face his father. He let his colored pencil go and it proceeded to roll off the chair to the floor. He rose from his knees. Placid, almost dejected, the boy shuffled toward Lincoln at the center of Gardner's sitting room.

But it was not Tad's gloomy behavior which worried Gardner now as much as the well-being of his father.

To Gardner, the president looked as frail a man as any able to still draw breath from this world.

There, silent and sagging in his chair, his skeletal fingers wrapped around Tad's waist, Lincoln looked up at Gardner above sad, dark-ringed eyes.

President Lincoln, photograph taken at Gardner's, February 5th, 1865

"Ok then, Mr. G, it seems we are ready and willing."

Over his shoulder, Gardner heard a pencil sketching. Perched upon a stool fifteen feet behind and to the left of Gardner's camera, the Connecticut painter Matthew Wilson sat with his pad. Hired by Secretary of the Navy Gideon Welles, he had come to watch Gardner's posing of the president. *I want to learn from the best*, the painter had confessed when he had arrived in the president's company.

It flattered. Even Gardner had to admit, he was well-practiced. By his tally, this was the sixth time he had photographed the president, beginning with those taken at Brady's studio in early '61.

It seemed so long ago now.

Lincoln cleared his throat. "I do admire your tidy production here. My apologies for not stopping by for a time. I have been busy."

Gardner smiled. "No apology necessary, Mr. President."

"This war, and I dare say you have seen more of it than I, it makes a man weary."

Gardner stood straight a moment. "A long road, Mr. President. Forgive me for saying, we're nearer to the end than the beginning. I can feel it. Every day now."

The president smiled ever so slightly. "Nothing to forgive there I can assure you. I am told it often these days, but I do not tire hearing it."

Reekie reappeared holding a wooden slip with a new plate. Gardner took hold of it.

Lincoln folded his stick legs and that smile then spread across his gaunt face; aged lines spread in every direction from lips to eyes. "Now where to, this boy and I?"

"Actually, I thought you and Tad might like to sit at the table," Gardner said, pointing to the northwest wall of his sitting room where a small table and single chair stood.

The president's dull eyes found the table across the room. He rose. Reekie stepped over to man the wooden frame holding the canvas backdrop behind the president.

Lincoln ambled forward, his long fingers engulfing Tad's hand as they moved past props toward the chair.

Gardner watched his slow gait, feeling almost guilty he had troubled the president so. *This was not the same man who sat before the camera in '61.*

Not even the one who sat for Gardner a little more than a year ago. He struck Gardner as a man who had stumbled away from a hospital ward in a feverish daze, exchanged his robe for a suit, and slipped away unnoticed.

Reekie wheeled the canvas background into its new position behind the subjects.

Gardner allowed Lincoln and Tad to get comfortable, then posed father and son, taking three final exposures.

"I think that will do, Mr. President. Thank you and thank you, Tad. You have been a delight."

"What do you say to Mr. Gardner, Tad?"

"Thank you, sir," replied Tad, swaying and staring at the floorboards.

President Lincoln and Tad, Gardner's studio, February 5th, 1865

"You are most welcome," replied Gardner with a smile for the doleful boy.

Perhaps Tad was just a little weary these days, like his father.

Across the room, Secretary Hay stood with some commotion, his chair legs screeching the floorboards. He was holding his watch.

"Well," said the president finding the floor with his boots and creaking to a stand, "I suppose I shall see you in a few weeks at my second grand coming out."

Gardner smiled.

A second inauguration. It had seemed so improbable just a few months before. Grant's bloody campaigns had deadened the people's optimism until Sherman came through in the south. On this very morning, the army was halted before Petersburg where the many thousands of Confederates remained dug in as if they had taken up permanent residence, clinging to hope for their cause.

But the great numbers of ragged men who now appeared every day in the streets of the nation's capital; in shabby grays and butternut uniforms, wearing tattered blankets, looking gaunt, almost emaciated, told the true story. They were beaten. Come to take an oath of allegiance. They were not the least threatening to those who passed them on the walks. They knew it was over. Lee's army was falling apart. It was being killed and starved out in every southern city and on every front.

Congress had already turned its attention to the nation after the war.

Just a few days before, on February 1st, the president signed the 13th Amendment that would rid the nation forever from the sin of slavery. But things were not all well. When Lincoln refused to sign their bill forcing harsh terms upon defeated Rebel states, he set off the spirits of rancor between the Executive and Legislative branches. Fiery congressmen such as Thad Stevens and Charles Sumner would not go away quietly. Looking back in later years, Gardner should have seen the coming storm with the nation's reconstruction.

"Yes, Mr. President. I will be there."

Gardner bid him farewell.

He would always remember the long handshake President Lincoln gave him in goodbye that day.

After escorting the president to the street and his waiting barouche, Gardner climbed the four flights again to visit the developing room to inspect the results.

He slipped in and shut the door.

John Reekie turned to him in the yellowish light; he wore a deep frown. The young man reached down to the table and showed Gardner what had happened. One of the plates, the final portrait before Tad had joined his father, had cracked. Broken in two at the top right.

Gardner took the pieces in his hand to inspect it.

The frail, once mighty commander in chief stared back from the negative glass; ghostly, black features against the reversed white of his coat, beard, and eyes.

Reekie, nearly in tears, explained how he had accidentally knocked it against the side of the tub of fixing solution.

"I'm sorry, boss. I don't know-"

"No worries, John," Gardner said, then patted him across the shoulder. "Tape it together and have it painted. It will mask the fracture well enough."

A frail President Lincoln, A. Gardner, February 5th, 1865
The original cracked negative was thrown away

He told Reekie to make a single proof from the plate. After that, the glass could be thrown away.

"We have four more years now," Gardner said, giving Reekie a reassuring smile. "Plenty of time to get it right."

∽

Gardner watched from atop the wooden platform, a few dozen yards from the East Portico where the crowd gathered upon a platform constructed for Lincoln's inauguration.

Gardner had received permission to erect the stand at his own expense, and so he had the carpenters construct it just as they had done for he and Brady four years earlier.

Stable, and with a good vantage, the wooden perch put the cameras tens of yards closer than the first time, when assassination plots of the new president filled the Capitol air.

He had both the large format and stereo cameras at his disposal and would make use of both, focused and ready for quick work which would come once Lincoln rose to the podium. James and an assistant would manage the sensitizing and developing from their van parked beneath.

The Capitol grounds were cleared of debris and the scaffolds that had blanketed her construction during so much of the war. Left behind were the mud and patches of dormant grass over which the crowds trampled to find their place. Freedom atop her dome, looked over them all.

A rain, light but incessant, had fallen from the drab sky all that morning of March 4th, 1865; the world all around the Capitol wet and cool. The president sat left of the podium; his gaunt face now clean shaven for the occasion. Seated next to him was Vice President Johnson.

Then, in the minutes before Lincoln rose to speak, the sky gave way to a sun that bathed the damp grounds in its warming rays.

Gardner, and surely he was not alone, found it a hopeful and perhaps prophetic sign. He and his crew worked over the course of twenty minutes to capture the seated president, his entourage; Vice President Johnson, Chief Justice Chase, and the many others.

A. Gardner, March 4ᵗʰ, 1865, Lincoln while delivering his address

James used a ladder against the scaffold to reach Gardner with sensitized plates and receive those just exposed by one of the two cameras.

Gardner managed four images in rapid fashion when President Lincoln spoke his brief address. His loud, shrill voice carried over the crisp air to reach Gardner's ears.

Fondly do we hope-fervently do we pray-that this mighty scourge of war may speedily pass away.

...so still it must be said "the judgments of the Lord, are true and righteous altogether."

With malice toward none, with charity for all, with firmness in the right as God gives us to see the right, let us strive on to finish the work we are in, to bind up

the nation's wounds, to care for him who shall have borne the battle and for his
widow and his orphan, to do all which may achieve and cherish a just and lasting
peace among ourselves and with all nations.

Gardner would cut the speech from the next morning's paper and
carry it with him in his billfold for weeks to come.

Saturday morning, the 20th

Gardner wondered where the time had gone, for four years was no brief
span.

1869 now. So much had changed.

One final year and the tumultuous decade would pass forever into history.

Gardner stared down upon the chamber below, he reminded and re-
committed himself to purpose. It was his historical record of those years
that should be preserved, so that future generations would never forget
their sacrifice.

He felt certain that his petition would be announced on this morning.

He turned to his side, away from his slung arm to stretch his aching
back. The ruffian, one row up and across, now a familiar sight to Gardner,
tipped his hat. A smile formed upon his stubbly face.

The gavel sounded and Gardner turned back around.

Reporters hurried down the balcony to gallery seats above the rostrum. Senators found their desks.

When a crowd of standing men dispersed, Gardner could see Senator
Pomeroy, seated, scribbling notes at his desk.

The parson made his way center. Gardner shut his eyes and was intent
to focus his mind on prayer.

O God

Amid the tumults of the people Thou art our strength and our refuge and the tower of our defense. Thy hand is on the helm of the universe. Thou rulest among the affairs of men. Thou settest up one and puttest down another. Thou raisest up kingdoms and overturnest thrones and powers and dominions. All things are subject to Thy control, and we bow before Thy divine sovereignty. We ask, O Lord, that Thy blessing may be upon Thy servants the Senators and upon the members of the House as they shall come to the consideration of grave and important matters.

The parson concluded and the day's business commenced.

A portly senator from Tennessee rose to address the body.

"This petition comes to us on behalf of the citizens of Lincoln County, Tennessee." The senator's words ran lazily together in a Southerner's drawl. "It asks that-" he continued on.

The Senate body listened and Ben Wade referred it to committee. Following this, another senator rose "to present the petition for the Cairo and Fulton Railroad Company, praying an extension of the time for building of the first twenty miles-"

Gardner saw Pomeroy shift in his chair, scrambling through papers at his desk.

"It shall be referred to the Committee on the Pacific Railroad," replied Wade.

Gardner watched Pomeroy begin to rise.

Senator Frelinghuysen of New Jersey shot up from his desk in the second row, rolled papers tight in his fist. "I ask the unanimous consent of the Senate to take up House Bill Number Nineteen Sixty-nine. It will not take but a minute."

"I hope that bill will be taken up. It is all right," returned Charles Sumner from the back row.

"I hope that we shall get through the morning business without interruption it will take but a few minutes," protested Senator Sherman of Ohio, who stood across the aisle in the row behind Pomeroy.

"Let us take this up first; and then I am willing to give way for morning business," replied Frelinghuysen, now holding his papers high.

The graying Sherman cleared his throat. "It will take but a few minutes to get through with the morning business, and the Senator can call up the bill."

"I hope the Senate will permit us to take up this bill now."

"I have no objection to it," countered Sherman. "I do not know what it is; but I think we ought to dispose of the morning business first."

"I will not interfere with the morning business as soon as the bill is taken up."

The two men stood facing one another across the chamber.

Gardner watched, helpless, as Pomeroy returned to his seat. The senator removed spectacles, folded his arms, and leaned back.

The blood ran to Gardner's head, he looked on as Frelinghuysen argued further from his desk. He was powerless to interject, to get Pomeroy back to his feet and announce his own petition, as he had surely been about to do.

The two senators; Frelinghuysen, Sherman, stood facing one another across the chamber.

They looked ready to argue the day, if necessary.

Many seated senators began to ignore them altogether.

Laughter peppered the galleries as a light rain upon the glass ceiling grew more intense, filling the chamber with its loud echo.

Upon some silent deliberation, President Pro Tempore Wade capitulated. He shifted forward in his chair.

"Proceed," he announced to the bill's champion.

Gardner sighed in exasperation, wondering what forces had conspired against him.

Gardner pulled the chain to his watch. Twelve minutes had passed since Ben Wade's consent. When the business finally completed, Wade spoke once more.

"Let's now move to the reports of the committees."

No more petitions today.

Gardner flew up from his seat. As if his feet were acting on their own, they propelled him up and out of that dreadful place.

If there had been some favorable action taken as a result of Brady's petition, Gardner could not bear to sit and hear about it.

XV

Margaret turned to him. "How do I look?"

She awaited a response as she stood before the table.

Gardner took a sip of his tea to wash down a mouthful of muffin. He set down the Saturday edition of the *Intelligencer* and brushed his open palms to let the crumbs fall to his plate.

"Lovely. I like blue. Is that a new dress?"

She smiled, then scoffed. "I've had this for years. Just goes to show you-"

She did not complete the sentence, but rounded the table and took the plate before him.

He leaned back as her right hand swept crumbs onto the plate she held just away.

"And you will spoil your dinner. You know the Bradys will serve a meal. My goodness, Alex. When Emily is away I can't leave you alone in the kitchen a moment."

Gardner watched her exit the room. He ran a hand down the length of his white shirt and took a deep breath through his nose before rising from the chair.

265

She reappeared, her shawl was about her shoulders, and she was ready to depart.

He went to reach for his coat from the hanger with his free arm. "How long do you think we will be? I'm awfully tired."

Gardner heard nothing at his back. He could feel his wife's stare. Then he felt her hands on his shoulders.

Turning his head, he received her kiss.

"I know better than to ask that you try and enjoy yourself. But thank you for enduring."

She squeezed him, then pulled away.

Gardner watched her to the door.

He could only shake his head, and brood over the recent days' misfortune. What a fine web he had weaved. His petition gathered dust in Senator Pomeroy's leather satchel; his fellow congressmen knew nothing of it.

And now, the dinner. Two men, obliged to fulfill the engagement out of gratitude for their wives.

"You and Mathew can talk politics," she turned and said. "Perhaps stop living in the past, if only a few hours."

He put on his long coat, gently over his slung arm.

"If only it were that easy, my dear."

Spring 1865

Gardner shot up from his campfire stoop at the rider's reckless approach. John Reekie stood as well.

The fellow wore civilian clothes; a dirty pale hat with wide brim to shield his face. One could not assume the intentions of such a man, and there were plenty of them slinking about the fallen city of Richmond.

Gardner scanned the road and his surroundings in search of others.

A late day sun cast long shadows upon the ruins of a city, the brick pilings and buildings still smoldering after so many days.

The man pulled up before them on his brown sorrel.

"I seen yous out here all by yourselves. And I suspect you didn't hear yet. And Good Lord you didn't hear, did yous?"

Gardner and John Reekie traded baffled stares.

The man drew a heavy breath, and his dirty fingers pulled the hat from his head.

"Lee surrendered at Appomattox yesterday."

"What?" Reekie asked.

"It's true. Word come in from the west. All the Union boys celebratin'." The man then stood in his saddle and waved his hat over the ravaged cityscape. "No more of this! No more, I say."

"Praise God," Gardner said.

"Indeed." The man returned the hat to his greasy head of hair. "Indeed." He touched its brim once, then kicked the horse.

Gardner's eyes followed him away, his sorrel kicking dust along the cluttered road.

Reekie beat his pant legs of dust. After a moment, he finally said "I guess that's it then."

Gardner looked at Reekie, then to their wagons, the mule and horse hitched to a post before the brick storehouse whose front had collapsed into the roadway.

"Let me think a bit."

Reekie shrugged. He sat again and began stoking their small fire.

Gardner sat.

They finished their beans in bacon grease. Gardner drank his tea and watched the dying flames.

Appomattox. Gardner knew vaguely of the place. Two days ride west for his wagon, maybe three.

The end had seemed imminent, a matter of weeks if not days, once Richmond fell.

Already well behind the army, Gardner could not have hoped to keep pace with Grant as he raced to cut off Lee's escape. Besides, a fallen Richmond was available to Gardner and his cameras.

Now, if to be believed, Grant had indeed caught Lee, forcing a surrender.

And Gardner had missed it. *Had Brady?*

≪≫

News had reached Washington on the morning of April 4[th,] and they set off for Richmond in two wagons.

Gardner's team had missed the fall of a besieged Petersburg two days before. He was not about to miss an opportunity in Richmond.

Gardner pioneered death views in the aftermath of Antietam and Gettysburg but contract photographer Thomas Roche scooped Brady and Gardner at Petersburg

Gardner and Reekie split ways on the old pike, with Reekie off to document what he could of Petersburg.

Gardner moved on to Richmond, arriving on the outskirts the morning of the 6th.

The last mile's journey, Gardner watched Richmond smolder on the horizon. His van crossed into devastated sections of the city with care, amidst scorched buildings and rubble spread over once quaint avenues.

Within that first hour, he set about photographing a city once regarded as one of our nation's finest. City blocks in stark ruins, as if the victim of some Old Testament reckoning.

Piecemeal, Gardner learned of Richmond's tragic tale from passing soldiers and those residents who dared to venture out of doors.

Jefferson Davis had fled on the night of the 3rd; leaving orders to sink any ship in the harbor that could not be commandeered south. Amidst the chaos, southern soldiers set fire to the tobacco houses. They demolished liquor stores that might fuel Union vengeance upon the population. The fire spread when looting began. Convicts free from the state pen lapped spilled whisky from street gutters. A munitions house exploded, shattering the windows of every building in the vicinity.

Dozens of square blocks, engulfed in flames, greeted Union troops arriving the morning of the 4th. The soldiers helped extinguish the blaze before raising the Stars and Stripes once more atop the capitol building.

President Lincoln, who waited in a tug upriver, stepped ashore that first afternoon. He and his small party advanced into town under the protection of a cavalry escort, to the cheers of former slaves who proclaimed him savior. Gardner was told the president even sat in Jefferson Davis' chair during his tour.

Gardner had just missed the president. But he would make good use of his time there.

He made camp with scarcely anyone to bother him amidst the shambles, the smell of tobacco fires still heavy in the air.

Blue coats posted guard at various points about the city. Many took a keen interest in Gardner as he lugged his cameras atop rubble and the surrounding hilltops to gain vantage. But most civilians kept to themselves, peering out from drawn curtains of the standing homes.

One of Gardner's many negatives of a fallen Richmond, April 1865

A glass stereograph, A. Gardner, 'Burnt District', Richmond, April 1865

Gardner took dozens of large format and stereos.

Free reign to record the terrible visage.

That Gardner did, for four days straight before Reekie arrived to join him early the afternoon of the 10th.

Gardner tossed the last bit of tea onto the flames and rose, dusting the seat of his pants. He tugged at his beard and stared up to a moon that now showed faint in the dusky sky.

"I'll take the negatives back to the studio. First thing in the morning. John, I want you to stay on a few more days. Then circle back through Cold Harbor and Petersburg. Back here once more to see what's come to pass. See who happens by."

Gardner stared down the stretch of road. He started for his horse, freeing her tether from the post. He began to saddle, trying to recall the roads that led to a telegraph house that still operated in a spared section of the city.

"I'm going to wire the studio. O'Sullivan should be back by now. I'll send him to Appomattox to photograph what's left."

Gardner mounted the saddled bay.

"Start transferring negatives to my van. Any remaining glass and supplies from my van go to yours. Whatever's unspent. Use all of it."

Driving back across the bridge at dusk on the 13th, Gardner found Washington still in the throes of a celebration that commenced the morning he had set out when news spread Richmond had fallen.

Now, with word of Lee's surrender, the carnival escalated.

At some risk to the special cargo he carried, Gardner took a longer, circuitous route back to his studio.

He took in the mesmerizing sights as daylight fell away; fireworks, illuminations and transparencies that hung from government buildings, the tall letters irradiated by gaslight, *Victory!* and *Union Saved by God's Grace.* Church bells clanged into the night.

He stole three hours sleep that night on a gallery sofa. He would allow himself no more than that before rising to work.

Lawrence would help manage the day's appointments as O'Sullivan prepared a wagon for a morning departure, as instructed in Gardner's telegram.

Gardner sequestered himself in his office and worked that Good Friday morning.

He took an hour's respite that afternoon to attend services as was only proper. By afternoon, he was immersed in the process of cataloguing his quantity of Richmond negatives. He plotted out next steps; copyrighting the images, contacting the newspapers, and getting them out to the printers. The public would never again be so interested in them as right now.

By day's end, Gardner was near collapse from fatigue.

O'Sullivan told Lawrence to take his father home to bed. Gardner was reluctant, but acquiesced.

Lawrence drove the horses north out Seventh Street.

Gardner lay down in his own bed that evening, trying to remember when he had last done so. His weary mind continued to race over what he would do tomorrow. But he felt good about the plans he had exacted.

He drifted off to a heavy sleep.

৵

A hard rap at the door startled Gardner from his slumber.

"Boss! Lawrence! You in there?"

Gardner shook his head to chase away the fog. *That was Tim's voice.*

He drew a long breath, turned and put his stocking feet to the floorboards. He pulled his watch from the table stand, stealing a glance from the window's moonlight. It was four thirty.

Gardner ran a hand down his nightshirt and started to his bedroom door. He opened it and stepped into the hall.

Lawrence was already standing in the doorway in loose shirt and shorts. O'Sullivan peered inside from the porch, hat in hand.

"Tim? What on earth is it?"

O'Sullivan opened his mouth, but Lawrence spoke first. "It's the president."

***

O'Sullivan steered the wagon south to where the capital streets began to fill with carriages.

People huddled on damp predawn corners and closed storefronts. No longer was it a celebration.

Gardner heard the sounds of women weeping. The word *president*. He heard the word *murder*.

O'Sullivan had told Gardner what little he knew enroute to Ford's Theater. Lawrence protested his father's order to stay behind and open the studio as usual in the morning, but complied.

They were soon stopped at 10th and E where wagons, riders, and foot-travelers crowded out every square foot of wet road.

A mist of rain wet sullen faces. A teary-eyed woman stared up at Gardner, black hair streaked across her face. She, like so many, had been there some time, without the aid of an umbrella. He studied the faces of wild-eyed men who seethed with angry words.

And so many others stood silent, as if shocked into stupor.

Gardner stared distantly across the road to the theater where blue coats had cordoned off a sector. O'Sullivan told Gardner that he heard the president lay in a bed across the street. Several guards now stood before that house.

O'Sullivan pulled up roadside. Gardner leapt down and paced into the crowd. He asked questions to any man who seemed in his right mind. It took but a few minutes to realize that little new information had been gleaned than when O'Sullivan had left the place two hours before.

A man had shot President Lincoln in the head. Rumors circulated that Vice-President Johnson was shot and killed, Seward too. Men clenched pistols at their sides. Some spoke with conviction that killing President Lincoln was but a precursor to a larger assault by defeated Rebels, who were surely on their way toward the city. One told Gardner the shooter at Ford's was Wilkes Booth the actor. Gardner recalled later how he dismissed it as another irrational rumor. Booth was an actor. Ford's was a theater.

The rain came on steady.

After half an hour, Gardner ran fingers through his soaked beard and went to find O'Sullivan. They decided it best to quit the hundreds, if not thousands, of people gathered in the street between Ford's and the house where the president lay, dying.

They drove to the studio. They boiled tea and waited.

It was nearly eight when Gardner heard church bells outside, first one then several from all directions.

They stepped out onto the walk and listened. After several minutes, a passing rider shouted over to them.

"Lincoln is dead. Just come from Ford's and saw it with my own." The rider drew closer to Gardner. "Soldiers carried his coffin out the boardinghouse and loaded it on a wagon to the mansion. It's headed there now."

Gardner knew it was true. He nodded in silent thanks to the man who then departed. He watched O'Sullivan wander down the street for Lord knows where.

Gardner stood a while. He went back inside and up to his office and wept behind its closed door.

XVI

Brady and Julia sat upon a posh blue settee in their room at the National.

He thought the place did not look half bad. The gas lamp on the table beside him turned at three quarters, cast a pale light on the furniture; the exquisite sofa, a fine mahogany table and its set of carved wooden chairs, two high crimson-backed chairs and a smaller beige settee at the window. Situated just so, it might as well have been theirs.

White china plates lay stacked upon the table, a row of crystal and saucers with teacups, ready to be set whenever Brady rang for the help.

Just as soon as the Gardner's arrived.

He felt Julia squeeze his hand. He turned.

"Thank you," she said, craning her neck to kiss his cheek.

"You look lovely as ever."

He put his other hand upon hers.

A knock came at the door.

Julia rose. "There they are."

Brady dreaded the fact that he was now required to host Alex Gardner for the next few hours.

She went to the door and opened it.

"Oh! Hello," Brady heard her say.

He came up behind her. He smiled, then introduced his wife to Truman Ash for the first time.

Brady seldom left the studio before six. Today he had done just that, having lunched at the Willard, visiting congressmen long enough to ask about their welfare as might a long absent friend and to inform them, *if they had not yet heard*, that they might soon hear of a bill upon the floor to authorize purchase of his works. He wrapped up his studio business and arrived back at the National at a quarter to four.

Julia had been quite happy to see him home at such an hour.

He sat on their sofa as she fetched her new black gown.

"Do you like it?" She stood holding it over the crux of her arm.

"Very much."

He smiled and took her hand. She sat beside him. Brady watched her smile fade. She read something in his eyes, through those blue lenses of his.

It was only yesterday that Brady had encouraged her to indulge in the purchase of a fine dress. It would be no issue, he told her.

He turned away. His eyes flitted about their empty room; their rickety table and chairs, the faded sofa, then finally up to meet her brown eyes and their troubled stare.

He pushed his glasses up the bridge of his nose. "There's something to tell you."

He told her about the proceeds from the Central Park property. He had obviously not purchased the new furniture he wanted, nor had he followed her suggestion and left it in the bank.

He confessed to her that the better portion of it was now gone, spent on drinks and meal tabs, many a small gift to congressmen, and other bills unknown to her. Where exactly it had all gone in such a short span of time, God only knew. He told her this, the truth. He watched tears of worry fill her eyes and her lower lip begin to quiver.

She laid her dress on the table and announced her intention to return it. But she did not seem angry, as he might have expected. Perhaps the result of having been let down so many times before.

"No," Brady pleaded.

He continued to beseech her, for several minutes, not to worry. "I'll make it right," he swore.

Eventually he managed to calm her. She even smiled a little.

"Now," he announced, "I must make this place do for guests. If even for the night."

For that he had a plan.

He went and rapped on the door of a room three down and across the hall. With the clink and rattle of a chain, the door cracked open. The silver-haired woman that peaked out behind it smiled for Brady.

"Mrs. Piedmont. How are you?"

She freed the door and Brady stepped in only enough for her to shut it.

He and the woman exchanged pleasantries. Neighbors for years now, he had helped the widow countless times with a meal or a pitcher of water when a porter was not to be found; he carried up with him what little mail arrived for her at the lobby desk. Her husband, dead now seven years, was once a respected tailor in the district, Brady one of his better customers.

Upon entering the widow's apartment on so many occasions, Brady had admired the furniture spaced across the room. Beautiful, lonely pieces situated upon that luxurious damask carpet.

"I must confess," he interjected after a minute of conversation, "I have a favor to ask of you."

Brady had a young porter assist him in swapping out the furniture which would be returned to Mrs. Piedmont in the morning. After inspecting the results, he decided he very much liked the new and vibrant look of the room. Something close to what they once enjoyed. Even though Julia thought it most unnecessary.

Brady washed his face and trimmed his goatee in the facility at the end of the hall. Already thinking ahead to the second difficulty that he must maneuver that evening; that of Congressman McCarthy's ball.

Capitol City had been abuzz over McCarthy's event for the last two weeks. The grand event of that winter season, one to rival last year's hosted in the senator's monumental west end mansion. Every politician and well-to-do who sat in Brady's chair in recent weeks had received their invitation. Dennis McCarthy of Syracuse had visited Brady's studio several times in years past. The two New Yorkers got along quite well.

Brady was joyed to learn the senator had accepted his recent offer for a complimentary sitting. Two days ago, upon the morning of his return from Manhattan, Brady made certain he was present for the appointment. As expected, McCarthy brought with him a card of admission to the gala.

Brady had his invite. But he knew Julia would say no.

Since the war, and even during the days of impeachment nonsense, the gaiety in Washington had only increased. The difference now being that Brady was no longer on anyone's short list, a painful reminder of his diminished role in this city.

The number of congressmen in attendance would give Brady a timely opportunity. He was determined to attend, with or without her.

When Julia proposed the Gardner's invitation to dinner, Brady sensed a bargain to strike.

They would entertain the Gardner's, wearing dinner clothes, and make a late appearance at McCarthy's. The ball would run late into the evening, well past midnight.

They could manage both.

She agreed, reluctantly.

Brady put on his best suit, and her the black gown, and a perfume that he had not enjoyed in years.

⌘

Brady showed Truman into the room. The three of them sat down.

It was not five minutes later and the Gardners arrived. Five of them now. Brady rang for the help, as they filled chairs around the mahogany table, four of the matching set and one of the high-back chairs for Truman Ash.

Two porters brought in dishes of veal and chicken salad, steamed potatoes, with water and a decanter of red wine.

Gardner, pious a man as there ever was, offered up Grace.

The meal commenced quietly as they ate. The Gardners commented on the tenderness of the meat and seasoned potatoes, compliments to the National's kitchen. They stepped lightly over politics, Grant's inauguration and the promise of winter's end and the spring season in Washington.

Brady and Gardner did not address one another directly. An unspoken heaviness in the air, their conversation reserved.

But if Truman Ash had any inkling of hidden tension at the table, he did not let on.

All the while, Brady could not help but think that inviting Truman was one of the better ideas Brady ever had.

He all but forgot he had even done so. And he would apologize later to his wife for not telling her.

It happened in the minutes after Gardner's departure from the Smithsonian the afternoon before; he extended the invite more than anything as a desperate means to deflect the strain of the impending, ill-fated affair. And it seemed to be working.

Brady could not help but notice the relieved look upon Alex Gardner's face when he stepped into Brady's room and caught sight of Truman rising from the sofa. It seemed clear now that Julia did not mind either, once she overcame her initial surprise at the sight of a stranger in her doorway.

Truman Ash was someone with whom Julia could take interest. No politician or portentous businessman. No capital elite. He was real, she might have said. Margaret Gardner, ever the endearing woman she was, likewise seemed taken with the young man.

To all, Truman Ash represented a most uncomplicated target of questioning as a means of conversation.

"Yes. I live in those towers. Several of us live there, actually. Scientists. Naturalists. Some for many years now. I have good company."

"I started collecting birds, oh, I'd say at twelve perhaps. Eleven."

"My brother and I. Yes. Senator Wilson encouraged us. That's how I came to know Professor Baird at the Smithsonian."

After another bite, Truman added to a moment's silence "I am glad you asked me here, Mr. Brady."

"Well," Julia said, "I am so glad my husband invited you."

A half hour after the main course, a waiter arrived at the door with tea and a tray of sweets, cookies and small cakes. After partaking in these, the two women retired to Mrs. Piedmont' beige settee, the drapes of the window pulled shut behind them. Brady proposed the three men retire to the chairs and sofa.

But a quiet now plagued the men. What Brady had most feared, their discomfited situation interrupted only when the waiter returned to collect tableware and pour everyone a cup of fresh tea from a silver kettle.

Their silence was made all the more conspicuous by the ladies' laughter, as they paged through an album of picture cards that Julia kept. Julia then went to her room and returned with a thin stack of tied letters, correspondence she had kept over the years. Margaret was touched to see so many of her letters. They read portions together and reminisced as if they had stepped back through those bygone years.

Brady drank his tea then cleared his throat. "Tell me, Truman, do you plan to attend the inauguration next month?"

"Perhaps I should. I suppose it will be quite an event."

"That it will be," replied Gardner. "You should come see."

"I might just do that. I guess it will be the second time now that General Grant will be my boss."

Brady laughed at the curious statement. "How so?"

"I served," Truman replied. "62nd Massachusetts." He blew his tea.

Brady caught sight of Gardner, who looked nearly as surprised.

Truman looked at the both of them and smiled. "Signed up in March of '65. Never fired a shot. Never broke camp."

Gardner nodded. He reached into his sling and scratched his invalid arm. "You were lucky."

Truman sipped. "I suppose I was."

Gardner exhaled. "I've been thinking a lot about those days. All those years of war. And when the end did come, things happened so fast."

Brady crossed his legs. "That it did."

Spring 1865

"Another grand day in Richmond, Mr. Brady."

Berger drove the wagon up beside the inn's porch where Brady stood. The white bay horse neighed.

"It's good to see you, Anthony."

Brady thumbed suspenders back over his shoulders and studied his surroundings. That part of town was clean and largely undisturbed, an oasis against the wasted part of that city. The sun showed bright upon the paved street. Soldiers and civilians entered a few of the shops open there. A freckled boy hawked papers on the corner.

Egbert Guy Fowx pulled up on his black sorrel. Fowx, a photographer whom Brady had recently procured from the Anthony's; a sweet morsel of retribution against the brothers, pinched the stubble on his chin and tipped his bowler at Brady.

Berger stole a glance at Fowx, then looked at Brady.

"You look set up mighty comfortable in there," he began to Brady. "I know you're itching to see what I brought you. But-" Berger paused. He removed his tweed hat and ran a hand through matted curls. "I think I've got something that will make you want to put that off a little longer."

Berger then showed a wry little smile, Fowx a grin of his own.

Brady stood, waiting. It seemed he was being toyed with, but his tired mind was in no mood for riddles.

⁕

Brady and Fowx had arrived that morning in their own van.

Berger had wired upon reaching Richmond two days earlier. He set up camp in the street and began his camera work.

Brady had missed Appomattox altogether.

Berger, nor any of his other teams, was closer than a hundred miles that fateful morning. Brady himself was in Manhattan. He had heard Gardner missed it too. Not a single photographer had been present when Lee signed papers in that Virginian's parlor, seventy-five miles outside Richmond.

It would have been the greatest of coups. *A loss for history.*

But if Brady could not photograph Appomattox, he had at least done the next best thing since leaving New York.

His ship took him as far as City Point. There, on the 12th, awaiting a tug that would take them to Richmond, he found Grant and his generals just returned.

The gruff general said little, nor did he seem jovial as his generals did in victory, but Grant did agree to photographs before he left for Washington as hero of the Union.

Brady and Fowx then started their way up the busy James River toward Richmond.

News reached the tug at a stop before the Confederate capital: the president was dead.

They arrived at Richmond where a stunned silence hung over the broken city, among the soldiers and even the secessionist inhabitants who ventured out of doors. Many a Negro wept openly in the streets.

Brady put his own sorrowful state in check. He and Fowx ventured to a part of town that had largely escaped destruction, where business continued albeit at a crippled pace. Brady rented a cramped room at a clapboard inn for the hefty fee of three dollars a night.

Fowx unhitched the sorrel and set off to find Berger in the city.

Now, staring at the pair of them, Brady could not possibly fathom what Berger was about to tell him.

"The old man is here," Berger finally said.

It took only a few seconds for Brady to work it out.

"Lee is here?"

Fowx nodded with a smile of his own. "Robert Lee," he said, as if further confirmation were necessary.

Berger continued. "He came in maybe an hour ago. I saw a crowd building through town, so I went to have a look. He's in a house on Franklin Street. I saw him go right inside. Four Union guards. No one gets as close as the front walk."

Berger then smiled once more. "But you, Mr. Brady, I am wagering you might do better."

They hitched the van and Berger drove Brady the city block to Franklin. Fowx trailed on his mount.

A small but stately two-story brick. Two of the Union guards stood before a wrought-iron fence, blocking steps that led to the high porch. A gathering of folk; children and adults alike, gathered on curb stones opposite the house, awaiting any comings and goings from the House of Lee.

Brady climbed down and approached. He announced himself to the soldiers. He chatted a bit with the young blue coats. He shared how he had known the general since Lee was a colonel in the Mexican War and commander at West Point, and how, on more than one occasion, he had photographed Lee in his studio in the years before the war.

All of it true. Impressed as the soldiers seemed, for both knew the name Brady, they relayed strict orders that no one was permitted to pass.

Brady returned to the van across the street and dictated a note which Berger drafted on a single sheet.

General Lee –

I request time at your earliest convenience for a sitting. I am in Richmond. I have my men and apparatus and it can be done discreetly at the back of the house. At this time the nation demands it upon us sir. Please let me know when I may call. I will leave a boy with instructions on where I can be found. Send word and you will find me ready.

Your friend for many years.

M.B. Brady

He provided it to one of the young sentries who promised he would deliver it but not until he was relieved of his watch. It was too late in the day for the camera anyway.

Brady accepted the offer and the three returned to the inn.

Brady awoke that Easter Sunday and at eleven in the morning, the three returned to Franklin Street.

After some minutes, the ranking blue coat agreed, begrudgingly; to allow Brady to scale the house steps.

He knocked nearly two minutes before he heard the clank of the inside latch and the door opened.

It was the general's wife. Mary Lee smiled at Brady, but looked fatigued, her eyes heavy, gray hair spilling out beneath her black bonnet.

"Robert has received your letter, Mr. Brady, but I am sorry, it is neither the time nor place for photographs."

"I beg to differ, madam," Brady said as he caught a slow closing door. Mary Lee's eyes widened.

"Forgive me," he said, straightening his posture. "I know it is difficult. But no mistake, now is the time. It has been decided not by me nor your husband. The nation is trying to make sense of all this, just as surely as he is."

She held him in her softening gaze, saying nothing.

It seemed another minute again before she spoke.

"Kindly wait below, Mr. Brady. Thank you."

This time she shut the door fast enough that she would not be denied.

Brady stood for more than a minute, pondering exactly what to do. He began to descend the series of steps.

He nearly reached the walk when the door opened once more.

Brady introduced himself, as if he needed to at this point, to Lee's eldest son, General Custis Lee, who stood there in full uniform.

Brady pleaded his case a second time.

Once more Brady was told to wait and the door shut until a Negro man appeared.

He told Brady to bring himself and his cameramen around the back gate.

They met the servant at the iron gate where they were allowed into a small yard.

They assembled their equipment beside a quaint garden surrounded by a low white fence.

Brady was occupied, helping Fowx adjust the camera upon its legs, when he heard the back door open.

There he was. Brady could scarcely believe his eyes. The old man stepped out from his back step in full Rebel gray, flanked by his son Custis and a uniformed aide.

Lee stepped toward Brady, slow and unsure as if he had just climbed off his horse after a lengthy ride.

He had not seen Lee in perhaps six years. A shell of that former man now, grayed and slightly bent. Brady crossed the stone walk and met him halfway to shake hands.

"General Lee. Thank you."

"Mr. Brady, I knew you would not be dissuaded and that you are just performing your duty. I admire that, sir. Here I am but only for a short time. I could not bear anything more right now. So please commence as soon as possible."

"Yes, General. We are ready to begin."

Brady did not engage in further conversation. The general wanted quick work and that he would get.

Robert Lee, sullen and defeated, allowed Brady to pose him against the rear of the house as Fowx operated the camera, Berger exchanging the thin plate boxes and shuttling between the yard and van at the street.

Lee said little the entire time, nothing of the war, and nothing of the tragedy that had befallen President Lincoln at Ford's Theater in Washington just days ago.

Brady then suggested photographs of Lee's group.

He went to the house to move a chair into position.

Brady caught sight of something in chalk upon the brick. He could read it now.

Brady lifted his arm and rubbed out the word *Devil* with the sleeve of his jacket. It seemed not everyone was so happy to see Lee return. Just as Brady did this, the general turned around.

Lee on the back porch of his Franklin Street home, Richmond, April 1865
A magnified view shows the word 'Devil' on the brick wall above the chair

"A bit of scribble on the house is all," Brady offered. The general, he was sure, had not been aware of it.

Brady returned attention to his subjects.

He posed the two men with Lee seated before the solid oak door. The defeated general's white head was centered beneath the raised wood on the door that formed the perfect shape of a cross.

Devil. The shape of the cross.

Brady's mind raced over these things as Fowx managed the final exposures that Sunday morning.

Whether the cause worthy or not worthy, Brady knew Robert Lee would surely suffer for it the remainder of his life.

Lee, his son and Colonel Taylor, by Brady's team, April 1865

Saturday evening

Nearly ten o'clock; Brady had been counting the minutes. He stood to stretch.

Gardner looked to Brady. He set his empty cup on the table and, with something of a smile upon his bearded face, he too rose. "It is getting rather late, isn't it?"

Gardner, for all his faults, was astute. Brady was grateful.

"A wonderful evening," Gardner said to the room. "Margaret?"

Brady turned to Julia, there close beside Margaret on the settee, an open album spread across their laps.

He watched as Julia's cheery smile fell away.

"Indeed. Thanks to these ladies," Brady inhaled. "But yes actually, Julia and I did have another invitation. Nothing that required our attendance naturally, but we had thought about dropping in. Isn't that right, dear?"

Margaret Gardner smiled. "No bother at all! Yes. It is getting quite late anyhow. Alex and I should make way."

Margaret began to bring half the book up from her lap to close it.

Julia's eyes followed this motion, as if trying to make sense of what was happening. Her hand came up quick to grasp Margaret at the wrist.

Julia then looked up at Brady, her brown eyes beaming.

"Mathew! I just had a splendid idea."

Brady swallowed.

"You know I am not one for these parties. You have our invitation to the McCarthy ball and you and Alex know so many more people there than we."

"Oh, that is not necessary," Gardner started.

"And I'm sure you could talk your way into allowing one more," she continued. "Truman might enjoy himself."

"Actually, Mrs. Brady," Truman interjected, "I have an invitation already." He fidgeted into his pocket and produced a card from it. "Courtesy of Senator Wilson. He hoped I might get out of doors and enjoy myself."

Truman turned and smiled at Brady. "He always does."

"Oh! There you go! The two of you take Truman for a little while. We will be here when you get back," Julia said.

She then turned and squeezed her companion's hand. "I would like to have Margaret a bit longer."

❧

The carriage pulled to a stop amongst a line of vehicles crowding the long cobblestone drive.

At the end of the lane, McCarthy's stately gas-lit mansion stood watch over the dark night.

Brady stared across the shadowy cab at Truman, then Gardner. It occurred to Brady that he could not have imagined a more dreadful outcome to this evening.

And now the waiting, trapped in this box on wheels.

Though Brady had insisted on the cab, he knew they would have been better off taking a horse car and walking the remainder. But even under present circumstances, appearances were important. As one notable Washington City columnist was fond of saying, *the carriages bring the cream, the street cars the skim milk.*

Ten quiet minutes later, they had moved but a few carriage lengths.

Brady opened the door. He paid the driver, informing him the three of them would go from here on foot.

Truman, then Gardner, exited the cab. Brady breathed the cold night air; it felt liberating.

The three moved up the walk to a line that led to the door of the mansion, smoke billowing from its brick chimneys. Granite piers surrounded the crowded front entrance and through its windows behind thin dra-pery, several figures passed between lit rooms.

It was another five minutes in the cold before they reached the interior hall. There the line started up the stairs where manservants waited at top. A crier announcing the latest guests. "Mr. and Mrs. Thomas Crown!"

Upon the staircase were many couples; men in suits of the finest cut, thick shawls and cashmere wraps covered silk gowns worn by ladies who shivered off the last of the cold. The pleasing aroma of lavender and a hundred perfumes.

At the top of the stairs, men wearing colored vests stood round, lead-ing women away to freshen in the room next.

When they reached that place, Brady stepped to the crier, with Tru-man beside him and Gardner a step behind.

"My good man. Here's my invitation card, given to me by the con-gressman. A dear friend of mine. We should like to pass through without announcement. Thank you."

The man glanced at Brady, at Gardner, then the card, and nodded be-fore turning his eyes to Truman.

Truman handed over his card. "No announcing for me either if you please."

The man exhaled. He glanced at the card then waved Truman through, turning his haughty gaze upon the couple next.

The three stepped into the spacious second-floor room.

A spindled six-burner chandelier set the elegant space aglow. Ladies in lace and jewel, gentlemen, those in suits or military uniform and others in bright foreign garb; they crowded every corner of the marble floor. A string quartet struggled at the far end against the din of laughter and con-versation. Couples danced; great hoop skirts kept their distance from one another as they spun about the center room as if bright planets in orbit.

Brady turned to Gardner, who looked uneasy.

"Well, I guess I will make the most of it and say a few hellos. Truman, if you would care to join me, I might make a few introductions."

Truman turned to Gardner as if seeking some permission.

"Very good. I will walk around a bit," Gardner said.

As Brady slipped into the crowd with Truman, he turned back to Gardner.

The Scot stood, hands clasped before him, staring pensively about the room. A man in black tails whom Brady did not recognize then stopped to shake Gardner's hand.

Gardner was well known and respected in these circles. He, like Brady, had photographed them for so many years.

Alex Gardner would be kept busy with conversation, whether he wanted the attention or not.

Brady turned to the room ahead, greeting the many he knew and leading Truman into a series of introductions as *a good friend and brilliant young naturalist at the Smithsonian.*

Truman leaned once to Brady between the handshaking.

"I seem to think that this isn't Mr. Gardner's favorite place."

Brady glanced over at Gardner, now cornered by a plump, red-faced man who looked quite glad to have happened upon his photographer.

"Truman, I think," Brady started between handshakes, "-wonderful to see you Mr. Nobles – that you may be right indeed. About Mr. Gardner that is. I suppose these scenes are not for everyone. And you may find after this evening that they are not for you either. But I submit that if you wish to make inroads in this town you had better learn to shake a few hands."

"I guess that it is so. Especially when there is a petition involved."

Brady turned suddenly to Truman. He smiled, then could not help but laugh. "Yes. Especially then."

He rapped Truman on the shoulder. "Come. Let's find Senator Wilson for you. Won't he be surprised?"

If Brady could deliver Truman to Wilson, that would not be the worst thing that could happen. He could further endear himself, were he required to call on Wilson again for immediate action in these coming days.

They paused at an alcove where two wide columns divided it from the main room. A grand fireplace with marble surrounds burned brightly at its center. They scanned its crowded sofas before continuing down along the south wall dotted with paintings as well as large Imperial portraits, many of them produced by Brady.

They found Wilson among a throng of guests there, holding a glass flute.

The senator was indeed astounded to see Truman. At once he pulled him into his present conversation, after thanking Brady for bringing him, and achieving what he could not.

Brady deflected praise. He replied simply that he would leave them for a time, resisting the urge to pull the senator aside to probe for any news on his behalf. He would let Wilson have his time with Truman.

Brady moved about the open floor, sharing pleasantries with no less than a dozen congressmen, among them the host McCarthy, in his broadcloth swallowtail over an embroidered blue vest. On mention of his petition, they each, in turn, remarked it a *marvelous* or *wonderful idea* and *long overdue*, just as so many had done at the Willard and about the town this past week.

But each time upon hearing their words, Brady was less affected by them. And a dreading now grew inside him.

Brady had finished his third glass of champagne, reaching the opposite end of the room, when he came upon a gathering, their backs to him. He could hear a man's booming voice as he drew nearer. Brady slipped forward into the crowd until he glimpsed the actor Peter Innant, standing in the open circle. Brady now remembered that Innant's *Macbeth* tour was stopped in Washington.

The stout man, with a black beard and slicked hair grayed at the temples, was in the middle of delivering a Shakespearean soliloquy to the hushed crowd.

Brady turned to his right.

Several yards away, standing there with a smile upon his lips, stood Timothy Howe beside his brunette wife. Brady slipped down toward the Wisconsin senator and member of the Joint Committee on the Library. He had last seen him a few days back in the Senate Reception Room, where the congressman had talked up Brady on a great many topics before the petition could be mentioned. Howe would surely have the news Brady sought.

Howe caught Brady from the corner of his eye.

"Mathew. Hello," Howe whispered, watching the actor.

"Hello, Senator. How are things?"

"Very well indeed."

"And in the Senate chamber I trust that holds true as well?"

Just then the actor closed his speech, his arm held out. A thunderous applause followed. Howe clapped, as did Brady, to the actor's bows.

"It does. It does! I have some good news to share indeed."

The actor threw up his hand. The crowd fell silent, and the actor soon began again. A different tone. A sad, despondent air. Brady turned full to the senator, but Howe was absorbed by the thespian.

"Life's but a walking shadow, a poor player that struts and frets his hour upon stage and then is heard no more..."

Brady pretended to listen as the actor continued, delivering the last words with a tear rolling down his cheek. More than a few of the ladies were now tearful in accord. Peter Innant lowered his head. The crowd cheered before they fell in toward him.

Howe's wife took her husband by the arm and whisked him forward in a rush to meet the actor.

"Oh! Excuse me, Mathew."

Howe had disappeared into the crowd. Brady lost him. He was left there to wonder just what good news the senator had for him.

Eventually, Brady strolled back through the room and into the hall.

After a few minutes, he spied Gardner down the corridor.

He was speaking with Senator William Fessenden, chair of the Committee on the Library.

Though he doubted the propriety of it, Brady started for them.

Senator Fessenden, a man known for staunch principals, had become a pariah in his own party last year when he had abandoned his radical colleagues and voted against Johnson's impeachment. Brady was surprised to see him at all in such a place. Not once could Brady recall finding Fessenden at the Willard or other social haunts. Brady knew his letter to him this past week had quite possibly gone unread.

Now, Fessenden was here. And Gardner had his ear.

"Senator Fessenden. How are you?" Brady asked.

Only then did Gardner appear to see Brady, his face turned white as if he'd been caught by the marm in a schoolyard prank.

Fessenden turned round slowly. He shook Brady's hand, all the while wearing that familiar scowl beneath the mounds of his thick gray hair.

"I am well. Thank you."

An uneasy second passed as Fessenden's eyes cut to Gardner, then back to Brady. His small eyes narrowed.

"Mr. Brady, you have a petition under my committee's review, do you not?"

Brady felt blood rush to his head.

"I do, sir. Yes. A petition submitted to the Committee on the Library for my war views."

"Yes." Fessenden paused. "And Mr. Gardner tells me he has a petition in waiting for the same. Quite intriguing."

"He did mention that, did he?"

"He did." The old senator cleared his throat. "Well, as you may know sir, I am not the sort to speak of such business outside the walls of the committee room. It seems I am now repeating myself as I just said the same thing to Mr. Gardner-"

"Of course, Senator," Brady interjected. "I did not come to bother you with that."

Fessenden's thick brows rose. "Oh?" He showed a coy smile, revealing dull yellow teeth. "Good! Then what shall we talk about?"

❦

Nearly two hours since they set foot inside McCarthy's estate on this misbegotten adventure, Brady found himself resting on a settee in the small alcove off the main room. Following the most uncomfortable encounter with Fessenden, Brady told Gardner he would find Truman, then find him. He spotted Truman, occupied with Senator Wilson, and decided he would wait. So, there he sat.

Then, scanning the crowd from his seated vantage, he spied Senator Howe on the other side of the great room.

He seized his chance. Brady shot up. His feet carried him across the marble tile, and he slipped through a maze of bodies until he reached the Wisconsin senator as he and his wife were about to descend the stairs. Brady put a hand on Howe's shoulder.

Howe turned; his eyes widened. "Mathew. There you are. Good to see you again."

Howe's wife stopped and turned with him, clutching his arm tightly. They both wore smiles.

"Senator. Madame. Hello," Brady said between breaths.

"Are you alright, Mathew?" Howe broke in with a laugh.

"Fine indeed. But I have been looking for you."

Howe's cocked his head. "Have you?"

Brady nodded, then "It was our conversation not an hour ago. I couldn't resist inquiring after what you had said."

A confused look came over the senator. He glanced at the tiled floor for a moment. "Well, I must apologize. I find myself quite ashamed as I can't recall the substance of our-"

"My petition, Senator."

Howe still said nothing.

"You said you had good news," Brady pressed.

Howe held Brady with a queer smile a moment then his eyes lit.

"Oh!" Then his smile left. "Oh," he repeated. The senator shook his head. "I am embarrassed now indeed, Mathew, for there was some misunderstanding. You see, the good news I was referring to came from the Committee on Public Lands. The land grant needed for the Superior and State Line rail."

Brady's smile was now a veil to utter confusion.

"The other day you stopped by," Howe began, "and, yes, now I do recall you mentioning your petition. But before doing so, you asked me about my railway bill. You seemed to take such an interest in it that it stuck in my head is all."

Brady nodded, recalling now his mention of one of Howe's bills as a means to conversation. How he had listened to the senator's rambling with affected interest.

"I am sorry for the confusion. As for your petition, Mathew. I honestly must say I do not know as we have not been called to that committee for some weeks now."

Howe held the look of concern as if he had an inkling of the damage he'd inflicted. He added quietly that "It may be better to ask Senator Fessenden or Senator Morgan about that."

❦

Brady glanced up from the settee to see Truman standing there. Brady brought the flat of his palm to the seat next. Truman sat down beside him.

"Has Senator Wilson shown you enough of the evening?"

"He has."

"Good."

The crowd's laughter mixed with the quartet heard around the wall of the room. A portly man across Brady snored off his champagne where his wife had abandoned him.

"You seem out of sorts, Mr. Brady."

Brady turned. "Just tired," he said with all the smile he could muster. "Tired is all."

Brady watched a Negro servant enter the space and scan the room. He held a small mahogany chest, twice as long as wide, in his kid glove hands. He met Brady's eyes and drew close.

"Gentlemen," the man began softly as he bent forward, peeled back its lid and tilted the box forward, "a cigar? Compliments of Senator McCarthy."

Brady stared down at the row of fine selections; blacks, darks, and tans.

The servant moved the box slightly to the left so that Truman might share the view. "They say these Cubans here are our new president's favorite."

"Do you smoke, Truman?" Brady asked, without taking his eyes from the cigars.

"No, Mr. Brady."

Brady nodded. He took a deep breath. "Nor do I."

***

Out on the stone terrace, Brady lit his cigar with one of two matches provided for him. He traded a puff of cold with his first pull on the smoke between his lips, turning it as it lit full against the small flame. He took it from his mouth, savoring its rich smoke. He blew out the matchstick.

The balcony spanned two double windows and a lone gaslight burned brightly above the center door. The narrow platform was bound by a wrought iron railing and men crowded the place, smoking and talking and admiring the dark night below them, tolerating the chill of that February evening for a time.

One of them opened the door and started into the warmth inside. A large group followed, nearly emptying the space.

It was only then that Brady saw the lone gentlemen remaining.

It was Gardner, who noticed Brady at nearly the same time. The Scot looked surprised for a moment before he gained his composure and smiled.

"Mr. Gardner," Truman said first.

Gardner stepped closer to them.

Brady held the cigar and studied the glow of its tip as he exhaled. "Truman agreed to accompany me for some cool night air."

"I was feeling a bit stifled myself," Gardner said to Truman.

Truman crossed his arms and ran them up along his coat. "So here we are."

"I guess so," added Brady unnecessarily.

A long silence followed which pained Brady increasingly. After a third continuous puff from his smoke, he could bare it no longer.

"Well, Truman. Tell me more of your family. We know now that you were not an only child," said Brady. "Tell me about this brother of yours." He puffed. "Taken up with your line of work, has he? A family of Massachusetts naturalists?"

Brady smiled a moment longer, then he caught Truman's face in the glow of the gaslight. Brady knew not how, but he knew that he had erred.

"No," Truman said into the quiet.

Brady cut his eyes toward Gardner, who looked equally confounded but seemed aware of something foreboding near the surface of this conversation upon which Brady had stumbled into.

It was then that Truman let go a small laugh. The young man fell silent again before he looked at Gardner, then back.

Brady watched Truman reach into his rear pocket and pull out his leather fold. He opened it, the tip of his index finger tripping over several bills then stopping.

"Actually, Mr. Brady," Truman began, "I had planned to show you something for quite some time now. At the café. At the castle. Then I thought the better of it. Well," he paused, "I guess I just decided not to."

Truman produced a card from his wallet. He held it out to the light.

"This is Seldon Ash. My brother."

Brady took the card between finger and thumb.

"The 39th Massachusetts Infantry," added Truman.

"Ah, I see," Brady said, to no reply, as he looked down at the card now in his possession.

In the glow, Brady studied the soldier on that worn carte de visite. A young man, with dark eyes set hard upon the camera, a bayoneted rifle in perfect line against the brass of his blue coat. The brother Ash.

Then, as if fitting the last veneer piece of a puzzle into place, Brady turned the card over to reveal its ornate stamp.

Brady's National Photographic Portrait Galleries. It was a faded black that ran stained where perhaps weather had touched it on more than one occasion.

"All this time I wanted to meet you," Truman said to silence. "I wanted to meet the man who gave me this gift."

Brady stole another glance at Gardner. He looked at Truman.

"We couldn't keep him from joining. Not a one of us," Truman said, almost smiling. "Not even Senator Wilson."

Truman took a step backward. He folded his arms again. "They broke camp at Lynnfield and went to Washington that first October of the war. And he came to your studio soon after. Since we were boys, Senator Wilson would bring us Brady cards on his visits back home to Natick. Seldon knew you well. We both did."

Truman then seemed to wait for Brady to meet his eyes once more, which Brady did. "This meant so much to him that day."

Brady smiled, staring back over the card. He could not find the words, a lump in his throat. The faces of so many thousand young soldiers who stepped before his camera, they flitted through his mind like flashes of lightning that peppered a dark and stormy sky.

To Brady's recollection, he had never known a one of them. He had never taken the time.

"To have it these past years," continued Truman, "has meant everything to me at times."

Brady looked to Gardner, who had stood silent among them, and handed him the card.

Gardner seemed hesitant to take it. But he did. He studied it front and back before he turned to Truman's stare.

"My brother died at Spotsylvania."

Brady glimpsed Gardner's fingers tighten on the card a moment. He studied Gardner's bearded face, waiting for some hint of emotion that never appeared. But Brady knew better. He could only fathom what passed for Alex Gardner's thoughts in those quiet seconds before Truman took the card back and placed it, gingerly, to the center of the left fold and returned it to his pocket.

The doors opened behind them.

"There you are, Truman!" exclaimed Senator Wilson. "I have been searching you out, my boy. I have been talking with our good Senator Davis about your work. He sits on the Board of Regents at the Smithsonian, you know. He has great interest in your work. Come! Come inside."

Wilson glanced over at Gardner. A moment of surprise stole across his face as he looked quickly at Brady, then back to Gardner.

"Oh, why hello, Alex," the senator began, then shook Gardner's hand. "Good to see you again."

Gardner nodded politely but said nothing.

Wilson forced a smile. "Excuse us, Mathew. Alex."

"Certainly," replied Brady as Truman stepped from his side and toward Wilson and into that warm and light-filled room.

Together, Brady and Gardner watched Truman's back as the door was shut behind him. The ash on Brady's cigar had grown perilously long and he tapped it into the iron tray fixed upon the railing.

Gardner gave a slight shake of his head from side to side and turned out to face the night.

Finally, Gardner spoke. "I sometimes think-" He stopped. Then, "We tried to tell the story of that war through our work. Do you think, perhaps, we lost sight of the real stories long ago?"

Brady said nothing. He knew it was not a question in need of reply.

XVII

Monday morning

The Senate Chamber, having slumbered its Sunday away as was custom, opened its doors once more.

Gardner took his seat in the gallery at the end of the first bench closest to the rostrum. Yes, he thought, it was *his seat* now, as many times he'd been there the past week; for all the good it had done.

A cold morning rain drummed upon the glass roof. The clerk was busy at the switches, lighting the gas jets along the ceiling. The galleries near empty, perhaps thirty men in all. Familiar faces; regulars who read their papers, napped, or held private session with one another.

Brady was nowhere to be found. He probably knew, as did Gardner, that there was a strong possibility that little in the way of business would be brought to the floor today.

It was quiet below. Pomeroy and the other senators sat behind desks with nary a word for one another. Reverend Gray gave a morning prayer and Ben Wade took his seat at the front.

"Mr. President," said Senator Henry B. Anthony, rising from his seat. The heavy-set former governor from Rhode Island ran a hand down his graying beard and cleared his throat.

303

"The supplication which has just been offered up to the Throne of Grace reminds us all that this is a holiday in the history of America. It is the anniversary of the birth of Washington. It has been the custom always, since I have been here, for the Executive Departments to be closed, and for both Houses to adjourn upon this day."

Gardner shut his eyes. He listened on as Senator Anthony moved that, at the very least, they recess until evening when the most urgent business could be considered.

Either way, Gardner knew petitions would not be among the day's business.

Senator Fessenden, subject of Gardner's, and Brady's, embarrassment the night before last, lifted his old frame from his chair and turned across to his Republican colleague. "I think we had better have the journal read."

"Oh no. It is not necessary," said Anthony to Wade on the rostrum.

Senator John Sherman of Ohio, a wiry man like his brother general, stood up. "I ask the indulgence from the senator from Rhode Island to allow me, before that motion is put, to take up the amendment of the House of Representatives to Senate Bill Number 440, and let a committee of conference be appointed upon it."

Sherman then turned toward Fessenden.

The three men now stood, forming an irregular triangle. "I desire to perfect the matter as far as possible now. The senator from Maine objected to it on Saturday."

Anthony turned. "I do not wish to interpose an objection; but if we give way to one thing we shall be compelled to give way to others."

Fessenden replied curtly that he had not yet read the bill and wished to before it was acted upon.

Sherman shook his head in frustration at old Fessenden and sat.

Wade pounded his gavel. "It is moved that the Senate take a recess until seven o'clock this evening."

Congressmen, including Pomeroy, began collecting papers and satchels, vacating their desks and filing toward the rear.

Others remained seated as they were, and took to their papers and pens.

"Wasted trip on this day, eh?"

Gardner turned round in his seat. One row back, the ruffian leaned forward in his heavy coat and smiled at Gardner through blackened teeth. "No action today." His breath smelled of garlic. "Not on the president's day."

The man leaned back then. He pulled his tattered hat low and prepared to nap.

Gardner turned back round. Reverend Gray crossed the rostrum. Gray glanced up a moment to the near vacant gallery and they locked eyes. The old Baptist smiled and tipped his black hat once to Gardner before he stepped down and proceeded up the aisle. Gardner's eyes followed him out the rear door of the half-emptied chamber. Gardner rose himself and started up the stairs, the good reverend now on his mind.

Gardner was reminded of a time. Somber days, when Reverend Gray had closed the service for Lincoln at the president's mansion. Like so many thousands, the president, who had led the nation through the fire, had not escaped it with his life.

The nation began to rebuild itself. But only after that final act was avenged, as if it could even begin to make things right again.

April 1865

Monday morning, April 17th. Lincoln had been dead two days when a man Gardner recognized from his days with Pinkerton's service walked in the studio.

Not five minutes later, Gardner was in the fellow's wagon, bound for the War Department.

Gardner had met Colonel Lafayette Baker on one previous occasion.

The man with brown locks and a piercing stare now rose from behind his desk and gave Gardner a firm handshake.

"Mr. Gardner, the Secretary of War has appointed me to run this manhunt. Sir, I need you."

He explained that Gardner would begin by making copies of the photographs of the suspected conspirators.

"Detectives have uncovered several photographs in their raiding of homes and hotel rooms; Booth, one David Herold, and John Surratt. Maxwell here will show you to your work. Thank you, sir. You will of course be compensated for your services as-"

"Money is no concern to me, Colonel," Gardner said. "It can be discussed later. If you need my help in any way, I am at your service. For as long as you need me."

The colonel's eyes fixed on Gardner. His lips turned up beneath his moustache slightly, as if almost to smile. But it was hardly a time for smiles, and it never did appear.

"Very well. Thank you. Let's begin."

That morning, Gardner made the first prints of the conspirators; a poster that would, in a few days' time, be pasted on walls and on doors far and wide.

Gardner rushed to Ford's that afternoon with a pass from the colonel.

He presented it to the blue coats who had held the theater secure since Friday night. Gardner had already photographed the brick exterior, draped in black muslin. He had photographed Howard's Livery Stable where Booth kept his getaway mount, the Navy Bridge where the actor crossed into Maryland, and even the telegraph office that carried the first news of the sinister crime to the world.

Gardner now stood inside the walls of Ford's.

He found the place cold and dark, a silent crypt to be forever haunted by the act. The attendant who showed him in turned up the gaslights.

Images of Ford's Theater, A. Gardner, April 1865

While taking his photographs, Gardner focused his stereo camera across the stage to the president's box with its disheveled flag that Booth caught in his boot spur as he leapt down.

⌒⌐

They held service in the East Room. Mary Todd Lincoln, Gardner heard, did not attend, too grief stricken she was.

On that 19th of April, silent mourners crowded every walk and corner along the avenue. Buildings swathed in black hung flags at half-mast. Cavalry and thousands of Union soldiers marched aside the funeral hearse driven by half a dozen white horses, along the cobblestones and over streetcar tracks toward the Capitol. A caparisoned horse followed, representing the fallen commander, as a drummer beat a solemn tap.

President Lincoln's funeral procession on Penn. Ave., 1865, photographer unknown

The next day Gardner waited nearly four hours in a line that started outside the Capitol and doubled through and around the coffin. He paid his final respects to a friend.

In a few days a train would leave on its tour through New York City and then east. The president and his beloved son Willie would be laid to rest in Illinois.

And all the while the hunt for the remaining perpetrators continued without abate.

The morning of April 27th, 1865, Gardner awoke to a hard knocking at his door. He took his watch from the stand. Not quite seven. He opened the door, tucking his nightshirt into hastily donned pants.

A short man stood cross-legged, wearing a large slouch hat and overcoat. Gardner guessed at once who had sent him.

Since Lafayette Baker commissioned Gardner in the manhunt for the assassins, he had been scarcely utilized at all. The colonel made it clear Gardner would be summoned when needed.

Whispers filled the city in recent days that men had been taken captive, including Seward's attacker, and that they were being held aboard two Navy ironclads. Gardner, like the multitudes, knew not rumor from fact.

That was about to change.

"I'm Camp," the patrolmen said, still-faced in the doorway. Gardner guessed that was not his Christian name. "Got orders to escort you to your studio, get your equipment into a wagon, quick-like. Whatever it is you need to make your photographs. Then to the War Department. And we've got to move."

Gardner knew there was no point in asking questions. This Camp fellow probably knew little himself.

"Give me one minute."

Gardner finished dressing, saddled his bay and the pair of them rode to the studio. Scaling the back steps two at a time with Camp at his back, Gardner was relieved to find O'Sullivan on the top floor, already readying the equipment for the day's appointments.

They loaded a wagon out back with two cameras, supplies and plates.

Within minutes, Gardner and O'Sullivan shared the wagon bench and followed Camp's horse at a fast clip through the cool spring air of morning.

Camp dismounted and entered the War Department building. Gardner waited with O'Sullivan. Morning birds sang from rooftops and branches in the small budding trees that dotted the yard.

A man came quickly out the front door.

"Morning, Mr. Gardner. I am Wardell". He pulled up his wide brim hat, revealing a sandy head of hair with wisps of gray.

"Good morning," Gardner replied.

Wardell looked at O'Sullivan. "Is there room in the back for you, son? Like to ride up front with Mr. Gardner here and talk a bit."

O'Sullivan looked Gardner's way. Gardner nodded.

Tim O'Sullivan climbed down and walked to the rear.

Wardell climbed upon the bench. "Navy Yard," he said.

O'Sullivan rapped the wagon side when he found secure footing at the back.

Gardner started the wagon down Pennsylvania Avenue toward the Navy Yard, a mile southeast of the Capitol.

No words were exchanged for several minutes, Gardner listening to the horse's clopping hooves upon the cobblestones.

Finally, Wardell cleared his throat and spat chaw. "Booth is dead. Shot through the neck in Virginia yesterday."

"My God."

Gardner's heart pounded as he steered past the Capitol and south along New Jersey Avenue.

"He's on board the Montauk just offshore."

Gardner felt Wardell's stare and turned to meet his eyes. "And you are going to take his picture."

Gardner nodded. When he imagined all the things for which he might be summoned during the course of this manhunt, this was never one of them.

"A picture only for us. The department," Wardell said sternly. "I am to see to that, Mr. Gardner. Understood?"

"Understood."

❧

At the Navy Yard one of the guards approached from the edge of the gated pier. Wardell climbed down to meet him and explain his orders.

The ironclads Saugus and Montauk were moored aside one another a hundred yards offshore. The calm morning waters like glass, they revealed sky clouds and shadows of the iron-plated vessels; the high turrets, and the soldiers in their billed kepis who swarmed the low decks.

"Sorry, sir. You may not pass," Gardner heard the guard reply to Wardell.

"Damn it to all hell!" Wardell exploded. "Colonel Baker's instructions."

"No, sir," the young soldier replied with force, apparently confident enough in his duties. "I have no confirmation of it. No one gets past without confirmation."

Gardner had to admire the guard's stoic nature as the gruff Wardell seethed, mere inches from his face. Delayed or not, Gardner was relieved to hear O'Sullivan making quick work in the wagon well, preparing plates.

The standoff did not last. A carriage rolled up to the gate. Inside it, Gardner could see Lafayette Baker sitting in the shadows. The colonel then stuck out his head.

Wardell explained the delay in both colorful and heated terms, obviously hoping to implicate the young guard.

The colonel said nothing for a moment, then offered his simple directive. "Follow me out to the pier."

Wardell climbed back aboard with Gardner, his fiery gaze still upon the soldier as two more swung open the gate.

Gardner drove the wagon onto the pier behind Baker's carriage. General Barnes walked out to meet them where puffs of light smoke billowed from atop a small river tug.

O'Sullivan climbed down. Gardner descended the wagon as did Wardell.

"You and your assistant," the general said, his eyes on Gardner, then O'Sullivan. "Carry only what you need. We must hurry."

"I need the van," Gardner said after a glance across the water to the ironclad Montauk. He explained how they could unhitch the bay from the wagon and ferry it across. It would save time and he would have a better chance at quality than trying to set up a hasty dark room on ship, risking the presence of actinic lighting and other elements that might ruin the work.

"Very well. Make it happen," replied General Barnes.

⌘

The horseless wagon was rolled onto the tug and the lot of them were ferried out where they crossed wooden planks to her deck. Gardner and O'Sullivan positioned the van to the side.

Gardner was led around the far side of the Montauk's turret where a great canvas awning covered that portion of the deck. He saw perhaps twenty men; Colonel Baker, Wardell, and others, standing there, beholding. Gardner stepped close to see the object of their attention.

It was a body. *The body.* John Wilkes Booth lay naked and wrapped in a white sheet upon a simple carpenter's table. A surgeon busy, probing a dried wound in the neck of the pallid corpse.

Booth looked much like the photograph in Gardner's poster except his hair was matted and longer. His full moustache was gone, replaced by a thin growth beard.

Colonel Baker then turned to Gardner. "I trust you can manage your photograph here, Mr. Gardner?"

Gardner nodded. "A little space and yes I can manage."

O'Sullivan set up the single plate camera aside the table, its legs spread and lens eighteen inches above table height.

Gardner took the thin plate box from under his arm, provided it to O'Sullivan who slipped the glass inside and removed the lens cap. O'Sullivan went to develop the plate. Gardner followed, with Wardell at his heels.

Gardner inspected the finished negative at the rear of the immobile van. It was good, unblemished and clear in detail.

Wardell approached Baker and they exchanged whispers for a moment. Wardell stepped toward Gardner.

"He comes with me," said Wardell, nodding to O'Sullivan. "An escort will follow me back to your studio. I need a single print made. Then I need that plate."

Gardner nodded his agreement. O'Sullivan, carrying the thin box and its negative, followed Wardell onto the tug.

Gardner crossed the planked deck to Colonel Baker. Baker led him away from the group to the railing where he looked out and skyward. A late morning breeze blew over the water and them. They watched as the tug reached the pier.

"I have arranged for the prisoners to be made available to you for the next three hours. They will clear Booth from here and you may photograph on deck. You must photograph them all. I assume you would do that anyways, but the images must be with a clear view of the face. Deliver two prints of each to the War Department by end of day tomorrow. The negatives and what you wish for them afterwards are for you to decide."

Baker then held up an arm and waved in the direction of the tug. In a few seconds, the vessel lurched forward, and its bow turned toward the ironclad. Baker began walking to center deck. Gardner followed.

"David Herold is here aboard the Montauk, as is Paine. In one hour's time they will be transferred to the hold of the Saugus where you may photograph them again if you'd like. The remaining prisoners you will find aboard the Saugus."

Gardner said nothing. The tug men tied off against the Montauk long enough for Baker to step aboard. He turned back to Gardner. "Any questions?"

"None."

"Good. And thank you, Mr. Gardner. Sergeant Wise here will see to your needs. Sergeant."

The sergeant nodded at Gardner, awaiting instructions.

⌒⌒

Gardner chose an area on the deck, on the north face off the turret where he enlisted guards to help him tie canvas across as a makeshift backdrop. The sergeant instructed two privates to start by bringing Lewis Paine on deck.

Paine emerged, up the steps toward the deck in shackles. A brute of a man in a dirty tan overcoat with great tufts of brown hair beneath his hat.

The sergeant ordered guards to remove the irons at his wrists which showed red and raw. The two guards and the sergeant stood ready but even so, Paine stared out with menacing eyes, like those of a wounded and dangerous animal. Were the troubled young man given to do something sudden and foolish, Gardner did not like his chances.

The sergeant explained to Paine what was to happen. Paine nodded his understanding. The sergeant moved the prisoner into place before the turret.

Paine was returned below deck after Gardner's fourth exposure.

When Gardner next returned from the well of his van, he found Herold waiting with the sergeant. Herold, the rogue who accompanied Booth across Virginia and to the stable where the actor was killed, was a scruffy man with oily black hair. He looked nervous and defeated. Gardner made three images.

Conspirators Lewis Paine and David Herold, U.S.S. Montauk, April 27th, 1865

The sergeant ordered the transfer of Herold and Paine across to the Saugus. A blue coat was enlisted to help Gardner with his van, taking it across and positioning it in similar fashion aboard that vessel.

Against the turret of the Saugus, Gardner continued his work. O'Sullivan returned on horseback and was transported to the ironclad to rejoin Gardner. Work resumed at a rapid pace over the next two hours.

He photographed the enigmatic Paine once more; wearing the shackles he would bear the remainder of his time on earth. A parade of men were brought upon the deck for Gardner's camera; Herold, O'Laughlin, Atzerodt, Spangler, Richter, Arnold. Gardner photographed each man from the front, as Baker requested, and had them turn in profile to complete a definitive proof of identity.

A few years later, Gardner would perfect that technique in his *Rogue's Gallery* work with the Metropolitan Police. Pinkerton continued this practice in the west, and it was not long before nearly every major city followed this standard.

Lewis Paine again, shackled and aboard the U.S.S. Saugus, 'mug shots' by Gardner

Gardner returned that evening and was rewarded with a sound sleep that night. The following morning, he made prints for the War Department, then delivered his negatives to the engravers at *Harper's*.

It was on May 13th that Gardner's photograph of President Johnson, and not Brady's, graced the cover of *Harper's Weekly*. So too did Gardner's photographs, taken earlier that year, of Sheridan, Sherman, Grant, and Meade.

The 1ˢᵗ of July, *Harper's Weekly* would feature Gardner's exclusive images of the conspirators.

꧁

The prosecution rested on the 23ʳᵈ of May in the military trial of the conspirators. The same day the Grand Review began along Pennsylvania Avenue; a majestic sight as Gardner had ever seen. The armies choked the streets of the city for miles. It took a full day to review the Army of the Potomac. The following day, Sherman and Sheridan brought their armies down the avenue.

The Grand Review of the Army, May 1865, this one is attributed to Brady's studio

Gardner's assistant photographed the days-long procession from windows and from across a wooden stage erected just outside the Executive Mansion where President Johnson, Stanton, and Grant sat and held watch. So many men, marching as soldiers one last time, before they exchanged rifle and sword for plowshares and hammers, returning to homesteads or forging new ones on which to expend the remainder of their quiet lives.

Gardner could not help but think of the late president. If only he had been there to see it.

❧

The defense rested in late June. Four condemned to hang: Paine, Herold, Atzerodt, and Mary Surratt. Gardner once more received the call.

Late morning simmered on July 7th. He and O'Sullivan set up two cameras in windows inside the Arsenal grounds facing the wooden scaffolds. O'Sullivan and his eight by ten large format at the corner of the building, Gardner operated the stereo camera from the window next.

The prisoners were led out the door and across the yard wearing sack hoods. A quarter after one. Intolerably hot, even in the shade, Gardner's airless room offered no relief.

The sentenced were led up to chairs upon the high scaffold and their hoods were removed. They shuddered and shut tight their eyes as their pale faces were exposed to the blistering sun for the first time in weeks. A soldier held an umbrella for Mrs. Surratt, who showed ghoulish white against her black hair and dress. Preachers accompanied and offered prayers inaudible to Gardner. All except Paine, who looked at ease, had terror upon their faces. Blue coats not on duty stood along the high brick wall behind the scaffold, but each man was silent under orders.

Many were certain President Johnson would send a pardon for Mrs. Surratt. A soldier manned the yard gate to give word when a rider was sighted. At twenty-six after the hour, they waited no more. Nooses were affixed and hoods returned to their heads.

Captain Rath gave the order.

The floor let out. The bodies plummeted.

The assassination of the conspirators, photographs by Gardner, July 7th, 1865

Gardner and O'Sullivan photographed feverishly in those next minutes. Most died quick, their bodies limp, swinging like so many sides of freshly hung beef. Herold did not. The skittish man who had trembled before Gardner's camera on the ironclad had his nightmare realized. His neck did not snap. He writhed for more than an anguished minute.

Four beings, who once lived and breathed air from this world, dangled, undulating in the hot July breeze. Another twenty minutes and most of the yard cleared. Soldiers lowered the bodies and carried them to boxes beside the earthen holes that would receive them.

⁓

On the 22ⁿᵈ of that month, *Harper's* showcased images of the execution.

Months later, Gardner would publish the first of his two volumes entitled *Gardner's Photographic Sketch Book of the War*: an ornate, leather-backed volume of contact prints with his own text as narrative on the war.

Gardner felt he had reached the pinnacle of success.

Gardner's Photographic Sketch Book of the War, published in two volumes, text and mounted prints; it is considered a landmark achievement in photojournalism

But even before the end of '65, the images were selling poorly.

He came to accept that his photographs only served to remind the country of what it so desperately wanted now to forget.

Gardner and son Lawrence journeyed west to bring the family home from Iowa.

He sold his farmhouse north east of the city and bought a quaint home in the heart of the city, a few blocks from his studio. The promise of a normal life was there, beckoning him.

Tuesday morning

The Monday celebrating Washington's birthday passed into the next day.

Gardner ate a light breakfast and took the omnibus toward the Capitol. Flurries dotted the green and vanished on the damp ground as daylight chased away dawn. Then the gray skies let open. White flakes began to fall on the wet stones and accumulate on the Capitol grounds.

Gardner purchased a paper and an apple from a vendor's stand in the rotunda. He ascended the steps to the gallery and took his seat. He read the paper for a few minutes as the galleries filled.

Below, the gavel sounded.

Wilson was there, below. Senator Pomeroy sat attentive at his desk in his row right of the rostrum as the parson led the assembly in prayer.

The ruffian behind Gardner spat into the brass pot at his boots, and was otherwise preoccupied with the unraveling ends of a coat sleeve.

Petitions were being read, a half dozen of them, when Pomeroy stood. The Kansas senator held a sheet of paper in his hand.

"I present the memorial of Alexander Gardner, a citizen of the District of Columbia-"

XVIII

Tuesday morning

There Pomeroy stood in the chamber, his paper petition in hand. "The memorial of Alexander Gardner, a citizen of the District of Columbia, representing that for some years he has been practicing the art of photography; that during the war he was with the army and has a large collection of negatives"

Gardner inched ever closer to the edge of his gallery bench.

"-representing army views and army scenes, incidents, etc., which he thinks would make a very valuable collection as a history of the war. I respectfully ask that this memorial be referred to the Committee on the Library. I think that is the most suitable committee."

Senate President Wade cleared his throat from the rostrum, the scribes below him writing with fervor.

"It will be so referred."

Petitions continued for many minutes thereafter. Gardner remained seated. He mused over what might happen next, in the scant days that remained for the 40th Congress. When next would that committee meet?

Had it already met, to confer upon one such petition already, that of Mathew Brady's?

Now, they had a second to consider. Gardner could only hope there was still time.

It could not have been ten minutes after Pomeroy's reading, less than that, Gardner would later recall, when petitions ended, and the body proceeded into the Reports on the Committees.

It was then that old Fessenden stood.

"I am directed by the Joint Committee on the Library, to whom was referred the memorial of Mathew B. Brady, asking Congress to take the necessary steps to procure a collection of war views and incidents photographed by him during the rebellion"

Fessenden paused. Gardner's heart skipped a beat. He breathed but it seemed he could not get enough air inside his lungs.

Had he come so far, with defeat certain from the start?

"- to report it back and to ask to be discharged from the further consideration of the memorial on the grounds that there is not sufficient time to consider it in this session of Congress, and without expressing any opinion thereon."

Old Fessenden sat down again with some effort, the next senator rising. Gardner's ears registered hushed banter down the length of the Gentlemen's Gallery, a woman's laugh across the chasm.

Brady's petition was dead.

Gardner sat still, stunned.

He stared down the length of gallery benches, and to those seated behind him. Searching the faces.

A few minutes passed before he managed to pluck free a single question from his muddled thoughts upon which to focus: *Where in God's name was Brady?*

Gardner's feet led him from the Capitol. He took a car west along the avenue.

He came to a place he had not ventured to in years, though it seemed only yesterday when he entered Brady's studio at 6th and Pennsylvania.

He stepped through the empty vestibule and climbed stairs to the second-floor gallery.

He scanned the long room, its papered green walls and its lot of portraitures, the tall windows at the far end shouldered in golden damask drapery.

A half-dozen discreet patrons dotted the oak floors. It saddened Gardner that the place seemed more a museum than the bustling fanfare he remembered. But even in its meager state, it brought back a flood of memories. The two years Gardner spent when he first came down from Manhattan in '58, building and shaping her. Gardner could not help but take pride in what he had accomplished here.

He crossed the floor, toward the far end of the room where a man with dark curled hair sat upon a cream sofa facing the north wall, bathed in the light of its towering windows.

Gardner stood there; with his free arm he took his hat in hand.

"When did you hear?"

Brady did not turn his head, but took a deep breath as he crossed legs with some effort. "News travels fast in this city. Someone always knows something before it actually happens. You know that."

Gardner rounded the sofa and Brady glanced up and showed him a half-hearted smile. Gardner sat and together they shared a view of the gray brick façade of a building across the alleyway.

They talked. Brady relayed the gloom of reality that had set in these past days, the countless conversations with uninterested and encumbered politicians. The encounter with Senator Howe at the party, when he knew for certain the Committee on the Library would not seriously consider his petition.

"I'm sorry. I didn't mean for this to happen. Not this way."

Brady raised his hand as if to dismiss the show of concern. He sat forward with his elbows to his knees. He did not take his eyes from the windows.

"The best of these lobbyists, they know how to get things done. They build up talk. Make sure their petition gets to the right committee member, someone to champion it. Then push it all the way through. The size of their retainer, the number of dinners and gifts depending on how lucrative that sought-after bill is to their benefactor. And oh, how often they succeed."

Brady then cut his eyes to Gardner. "But not always. They also know when they've been beat. When it's time to cut out and go home."

Gardner nodded. He thought he understood. Brady looked toward the window and sighed. "I will see to it that my life's work is not forgotten. My negatives sold off as scrap, to become the makings of some gardener's glass roof. You and I, we won't be around to protect them. They need to be preserved. That is most important. As much of it as we can. If not by this Congress, the next or the one after it. If first not my photographs, then yours."

Gardner stared until Brady turned his way. It occurred to Gardner only then how he had missed the man these years. Gardner smiled, then asked "And just how do you suppose we do that?"

Brady laughed. He lifted his arms and stretched his hands toward the sky and brought one down upon Gardner's knee. "I could use a roll and cup of tea. How about you?"

Tuesday evening

Gardner looked at Margaret from across their table, she wore a heavy shawl over her shoulders. In the room next, the fire from the hearth burned low but warm.

"And we sat there in the café the longest time. Talking. The first time in a long time." Gardner sipped his tea, then added "It stung him. That I know."

He glanced at the fire then to Margaret who it seemed had never taken her eyes from him. She set down her tea. She did not smile but there was nevertheless something comforting in those blue eyes.

Gardner shrugged. "But he seemed-" He ran fingers over saucer and cup. "He seemed content."

She nodded and they left it at that.

She soon rose, kissed Gardner good night, and climbed the stairs toward their bed.

He sat to watch the fire burn down.

He stood and crossed the room to the bookcase.

There, among forgotten entries on the top row, Gardner pulled free a blue leather-bound volume and returned to the table.

He blew dust from the gold lettering on the cover of his *Sketch Book of the War*.

He had printed a mere two hundred of the costly two-volume series; an expensive gamble in which Gardner was lucky to recover costs.

He had gotten the message even back then. They wanted to forget the war. They needed to forget it, at least for a time. Fine. But surely not to be forgotten for all time?

He turned up the light at the wall and opened the book.

He began paging through it, studying the gloss prints affixed to each page, his own words the text and title to accompany them:

Dunker Church Battle-field of Antietam
A Harvest of Death
Slaughter Pen, Battle-field of Gettysburg

328 | MICHAEL KLAENE

Gardner's thoughts turned back in time, to when he was but a boy. His mother ushering he and James to the Hunterian near the towering Glasgow Cathedral, where they visited on so many rainy Saturday afternoons. Magnificent galleries, long walls in well-lit rooms where he marveled at the grand colors upon canvas. His mind conjured vivid recollection of the oil paintings depicting great battles of Britain's past wars. He remembered the excitement they elicited in him, the grand adventure of war.

He shut his eyes and saw them, as if he stood before them now.

Intense, illuminant works; the soldiers in broken lines giving battle with bayonet, confident generals on horseback showing the glisten of immaculate swords. Men fallen upon their backs with hand over the red blemish of their shirts, and a soft smile upon their lips before departing, sweetly, from this world.

Gardner rubbed his tired eyes.

When he closed them again, the paintings were gone. Their visitations replaced by a dark and menacing imagery; the corpse-strewn field at Gettysburg, severed limbs and bowels scattered for yards upon the shell-pocked earth, the sunken road at Antietam choked with dead. A man's severed head torn away, a boy's lower jaw shattered by a minie ball.

These things plagued Gardner's weary mind as he returned the book to the top shelf and clambered off to bed.

They would not let Gardner forget.

And it was rightly so that he should not let the world do so in kind.

Brady awoke from his fitful night's sleep. He stooped over the edge of bed to stretch the tightness from his back. He stood and dressed. Julia was already in her chair, reading George Eliot and sipping tea. He ate a single piece of toast from the morning tray, then went to her.

He bent forward, took her chin in his hand and held it up to meet her lips with his.

"I won't be late."

Brady took the horse car to the Capitol and stepped into a stiff and wet westerly breeze. A light snow fell on her sloped grounds, leaving but the brown tips of dormant grass in view. He climbed the slick steps with care.

Inside the warmed rotunda, he purchased a copy of the *National Republican*.

North across the hall he found a young page among the crowd. He handed the page a dime with the letters from his overcoat. He gave instructions to deliver them each according to names scribbled on the back fold.

Brady ascended stairs to the Senate's gallery and took a seat in the top row. He read the paper with minutes to spare. There on page one, in its complete review of Senate proceedings from the previous day, it was printed that Congress had discharged the petition to purchase *Brady's War Views*.

He peered up at intervals to watch the galleries fill. Flurries seemed heavier now, covering the high ceiling windows; wind cast them into curious shapes, only to scatter them again.

He reached the final page when he spied Gardner taking a seat at the foot of his section, where Brady had seen him in the days before.

Brady made his way down the aisle steps. Gardner had yet to see him.

A lanky man sat in the row above Gardner's, wearing his heavy coat as a blanket over him. He turned to Brady and slid a hand free to tip his weathered topper. A smile lit across his whiskered face.

Brady tipped his own hat as he stepped past and into Gardner's row.

Gardner turned his way.

The Scot's startled gaze soon gave way to a smile and silent nod, Brady took to mean, of appreciation. Brady sat, setting his cane in the space next. The gavel sounded. The pair of them watched senators find desks. They watched the sergeant-at-arms below, working the last of the lobbyists out the rear doors so the session could begin.

"Look at all of us," Gardner said. "With our hands out."

Brady cast a sidelong glance at Gardner. Down the aisles of the Gentlemen's Gallery, to the Press Gallery, and across the chasm to the Ladies' Gallery. More souls gathered than in past days, as many as he'd seen since the days of impeachment. The day was drawing near, the end of the 40th; time running out for those of want and need; railroaders and contractors, the desperate souls; failed businessmen, the veteran pensioners and war widows.

"If you don't ask," Brady said, "you are guaranteed nothing."

Gardner gave a trifling nod, perhaps in it some acceptance of that reality.

They listened to petitions. Two by Pomeroy, another by Senator Trumbull, then several from Nye of Nevada, the first of them on behalf of a Mary E. Hill, praying "for reimbursement of moneys to aid suffering soldiers."

Brady decided now was a good time to relay, in hushed tones, his course of action since yesterday morn; his visit to the Willard and the senators who listened to him call attention now, not to his own petition, but to Gardner's. His drafting of three letters that were delivered to a Capitol page last night as the Senate met in evening session under the glow of gas light. And still more letters drafted this morning and delivered to a page before he took seat.

One note to Henry Wilson himself, to see what he might do on behalf of Alex Gardner.

"What's that, Mathew?"

It startled Brady back to the here and now. Whatever he had begun to say, he did not get far.

Gardner stared at him and seemed to be waiting for him to speak.

Brady cleared his throat. "The committees are now reporting."

Gardner nodded and turned away again.

Senator Trumbull, on behalf of the Committee on the Judiciary, began with his list.

"Colored voters of Georgia, in relation to the act of Legislature in expelling twenty-nine colored members from that body-" Then an "L.P. Gruder of Georgia, praying such legislation as will protect Union men in that state-"

The congressman summarized the substance of the petition, then the others in his committee's charge, until he announced their singular fate.

"We ask to be discharged from their further consideration."

It continued on. Senator Williams on behalf of the Committee on Private Land Claims, Chandler from the Committee on Commerce.

Petitions of private citizens and those on behalf of states were dealt their unceremonious end: "They have instructed me to report it back and to move that it lie on the table, upon grounds that there is not sufficient time during the present session, owing to the pressure of business."

The reports ended on the floor and the Senate body pushed into their next item on the agenda.

Brady was satisfied with his decision to not tell Gardner of his efforts as he had watched the page circle the floor to visit desks in recent minutes; Howe, Fessenden, and two others on the committee. Each one of them tucking Brady's note into their stacks of papers without so much a glance at the content.

Gardner would never know. And it was because of that he found the man's next words to him ironic.

"Thank you, Mathew. You have done more than enough."

Brady offered his hand. "If only that were so."

After another minute, Brady quietly gathered his cane and rose. "I must be off, Alex. I told Julia I would not be long."

Thursday

Gardner took his gallery seat the next morning. The 25th. He had come this far. He would see it through.

Snow blanketed the glass windows above, forcing pages to light every last gas jet in the darkened chamber. Heaters knocked and clacked before they would churn warmer air into the room. With the ruffian behind him letting go of an occasional snore, Gardner listened as the Senate rushed forward with business.

Petitions were only a few. Then the reports from committees.

Nothing. They began to discuss the first bill. The trip a waste.

He bundled up and left, sloshing his boots through wet snow to the next horse car down at the avenue.

Friday

Gardner returned on the 26th.

He sat, watching and listening, as if paying respects to a dear friend, stopping by his bed each morning to take part in the death vigil. The roiling heaters had made the room insufferably warm, a condition worse than the cold they were made to eradicate. Gardner's brow was moist, his ears red as he watched Senator Morgan rise, notes in hand.

"The Committee on the Library have had under consideration the petition of Alexander Gardner, praying Congress to purchase his collection of photograph incidents of the war."

Gardner inhaled. For that instant, anything was still possible.

"The committee asks to be discharged from the further consideration of this petition, it being of the same nature as the one presented a few days since by Mr. Brady, because there is not sufficient time for Congress to consider it."

Senator Ben Wade put it to rest. "Discharged."

Gardner leaned back. He scratched his kept arm.

A strangeness then came over him, his head lighter.

He looked about the People's room in which he now sat, the body below, the faces in the galleries, and, strangely, felt a certain satisfaction in his defeat.

He turned round; the ruffian there, a wry smile upon the man's whiskered face as he put an old pipe between his lips, leaving it to dangle. He twisted forward to remove his hefty coat. Gardner watched him do so; the man pulled free his left arm and the coat fell away behind him, a stump beneath the pinned flannel where his right arm had once been.

After a moment, Gardner stood up and readied to leave.

"God bless," said the man.

Gardner smiled. "I will see you around."

"I'll be here." He tipped his ragged silk hat as Gardner started toward the open aisle.

Gardner walked out the wide Capitol steps; he took in the avenue ahead. Fat flakes, pure and white, falling heavy upon the cobblestones and awnings, upon the brims of men's hats, layered high now on the black roofs of the busy hacks, the manes of horses and horse teams, and the crown of a streetcar that coursed its metal track down the thoroughfare. He started out, deciding he would walk a ways.

❦

That evening Gardner and the lot; Margaret, Eliza, Lawrence, his mother, and Emily remained at table long after the meal.

They talked. Laughed as they had not done for some time.

Gardner surprised Margaret with tickets to a music house tomorrow evening before he and Lawrence retrieved wood from back and put many pieces of aged oak toward a generous fire. Emily made hot tea and cakes. Gardner wheeled them all to the front porch for a few minutes to watch a heavy snow fall before they settled in again round the fire and spent the evening's remainder in each other's company.

The last days of February 1869

The small cutter led by a tall Shire draft horse, its white stockings beneath a jet-black coat, plodded through snowfall drifted a foot and more in places. Cedars bowed with heavy white and spindly maples struggled with their own slender loads.

They glided across the hillside amongst larger sleighs and in view of the children who tobogganed down the grander slopes.

Brady and Julia sat nestled inside, the cold upon their faces, a heavy blanket across their laps.

They pressed close to one another. They kissed and watched as the afternoon winterscape of that young year slipped past them.

Gardner scratched his suspended arm that night as he sat on the edge of bed. He looked forward to its freedom in two days' time.

On the stand lay a folded copy of that morning's paper, as yet unread. He emptied his pockets upon it; keys on chain, pennies and several dimes. He sat there a moment, repositioning the coins as he ran fingers over the dates; 1858, 1860 and 1864 among them. He allowed himself a moment to wonder where the time had gone.

Gardner lowered himself into bed. He capped the lamp and laid down his head.

When sleep finally greeted him, he dreamt colorful dreams. Of boyhood places, thick summer woods and hideaway nooks along the banks of the River Clyde; evening walks with Margaret the first summer they met, before they married and before the children. Before he was himself. Days past and never to return. Cherished moments, memories that would one day die with him.

Gardner then found himself upon a ship's deck, the Atlantic frothing below. Her dark waters beat angry against iron walls as an ethereal New York harbor took shape through the morning mist.

Lawrence stood before him. Gardner's coated arms stretched over the boy's shoulders with hands fisted tight against the rail. White gulls flitted past one another at great speeds, bounded by nothing. Swooning and climbing steep against the vessel, barely missing another, as father and son watched, breathing the briny air and counting waves upon the waterline.

From the Author

My fascination with Civil War photography began at an early age, with a pictorial history book on a family room bookshelf.

As a boy, I remember thumbing through its pages on rainy days. I do not remember the text, with its details of Civil War generals and the battles. Perhaps I was too young for all that. I do, however, have very distinct memories of the photographs within its pages, many of the same that appear in this book. They are the famous photographs of Brady and Gardner and the teams of men who helped pioneer photojournalism.

These photographs impacted me in two ways.

First was the realization that these photographs were, already at that time, one hundred and twenty years old. The boys I saw, not much older than myself, had by then, assuming they survived the war and lived to be old men, likely been dead some fifty or more years! Their great-grandchildren were now older men. Yet, there they were. Young and vibrant and off to war.

The second way these images impacted me was the shock I felt viewing the death on display. Stark views of dead soldiers in the field. Since that war, there have been many such photographs taken; from the World Wars, Korea, and Vietnam. But this was my first experience with such imagery.

Ironically, they were the first photographs of this kind which were widely revealed to anyone.

Mathew Brady and Alexander Gardner are most definitely real, their influence on history momentous. Rarely will you find an article or documentary about the American Civil War that does not feature one or more images associated with them, even if they make no mention of the photographer. Their work in many ways has defined our perception of the war.

I do not remember when I first became aware that Mathew Brady (spelled with 1 *t*) was the man linked to so many photographs in that book, but I think most people with a penchant for American history are at least familiar with his name. He was *the* photographer of the Civil War. The story of how he earned this unofficial title, and how his name so long overshadowed others, is complicated. In recent decades, many photographers, most notably Alexander Gardner, have been given their just due. Historians such as William Frassanito, with his landmark works on Civil War photography, have provided clarity to their work. I am certainly indebted to those who have mined this topic well in their studies and non-fiction writings.

Neither Gardner nor Brady left a diary or journal. Most of what is known comes from limited scholarly research, stories passed down through the generations, and the images themselves. They were dedicated men, yet different in many ways; Gardner was a creative yet conscientious businessman, Brady a flamboyant big picture man lacking, some might say, in the capacity for self-control. As I hoped to portray in the book, they were remarkable people. They were also human and, therefore, were not without their shortcomings.

They were partners, then competitors. This competition is clear based upon their actions. One such unmistakable action, in this author's mind, being their submission of competing government petitions, a mere four days apart, in the late winter of 1869.

As for Brady and Gardner, their lives diverged in the subsequent years.

After the failed Senate petition, Brady submitted another, this time to the House of Representatives, during the next Congress in 1870. It too failed to stir sufficient interest. In 1875, Congress finally paid Brady $25,000 for a large collection of plates, with help from the influential, including congressmen and future President James Garfield. As a result, many images were procured for safe keeping. But, this financial windfall was not enough for Brady, who died in poverty in 1896.

Gardner left photography in later years and pursued a number of ventures that allowed him a comfortable life until his death in 1882.

Many of Gardner's negatives, and still more from Brady, eventually made their way to the government, but only after they changed hands privately over the years. Unfortunately, thousands of images from this era have likely been lost to history. Those that survived have since been well cared for and are now easily accessible via the Prints & Photographs Online Catalog of the Library of Congress. The majority of images that appear in this book came from this excellent resource.

Proof is my attempt to bring these men and their work to a wider audience, in dramatic form. Liberties were taken to be sure, but I attempted to align with historical fact whenever I felt it was possible. If readers are encouraged to dig deeper into the real and intriguing aspects this story addresses, I feel these liberties will be justified.

Thank you for reading. If you enjoyed reading this book, please check out my novella _A Bird in the Castle_, a fictional tale of Truman Ash and his adventures at the Smithsonian.

It is a story that pays homage to the many real-life 19th century naturalists that once called _the castle_ home.

About the Author

Michael Klaene was born and raised in Cincinnati, Ohio. He graduated with his BA in History from the University of Cincinnati.
He now lives in Northern Kentucky with his wife and two sons.
Proof is his first novel.

Made in the USA
Middletown, DE
19 December 2024

67725353R00205